"Lee Norman, drawing on his own deep life experience with loss, has given us a highly unusual novel that is at once sweet, tender, gut-wrenching and philosophically bold."—Bob Kamm, author, *Love Over 60*.


"To the unbeliever death is the end, to the believer, the beginning." Unknown

# The Grand Creation

Lee Norman

authorHOUSE®

*AuthorHouse*™
*1663 Liberty Drive*
*Bloomington, IN 47403*
*www.authorhouse.com*
*Phone: 1-800-839-8640*

*First published by AuthorHouse 5/31/2011*

*ISBN: 978-1-4567-2763-5 (e)*
*ISBN: 978-1-4567-2764-2 (sc)*

*Library of Congress Control Number: 2011900553*

*Printed in the United States of America*

# Dedication

*To*
*My high school sweetheart*

For over forty years, you were the essence of my life and the source of my energy as I sought a visionary future that gives our lives meaning. Even in your passing, you continue to be the driving force that created this book. Without you, I would never have pursued a life after death. Nor would I have found Barbara, the perfect mate who also lost her husband after 35 years, and understands my love for you as I understand her love for him.

# Chapter 1

DECADES OF DUST SCATTERED in the relentless Phoenix sunlight that streamed through the high gym windows. The light glistened on the single drop of sweat that slid down Mark Stephens' 16" bicep onto his old, tattered football cleats. The stifling August heat and three days of double day practices contributed to Mark's slow measured movements as he picked up his new varsity Ryddell helmet. His old leather helmet and the headaches it caused were gone forever.

Just as Mark straightened his broad shoulders, Juan Barrio, the rock solid 175 pound running back on the winning 1956 Panther football team and Mark's best friend, couldn't resist giving him a fake tackle, his well defined thighs rippling with the effort. The corners of Mark's usually serious eyes crinkled as a smile spread past his high cheekbones showing his straight white teeth and the dimple in his strong, square chin.

Lockers slamming shut and groans caused by stiff, sore muscles competed with Juan's question to Mark: "How's your old body holding up?"

Without looking up, Mark continued to lace up his cleats. "I may be four months older than you, but the difference is better measured in my superior brain power."

Juan, who matched Mark's 5'9" athletic build, answered, "So you agree that you are physically inferior?"

Mark stood up straight, and did trunk rotations while responding, "No, I'm calling attention to your poor judgment. You are ticking off your pulling tackle. Don't forget I am the one who takes out the linebackers waiting to crush your ego."

The two had grown up together in the same low end neighborhood on South Tenth Street. They were very competitive with each other. They couldn't walk down the sidewalk without seeing who could jump the farthest. When they were just ten years old, they pushed each other to see who would go off the high diving board first. Everything was a contest, even their age.

"Okay, Mr. Debator ," Juan said, "you got me there, and I really appreciate it when you hit those holes first." Juan never missed a chance to razz Mark about his good looks, and excellent public speaking ability. It was Mark's fierce debate with his opponent about doing away with caps and gowns for the graduation ceremonies that got Mark elected Student Body President of Phoenix High School.

Juan continued, "And I really appreciate those freshmen girls who come to watch us practice. The heat almost got to them on the first day, but now they bring umbrellas. That's real dedication."

Juan's handsome face and easy smile always hinted of mischief, but it was the dark Don Juan eyes that assured he was never without a date on Saturday night. It helped that he always found a romantic setting to practice the chivalry that brought that dewy look into so many coeds' eyes. The girls loved the way he opened doors for them and how he always spoke respectfully in that low, smooth voice. The dancing was the thing that cinched it though. When he held them in those strong arms as he glided them across the floor or showed his moves with the latest swing craze, they always fell under his spell.

Mark said, "You need to keep your eye on the ball more."

Juan replied, "Oh, yeah, and you need to get a life."

Mark's reputation after his successful election was that he seemed "stuck-up" and not interested in other people. He was a good student but was too serious, and he seldom dated.

As he closed his locker spinning the lock with a practiced flair, and started for the tunnel entrance to the field, Juan called over his shoulder, "I heard that there's a cute little freshman who really has the hots for you." When the broiling sun slammed into them as they entered the field, Mark squinted and pretended to be disinterested. In disbelief, he asked, "Oh? What makes you think that?"

Juan answered, "Word gets around. Why don't you find out for yourself? I'm going to the Mormon dance on Saturday night. That's where I heard about DeeDee. You should go to your church's dances more often. She's an amazing dancer, took a lot of lessons or something. She has a smile that could even make the corners of old lady Kravitz's mouth turn up on test day."

Mark asked, "Is DeeDee her real name?" Juan said, "No. It's Dianne, but everyone calls her DeeDee."

Mark showed a little interest. "Did you dance with her?"

Juan said, "Yes, twice."

Mark, knowing Juan's reputation for holding back on

3

any information regarding his dates, asked anyway, "Did you ask her out?"

Juan answered, "Carmen, my date that night, wouldn't have appreciated it. Why don't you go to the dance tomorrow night?"

Mark said, "My blunderbuster Nash isn't very reliable right now, and the front seat falls back at the most inopportune moments. If I don't grab the steering wheel in time, I find myself in the back seat trying to drive the car."

Juan suggested: "Then go with me. Carmen is on a weekend trip with her parents. I'm on my own. What do you say?"

Mark didn't know why, but said impulsively, "Okay, but I don't neck on the first date." Juan said, "Mark, you really need to get a life." Then after a pause, he added with a smile, "Everyone on campus knows that I do."

Taking deep breaths, both athletes trotted out to the field prepared for another rigorous, hot, body-odor producing two hour workout that would leave them beyond exhausted, but convinced that another state championship would be theirs.

The previous year, schools had been desegregated, and PHS got many talented black athletes when Washington Carver High closed down. Coach Willingham made sure his football players had no room for white vs. black arguments. They learned from him how to put human values and the team's success ahead of all else. That made them an unbeatable force.

"What time Saturday?" Mark asked Juan as they approached three other team members who were limbering up.

"I'll pick you up at 7:30. You won't regret it," Juan replied.

One of the three team members stood up and said, "We didn't know you jocks were dating each other." Juan realized the other team members were misreading his intentions. Juan quickly added "I'm setting Mark up for a date with DeeDee. She's a cutie! He won't regret it."

# Chapter 2

J UAN CHECKED HIS WATCH. It was almost 7:30 and he was a block away from Mark's house. Mark's family had to move to the South Phoenix ghetto when his father lost his gas station nine years earlier. The owner of the lot in downtown Phoenix had decided to cash in on the growing need for parking lots. This left Mark's Dad fixing tires in someone else's gas station. The dirt road leading to Mark's neighborhood was lined with small cinder block houses, some with a dirt floor, most in need of paint. The fans blowing the tattered curtains in the windows did little to break the incessant heat. Mark's house was the only wood framed house on the block. Although it had no insulation and a cement floor, the lawn and the garden added a touch of color to the otherwise drab neighborhood.

As he drove, Juan was thinking how great DeeDee would be for Mark. Her ready smile, her excitement for life, her joy at being around people would be the perfect balance for Mark's serious, introspective side. Juan was pleased with himself and the possibility of bringing them together.

Juan drove into Mark's dirt driveway and honked the horn. Mark came out just as the Platter's began singing

"The Great Pretender," on the car radio. Juan motioned for Mark to come and listen. Mark could hear Juan's voice mimicking the singer. He stood outside shaking his head. When Juan turned off the radio, Mark opened the door and said "I hope you don't do this with all of your dates."

Juan replied, "This song is about you. You are a great pretender pretending you are living well, but you're lonely and no one can tell, but me. And that's why we are going to the church dance tonight. You are going to meet DeeDee. You can kiss loneliness goodbye."

Mark said, "All I want to kiss goodbye is your singing."

Juan backed out and put the car in first gear so he could peal out leaving a cloud of dust. "Your problem is you don't recognize talent." Juan said.

"Not so," Mark replied. "I recognize a lot of your talents, such as your way with Carmen, Rose, Janine, Alice, Rachel, and …:

Juan interrupted Mark. "Wait a minute, what's wrong with dating some nice looking ladies?"

"All at the same time?" Mark asked.

"Yes, and soooo?" Juan asked incredulously waiting for Mark to deliver a serious objection.

"You are the great pretender, not me." Mark said.

Juan replied, "And you are just a dreamer. That's why I have you out of the house on a Saturday night. There is a real life waiting for you besides football and politics."

Mark responded, "Don't pretend you put football in second place. You know there is a scholarship at Tempe waiting for you at the end of the year."

"Sure, I know I have a good chance, and it is important

to me, but there needs to be balance. As the Bible says, "Man does not live by bread alone" Juan remarked.

"I'll run that by God when I get to heaven," Mark replied.

"You don't have to. Didn't Brigham Young have a bunch of wives?" Juan said, believing he had won the argument.

Mark conceded the point. "Yes, he had 26 wives." To add a little humor he asked, "Do you know what Mark Twain said about him having all those wives?"

Juan thought there goes Mark again trying to trump me with a reference to literature. "No, Mr. English Major, I don't know. What did he say?"

"He said Brigham Young had that many wives because when he got home at night, he wanted to find at least one in good humor." Juan had never heard it expressed as "good humor," but he caught the meaning and laughed.

"Tell me about DeeDee." Mark asked "Why do they call her that?" "DeeDee stands for 'Daddy's Darling.' She is an only child. Her mother couldn't have any more children after DeeDee was born. As I told you, her given name is Dianne. Dianne Henderson. You should know her. She is a Mormon, goes to First Ward."

Mark's ward, the Fourth Ward, was in his gang ridden neighborhood. He lived and worked in that environment and never went to the uppity north side. "I don't know all the Mormons in Arizona," Mark said somewhat condescendingly to Juan. "Why are you hanging out with Mormons any way? You're Catholic."

"Because that's where all the good dancers are – duh." Juan said.

Within twenty minutes, they arrived at First Ward. The dances were held in the church multipurpose gym.

Folding metal chairs surrounded the gym floor with the guys congregating on one side and the girls on the other. The DJ, provided by the church, was announcing the first dance. The chairs began to scrape, hearts began to race as the girls on one side of the gym waited in anticipation as the boys on the other side began to make their choices.

The church monitors moved about the dance floor checking for improper attire, records with questionable lyrics, or dancers who violated the rule about keeping "daylight" between their bodies.

Juan's eyes roamed over to the girl's side of the gym. He didn't see DeeDee, but he did notice the ladies ogling Mark and him as soon as they entered. A new song invited the dancers to pair up for another swing. Juan concluded that DeeDee must not be there. Mark felt a little dumb and rejected. All this business about how "she has the hots for you" from Juan, he thought to himself, and now she isn't even here. What a let down!

Mark asked Juan where the restroom was. Mark really wanted to check out his appearance - an egocentricity he didn't admit to.

Juan pointed to a wide hall. "The girls are on the left and the boys are farther down on the right." Juan directed.

As Mark was about to pass the ladies restroom, two oversized junior high kids were having a race to the men's room. They carelessly knocked Mark toward the ladies room side. At that moment, a younger girl was leaving the ladies room just as Mark was pushed toward her. He grabbed the door frame to keep from going into her. At 5' 3" she looked up at Mark. Their eyes met. Mark had a strange deja vu that he had seen her before. A knot tightened in his stomach as a flicker of recognition brought back a distant memory of when he was in the sixth grade.

She knew he was the President of PHS, but now looking up close into his eyes, she, too, had a flash of familiarity about him. She said, "I'm sorry." even though the near collision was not her fault. It was then that Mark remembered their first meeting.

# Chapter 3

MARK APOLOGIZED, "No, IT wasn't your fault. It was my body that created the problem, not yours. Two kids pushed me. Are you all right?"

Timidly, the girl said, "I'm not hurt." Mark excused himself and headed for the men's room. He used his hands to smooth his thick dark brown hair into his usual Fabian style. He raised his arm to the mirror. No sweat signs yet. He checked his teeth to be sure no lettuce from his usual evening meal was stuck and visible, reducing his flashing smile to green teeth.

When he got back to the dance floor, Juan just finished dancing and was returning to his seat. Juan asked, "What took you so long?"

Mark said, "Two rowdy kids almost knocked me into the ladies room. I was able to stop just as a young girl was coming out. Our eyes met, then she apologized."

"So what's the big deal?" Juan asked with little interest.

"Both of us," Mark said pausing as he gazed down toward the dance floor, "I'm sure that both of us registered signs that we had met before. Then when she said 'I'm sorry!' it came to me when that meeting was. I attended

Wilson Elementary School. The grades there were first through the eighth grade. The first to fourth grades were separated from the fifth to the eighth grades. Each section had separate bathrooms."

By now Juan lost all interest. "Get to the point." Juan said. "I'm missing out," he sighed as he stared at the dancers.

"I am. I am." Mark said. "Our sixth grade P.E. teacher asked me to take some softballs over to the fourth grade section. After doing that, I needed to use the restroom and I made a sharp turn toward the boys' room and ran directly into a little second grader. She fell down, but quickly got back up and looked up at me and said, 'I'm sorry.' We both stared into each other's eyes. Did we know each other? There was a strangeness about the whole thing because in the six years since that meeting took place, I have dreamed several times of looking into that little second grader's eyes. I remember her smile was full of energy. It was the kind of smile that makes it difficult not to smile back."

"What did you do?" Juan asked.

"Nothing." Mark said. "I mean, I remember thinking, 'Great, now I'm in trouble. Sixth graders aren't supposed to use restrooms for second graders and the little girl got knocked down. But she apologized to me so maybe she wouldn't tell on me.' But why that meeting? And those dreams? And then I saw those eyes again tonight. I… I don't know what to make of it. I think it is the same girl. I had the same strange feeling when I looked into her eyes."

Suddenly Juan yelled out, "There she is going across the dance floor."

Mark looked up. "Yes, that's her. How did you know?"

"What do you mean how did I know. She is who we came for. That's DeeDee." Juan explained.

"Oh, my gosh!" Mark's face drained of color. He sat down. "That's the girl I bumped into twice in my life." Mark remembered the second grader with dark tousled hair wearing a long, brightly flowered jumper and black patent shoes. Now he looked at her light brown curly hair escaping from her stylish pony tail. Her cream colored blouse clung in just the right places, and her simple plaid pleated skirt fell below her knees, but it showed the promise of curves of a well defined body. She was a fit and supple dancer whose every move exuded a wonderful energy and grace. And then there was that smile.

# Chapter 4

A T JUAN'S URGING, MARK started the long walk to the other side of the dance floor. He didn't wander. He walked straight to DeeDee, but it seemed as if ten minutes passed as he walked the fifty feet. His thoughts raced: I have to make sure there is daylight between us. It's a church rule. My right hand has to be high above her waist. What if I don't start on the right beat? Maybe someone else will ask her before I get there. Ok, breathe. Slow down. She sees me. What should I say? Of course, stupid, just ask her for a dance.

DeeDee saw Mark coming her way. Her heart beat began doubling. DeeDee was worried she would say something stupid. She became self conscious. Before Mark got close enough to say anything, she started to stand…No, sit, stay. He may not even ask. Maybe all he wants is to talk about us bumping into each other.

"Would you like to dance?" Mark asked as he bowed toward her and extended his hand.

DeeDee's usual smile turned to pure joy as she took Mark's hand and floated out of her chair into his waiting arms. As they touched, DeeDee's body trembled. Mark felt tingling warmth that stirred some dark feelings of long ago.

"You have a reputation for being the best dancer at P.H. I can use some lessons," Mark said as he carefully abided by the church rules and prepared for the first step. They stood there poised to start.

DeeDee instantly entered into her comfort zone. She knew her body would respond to the confidence she always exuded when it came to anything regarding dance. She knew the steps and their terms whether it was jazz, tap, ballet, or ballroom, and she knew her music.

Mark seemed frozen. He was afraid of taking the first step. He hesitated, and then admitted his fear to her. "I can never hit the first beat at the right time. If you can help me out I'll probably be good to go from then on."

DeeDee said, "The first rule of dance for a good female partner is to be a good follower, but you took the lead when you asked me."

DeeDee squeezed his hand. "Okay listen" nodding her head. "Ready: five, six, seven, eight," and the dancers started their dance with life in perfect rhythm.

When the music stopped, Mark interlocked fingers with DeeDee as he walked her to the girl's side of the gymnasium. He felt her hand trembling again, and gave it a squeeze. "Everyone is right about you being the best dancer." Mark said.

"I don't know about being the best, but I do love dance and I know you have good rhythm." DeeDee said.

Mark felt relieved. He thought he did well, but then it was just the two step. His relief was short-lived. Before they reached the other side, the D.J. started another record – Bill Haley's "Rock Around the Clock," and DeeDee started rocking to the music. Mark initially felt fear. A two step was easy, but a complicated swing dance was beyond his ability. DeeDee gave Mark a big smile with an enticing point of her head toward the dance floor. Mark hesitated, but DeeDee loved to dance, and he was feeling the rhythm coming through her. He let the beat flow in, and everything seemed so effortless even though he had no plan what he would do first.

DeeDee, with a nod of her head on each beat, five six, seven, eight, clued Mark who barely lifted his left arm as he held her right hand while she glided under and returned to face him in perfect synchronization with the beat…That was so easy thought Mark, almost like power steering. DeeDee made everything look graceful, easy, smooth, and natural.

When the dance was over, Mark pulled DeeDee in close to his body and gave her a big hug. He made sure the squeeze was short and did not linger long enough to catch the church monitor's attention. He felt the firm body of a dancer, but her sweet innocent smile was that of a young teenager in seventh heaven after dancing with Phoenix High's student body president.

Mark didn't want to push his luck. He got through two dances without falling down, and DeeDee, at this point, thought he was a better-than-average dancer. The air conditioner wasn't keeping up with all the warmth coming from the dancers. Beads of sweat ran down his temple. He picked up a BYU magazine and began fanning himself.

"Me too, please." DeeDee said as she leaned her head toward Mark for a few fan repetitions.

"Let's step outside for a moment and cool off." Mark said.

DeeDee said, "A good idea." Mark guided her to the nearest exit.

Outside, the temperature had dropped to 90 degrees as the full moon rose. The shadows flickered while the breeze played in the trees, hiding their faces one moment and making their eyes sparkle the next.

"That feels good." Mark said. When DeeDee turned toward the moon coming up behind Mark, her perfect teeth glistened.

"Do you ever stop smiling?" Mark asked. "I mean you have a beautiful smile and perfect teeth." Now it was Mark's turn to become self conscious…What a clumsy stupid thing for me to say! What's blocking my brain from creating a simple sentence? She is so young. Everyone is going to be wondering about me standing outside the church with her in the moonlight.

"I get my smile from my dad," DeeDee said. "He always has a smile for everyone."

"Do you have brothers and sisters?" Mark asked, feeling a little better about this question even though he knew the answer.

"Nope," DeeDee replied. "After I was born, my mom couldn't have anymore children."

Mark nodded that he understood. "That's a real shame." Mark said. "Your mother was working from an excellent blueprint." That comment made DeeDee smile bigger, but then she blushed.

DeeDee continued, "I know you have a sister and a brother." Mark nodded yes, "And that you are older, I mean older than they are, I should have said oldest, and that you are our Student Body President."

"I don't think I'm everyone's president," Mark said.

"Yes you are! You got elected," DeeDee protested.

Mark was feeling sensitive to the word "older" and was uneasy about staying outside too long with a bubbly little freshman, but he wanted to ask her a very important question. "Did you ever go to Wilson Grade School?" he asked.

"Yes!" she said, "Why?"

"Let's go back in. Juan wants to dance with you." Mark said without answering her question. He didn't take her hand but walked shoulder to shoulder with her. He was perfectly in sync with her as they walked to the front door. He opened it for her and made a sweeping gesture for her to enter.

"Thank you, Mr. President," DeeDee said.

Mark looked down at her and smiled broadly...I like this little girl...he said to himself.

# Chapter 5

DEEDEE WAS THINKING ABOUT the question. She looked up at Mark's eyes. The deja vu rushed past her. She remembered that day at Wilson Grade School when she bumped into a bigger student and looked into his eyes as if she knew him from somewhere. "I think I...." Her thoughts were interrupted when Mark stepped into the dance hall with DeeDee at his side, and Juan met them by bowing and motioning DeeDee to the dance floor.

"May I have this dance, or are you already taken?" Juan asked.

DeeDee took his hand saying formally, "I would love to dance with you." With her hand on top of his, Juan led her to the floor, and waited for the right beat to start his swing.

Mark sat on the sideline pretending not to notice DeeDee and Juan laughing and making eye contact as they executed a complicated but smooth east coast swing with moves that looked choreographed and rehearsed. Juan was the striking figure on the dance floor and he knew it. With DeeDee, he could show off dance steps that even American Bandstand dancers would have found novel and beautiful. DeeDee loved the challenge, and put more energy into following Juan's lead.

Other dancers stopped dancing, and pulled back to give DeeDee and Juan center stage. Soon everyone encircled DeeDee and Juan as they put on a show. The church dance monitor hurried through the crowd to see what was happening. To his surprise, the two teenagers were demonstrating dance expertise that obeyed all the church rules. He smiled and applauded along with all the other observers when the dance song was over, and Juan and DeeDee returned to where Mark was sitting. Both perspired profusely. DeeDee's hand was sitting on top of Juan's as he returned her to Mark.

Mark stood up. "That was an amazing performance. How long did you guys have to prepare to do a dance like that?"

"No prep at all," DeeDee said as she sat down in the chair next to Mark. He read the gesture and smiled at DeeDee's choice.

Juan asked DeeDee, "Who are you with?" Mark's hair on the back of his neck started to bristle. His muscles tensed, and then he realized that the question meant how she got here, not who she was with.

DeeDee never thought otherwise. "Spacia's older brother brought us on his way to his girlfriend's house. Spacia is my best friend and she gets her brother to give us rides. Robert is twenty-three and studying to be a lawyer."

Juan said, "We can give you and Spacia a ride home tonight if you like. It's just me and Mark. Lots of room."

Dee Dee answered quickly. "No, but thank you. My parents have rules. They know Spacia's brother, and we come and go with him."

Mark liked a girl who would obey her parents even though he felt DeeDee would have wanted to go with him in Juan's car. He wanted to be able to visit more with her, but would like to double on the first date. It would ease the burden of having to keep up the conversation if it started to get thin.

Mark asked, "If your parents knew me, do you think they would let you go to the next dance with me?" It was a bold question and risky.

DeeDee answered, "I'm sure if they got to know you, they wouldn't mind." Mark weighed her choice of words and decided they would not be thrilled to have an eighteen year old dating their fourteen year old daughter unless there were certain conditions attached. Even then, their consent would probably be given reluctantly.

For the last dance of the evening, Juan danced with Spacia, and DeeDee danced with Mark. The church did not play slow dreamy music for the last dance because it encouraged teenagers to droop all over each other in physical embraces. Instead, the two step music had a little hop to it. Mark took his cue from Juan when making turns. The bodies could make legitimate contact for balance while turning.

Unfortunately, Spacia's responsible older brother was right on time in his black Belair when he honked his horn twice to catch his sister's attention. Mark and Juan gave the girls a hug, and as the girls entered Robert's car, it was Juan who yelled out, "We will call you."

When Mark got into Juan's car, he blurted out, "By 'we' you mean you and your multiple personalities? You didn't consult me before you asked to give them a ride home, and then you didn't consult me about giving them a call."

# Chapter 6

Juan ignored Mark and pulled away from the curb right behind the black Bellaire driven by Spacia's brother. "If that got your shorts in a bunch, you're really going to object to what I am going to do next." Juan had a devious, cunning smile. "I'm going to follow them home."

"Why?" Mark yelled.

"To find out where they live, of course." Juan said.

"Now you sound like a stalker. Don't do it, please!" Mark pleaded.

"You take the fun out of it." Juan objected. "Watch!" He then sped up to the side of the black Bellaire. He waved to the girls. Then he fell back behind them, making every turn they made.

"Don't do this! You make us seem so pathetic and hard up." Mark tried again.

Juan then passed them and pulled in front. He stayed there for two blocks and then turned up 16$^{th}$ Street. Spacia's brother followed them.

"Now you've done it!" Mark said. "He is stalking us!"

When Juan came to Diamond Street, he turned left. The black Bellaire followed.

Mark, fully irritated, asked, "Now what are you going to do? Ditch him? How are you going to explain this behavior to Dee Dee's parents after Spacia's brother tells them about us?"

Juan let out a maniacal laugh for the next two blocks and then pulled suddenly over to the curb, stopped, and turned off the car.

Spacia's brother pulled into the driveway next door, stormed out of his car with his fists doubled and fury blazing in his eyes. Spacia and DeeDee rushed out of the car behind him, trying to stop him as he marched toward Juan and Mark.

Mark reluctantly got out of Juan's car ready to use his debating skills to diffuse the situation. He began, "We're sorry if…." Suddenly Juan and Robert began making muffled nasal sounds as the girls were unable to contain their smiles any longer and everyone but Mark began howling with uncontrollable laughter. Mark was confused.

"It's called reverse stalking." Juan could barely get the words out of his mouth.

Mark then realized, "You knew where they lived all the time!" Mark said half angry and half smiling. Juan gave it all up. "I found out who Dee Dee's best friend was and that they lived next to each other. I got the address from the phone book and drove over earlier today.

Spacia took over. "This afternoon Juan knocked and introduced himself. I already knew who he was. He told me about reverse stalking and asked if I wanted to play it on you tonight. It sounded like fun, and it was."

At that moment, Dee Dee's front door opened. Her

parents wrapping robes around themselves came running outside. "What's all the noise about? What's going on?"

Spacia's brother stepped forward. As the oldest person there, he felt it was his responsibility to explain what happened. DeeDee's parents waited expectantly as Robert started to explain.

Robert began with assurance. "I dropped the girls off at the church and picked them up at 10:30 as planned. The two boys were at the dance. This is Juan Barrio, maybe you've read about him on the sports page?"

Dee Dee's father stepped forward. "I have. So you're the star running back for P.H.S.!" He grabbed Juan's hand and gave it a vigorous shaking saying, "I liked what you did to West High. You ran through their line like it was paper."

Juan acknowledged Mark standing next to him: "This is my teammate. I have to give him most of the credit. He's the one who punched holes in the line. All I did was run through."

Mark, with his impressive voice and good diction, was once again feeling comfortable about himself. "Juan is being modest. I am Mark Stephens, a pulling tackle for the team." Mark went over to DeeDee's father and shook his hand and then turned to DeeDee's mother. He let her offer her hand, then took it and with a slight bow said, "It's a pleasure to meet DeeDee's parents."

DeeDee announced," Mark is our Student Body President at P.H.S."

Her mother paused, and then said, "That means you are a senior there." She couldn't hide a sudden consternation when she realized that this handsome popular boy was four years older than DeeDee, her baby girl.

"Yes, Maam." was the polite reply.

Robert began again. "Anyway, Juan here wanted to pull a prank on Mark. He got my little sister to go along with him." Robert then explained the object of reverse stalking and how successful it was. Mark agreed he was duped. Everyone had a good laugh at his expense.

Then DeeDee's father said it was past curfew and that everyone better be getting to sleep. DeeDee's mother was thinking about something else: all of this was planned. There wasn't just a chance meeting of boys at the dance. She mentioned these concerns to Ray, DeeDee's father, when they got in bed.

Ray concluded, "But they are athletes with good character. They seemed like fine outstanding boys. I wouldn't worry much about DeeDee."

But Ann was.

# Chapter 7

Later that week, DeeDee's father got a call at his office. Ann met him with a serious tone. "DeeDee called. She said Mark asked her out for Saturday night and wanted to get our permission. I told you this was going to happen."

Ray didn't remember who Mark was. "What's so wrong? Have her bring the young boy over and we will meet him as we always do and make sure."

"You already met him." Ann interrupted. "He is eighteen years old and has his own car."

Ray realized his mistake, "Oh, you mean that Mark. Well, I… aw… aa… I…what do you think?"

Ann voiced her concern again. "She is fourteen, and he is eighteen, and he has a car."

Ray countered, "I am eight years older than you."

"That is different," Ann's voice couldn't hide the exacerbation. "I was almost eighteen when I met you."

"Did we raise our daughter with good standards? It is one date. She always follows the rules," Ray presented his case.

Ann argued, "Maybe this relationship will dissolve on

its own, or it could be her first heartbreak. I don't want her heart broken."

Ray, with assuredness said, "What relationship? You mean heartbreaks like all teenage girls have? And don't most of them learn from it and become more mature about relationships when they are old enough to start getting serious about someone?"

With a sigh, Ann said, "I don't want her heart broken, but I guess we can't choose her dates for her. He seems to be a respectful, good young man."

"At its worst," Ray said, "this could just be one of the learning bumps in a girl's life. We will be there to help her get through it.

"You are probably right," Ann conceded.

When DeeDee got home after cheerleading practice, she asked her mother, "Well, what did Daddy say?"

DeeDee's mother asked, "Where will you be going and who else will be with the two of you?"

DeeDee was eager to respond with all the right answers. "The church dance! Juan and Spacia are going and we thought we would double date and then go to Bob's Big Boy for hamburgers afterward."

"I have a thought, " DeeDee's mother said. "Why not have everyone come over here at say 6 p.m. for a barbeque before you go to the dance?"

There was a pause and then DeeDee said, "I'm not sure Mark can get off work. I'll call right now and see." DeeDee wondered if her mother was making this new proposal as a condition of date approval, but she didn't want to take a chance and antagonize her mother.

Mark answered on the fourth ring. He was outside trying to make his old Nash shine enough to remove his usual embarrassment just being in it. The army blankets covering the torn seat covers, however, could not be shined away. He would have to stay with plan A and double date with Juan.

"Mark?" DeeDee asked, "Is that you?"

"Oh, hi, DeeDee. Are we on for Saturday night?"

"I think so. My mother wanted to know if you would like to come over to my house first for a backyard barbeque before going to the dance." DeeDee didn't want anything to ruin her date with Mark. There was apprehension in her voice.

Mark sensed it and put those fears aside. "Sounds like a great idea. I'll see if I can get off work. I don't think Juan will mind. What time?"

"About 6 p.m." DeeDee answered, relieved that Mark was so positive.

"Can you call me later?" she asked.

"Let's say I will call you if there is a problem," Mark said.

"You mean if I don't hear from you, you will be over to my house at 6:00 on Saturday?" DeeDee asked as if she didn't expect Mark to come.

"You've got that right." Mark answered.

"Then I hope you never call me. I don't, I mean I don't want to hear from you." DeeDee stumbled on. "I don't mean I never want you to call. I do want you to call but not about, anyway, see you Saturday." DeeDee said and hung up the phone. She was feeling so stupid. "I'm going to blow this date." she said to herself.

"What did he say?" her mother's voice came from the kitchen.

DeeDee thought about all the fears going through her mind and then took time to collect her thoughts before she answered her mother.

"He said yes, and that he would call if there is a problem." DeeDee yelled back to her mother.

Her mother thought...that's a good sign. If his intentions were dishonorable he would not want to face her parents before committing a crime.

That Saturday the boys arrived at DeeDee's five minutes early. Most of the houses in the neighborhood were modest two bedroom brick tract homes, with large manicured lawns and connecting sidewalks, an upper class neighborhood by Mark's standards. Juan went next door to collect Spacia. Both boys brought their dates flowers. Juan went inside Spacia's house while Mark knocked at DeeDee's door. Dee Dee's mother looked out the window through the blinds.

"It's Mark and he has flowers for you. How gallant! Wait for a minute, don't rush to the door, and think what you are going to say."

DeeDee slowed to a walking pace. "What should I say?"

"Thank him, of course, and then look for a vase to put them in."

When DeeDee opened the door, Mark had one hand behind his back, and extended the other holding the bouquet. She was delighted to see the professionally done bouquet with pink, purple, and white carnations.

"Oh, Mark, thank you! They are beautiful!" DeeDee said. Ann came forward to see. Mark then brought his other hand from behind his back and presented a second bouquet of flowers to Ann. Ann was taken by surprise. "Two bouquets for DeeDee. That's..."

"No, Maam." Mark interrupted. "These are for you."

Ann's eyes enlarged, her mouth dropped open. "For me?" she asked in disbelief.

"Yes, Maam," Mark said, "to the lady of the house for inviting two teenagers with large appetites into her home for supper."

"But you shouldn't, I mean, it wasn't necessary, that is I wasn't expecting…

DeeDee helped her mother out, "Mom, do we have two vases?" Then she turned to Mark, "We both thank you for the beautiful flowers."

"Yes! We most certainly do." Ann said as she took the flowers and went to the kitchen. She stepped out on the back porch and called to Ray, "Mark is here and he brought DeeDee flowers."

Ray motioned for her to step outside, "He did what?" Ray asked.

"He brought her flowers. Isn't that sweet?"

"Too sweet if you ask me," Ray said bending over to Ann's ear. "It means he's courting her for marriage. She is too young. That's too serious. I don't like it."

"Lighten up." Ann whispered back. "He gave me flowers too. Does that mean he is courting me?"

"Well, I don't like it." Ray said.

Ray was from the old school. Out on the range in Wyoming where Ray spent his childhood riding instead of going to school, he was taught that flowers meant a serious courtship.

As he turned back to the barbeque, Ray's thoughts were on how he could get rid of this boy.

# Chapter 8

JUAN AND SPACIA ARRIVED. The aroma of tri-tip on the grill whetted everyone's appetite. The girls helped Ann set the table and bring out the food. Mark and Juan went over to the brick barbeque pit.

Mark said, "Boy, it sure smells good!"

"It will be ready soon," Ray said without greeting the boys or looking up.

Juan said, "Well, it can't be too soon for me." And he walked away.

Mark was concerned. This was not the same Ray he met last week. Juan's quick departure confirmed Mark's observation.

Mark said with a smile, "Don't worry, Mr. Henderson, I've already talked to Juan. He knows it's impolite to ask for sevenths and eighths."

Ray did not respond.

"Is there anything I can do to help?" Mark asked.

Ray hesitated, then said, "Maybe there is. DeeDee tells me you're a meat cutter."

"Just a counter hop in the meat department. But as a first year apprentice, I have picked up a few skills," Mark said.

"Maybe you can butterfly that last tri tip for your hungry friend," Ray softened. Mark picked up Ray's butcher knife and examined its quality, then picked up the steel and began sharpening the knife to give it a haircutting edge. Ray was impressed. "It looks like you know something about it. What other jobs have you had?" Ray asked.

As Mark quickly and expertly opened and sliced the tri tip, he said, "My Dad taught me the value of work. No, the fact is, because of lack of food, he had my brother and me working early on. I was eleven the first time I went out picking cotton with what my Dad called 'the darkies.' Then he got my brother and me paper routes. We were 12 years old. Seven days a week for the next three years, up at four A.M. everyday folding and delivering papers. One day my voice changed, and I knocked on someone's door to collect subscription money. A little boy yelled to his mother, 'The paper man is here.' For a whole month of work," Mark said grimacing, "I made two or three dollars. A man gets paid more than that."

"Why so little?" Ray asked.

"People wouldn't or couldn't pay, or they would move owing me money. One morning I went to deliver to a house, and the whole house was gone. It was time to find another job."

Ray nodded, "What did you do then?"

"That summer I pitched watermelons with a crew of hard working wetbacks. We worked well together. In fact, they had a sit down strike one day and I joined them. They wanted a raise from 20 cents an hour to 25 cents an hour. We won." Mark could see more interest and a more cordial attitude coming from Mr. Henderson. "Then I got a job sweeping the parking lot in a small shopping center with just a few stores. Every morning before school, I swept it clean with a wooden broom for $5 a week. Finally, I got a good job at Food Town's Meat Department. I started at 81cents an hour and I'm up to $1.25 now."

"That's more like it. So how is it working there?"

"It's a good job. But do you mean do I like cutting meat?"

"Yes," Mr. Henderson replied. "Becoming a journeyman meat cutter."

"My boss is a great guy," Mark answered. "He is going to help me get through college. We already talked about it. He will let me work my hours around school."

"What are you going to study in college?" Mr. Henderson asked.

"I'm thinking about becoming a dentist, but I haven't made up my mind yet."

"What does your father do now?" Mr. Henderson asked.

"He is 74, not in the best of health, and he is retired. He gets a government check for $50 each month, but after his cigarettes and doctors, there isn't much left. My brother and I buy our own food, all of our clothes, and whatever else we need."

"I guess that's a pretty complete story about where you're coming from and where you're going," Mr. Henderson said, satisfied with Mark's character.

Mark nodded yes knowing that he left out the death of his sister and other details. In his childhood, he went to bed hungry because there wasn't enough food for the family. A big meal at his house was sharing a can of pork'n beans with two hotdogs cut up in it for all six members of his family. When he was ten years old and there wasn't any more food in the house, Mark's parents took him to stay with his half sister and her husband who smoked four packs of cigarettes a day. In their household, Mark was a daily babysitter for his 3 and 5 year old nieces.

On the day he was left with the half sister, who lived miles away, his mother told him to be brave and not to cry, and that they would come to visit him on weekends. They came the first weekend, and she repeated her words about being brave, but no one came the next weekend, and the following weekends, and he cried silently into his pillow every night for a week. Then the tears stopped and Mark withdrew into himself. He played alone at his new school and fought with anyone who tried to intrude on his silent lonely world. He was a heartbroken ten year old boy who missed his family terribly, especially his brother, but the world would never know. His young psyche began drawing some conclusions, and forming a barrier of protection that would never let him feel this pain again.

Six months later when his father found a better paying job changing tires and washing cars at a used car lot, Mark returned to his family. His brother was happy to see him, but Mark was not ready to bond again. Mark ran with the older kids and would not let his brother join him. He threw rocks at him to make him go home. A year later when Mark's sister was killed in an auto accident, Mark did not shed a tear.

Mark did not know it, but he was on the edge of bonding with another person for life. He wasn't aware of all the implications this bond would have. He couldn't analyze this new relationship because those childhood memories remained locked away deep in his unconscious. He was drawn to DeeDee, yet he felt something ominous, something frightening. But, as he often would do when in a dangerous situation, he would turn and face the danger, not run away. He knew he needed to explore these feelings. DeeDee was the catalyst, the energy that would not let Mark ignore her.

The barbeque was delicious, but the most warming part about it was Mark's connection to DeeDee's parents. Ann saw him as gallant, sweet and romantic. Ray saw him as industrious, hardworking and appreciative of life's opportunities and challenges. DeeDee was falling in love. For now, it was an innocent, genuine, heartfelt bond.

# Chapter 9

Later at the church, Mark danced with no one but DeeDee. Juan danced with Spacia most of the time. He created opportunities to show off his skills by coaxing DeeDee twice to join him on the gym floor and then again with two other skillful young ladies who were also willing to be his partner.

At one point, the two couples went outside to cool off. The breeze evaporated the perspiration on their heated bodies. Juan remarked, "Think about it. Two weeks ago we didn't know you girls. Now we are good friends. Do you ever wonder if all this is planned?"

"What do you mean?" Spacia asked.

"That there is some big plan that we are all following." Juan replied.

Mark asked, "If there is a plan, what is the purpose?"

"To find out about each other," Juan said.

"If that's true," DeeDee said, "then I am missing out. I don't know much about you, Juan."

"I'll tell you all you want to know. Ask away."

"Tell us where you're from, about your family, and all that."

"I'm from my mother's womb." Juan said with a smile. "She happened to be in Madrid at the time. My two sisters and brother got there first. My father always wanted to go to el grande y bella pais el Estados Unidos de America." Juan said in perfect Spanish. "My father insisted that the whole family learn English. He was a teacher in both countries. When I was five years old mi padre got el officio in el gobiermo and we moved to become permanent citizens. My older brother died for this country fighting in Germany. My two sisters have married. I'm the baby, still at home, and very spoiled."

"You took the words right out of my mouth," Mark said smiling. "Thanks for filling us in. I remember the day the neighbors found out about your brother. Everyone felt your loss. The official German surrender was the next day. That had to be a bitter pill to swallow. If there is a plan for everything that happens, I don't think I want to see it." Mark stated.

"Why not?" Spacia asked.

"Okay, let's say you knew you were going to die in a certain way on a certain day in the future because that was the plan. What would you do? How would knowing that change your life?"

Spacia was nodding up and down as she thought of different scenarios and how she would deal with them in her life. She wondered if she could cheat fate out of her death by hiding, or if she should become super religious, or try saving other lives so hers might be spared. She could not imagine a normal existence with that new knowledge. It would consume her.

DeeDee said, "If I were going to die, I couldn't stop it, so I would make plans to enjoy all the people I love until the time came for me to go."

"Where would you go?" Mark asked.

"I don't know," she answered, "but we better get back in. The last dance is coming up soon."

"Yes," Mark said, "you are probably more right than you know." Juan looked at Mark. The girls missed Mark's meaning. No one knows when their last dance will come.

Inside, they knew the D. J. was setting up the final dances. A slow dance would come first, followed by an upbeat song that would force the dancers apart. Church policy!

Mark took DeeDee by the hand and walked to the beat. When he reached the center of the dance floor, he brought her in close and began a series of turns which allowed them to be closer together. The continuous twirling caused Mark to get a little dizzy. DeeDee said, "I've got to teach you how to spot. It will stop the dizziness." She slowed them down to keep Mark from looking like a baby taking its first steps.

"Thank you, partner." Mark said. "I couldn't stagger very well without you." He wanted to sit out the last dance, but sitting out the last dance to DeeDee would be like forfeiting life. He danced to the end and took the opportunity to give her a big hug when it was over.

That night when Mark walked DeeDee to her door, he held out his hand. DeeDee took it as a hand shake. He placed his other hand over the back of her hand so that her hand was inside both of his as if he were holding a delicate bird that he didn't want to fly away. He pulled her in closer, released her hand to go around his neck and dropped both of his hands to circle her lower back. She wrapped both arms around his neck. Together they pulled each other close for a hug that lasted less than five seconds. Neither of them noticed the parted Venetian blinds. When Mark stepped back, he said, "It was a lot of fun. Would you like to go out again next Saturday, maybe for something a little different, say swimming?"

DeeDee was overwhelmed and couldn't get her mind to wrap around what just happened. Her thoughts were going full blast... Mark Stephens P.H.S. Student Body President, and a senior, and a football player, and handsome, and he wants to go swimming with me, and the last time I went was after work at the Inn where I worked and it had a slide and... DeeDee blurted out, "Yes, we could go to the Inn. I worked there last summer. I know Alice, the manager, and we could go there for free and the slide is a lot of fun." In the back of her mind, DeeDee knew her mother would say yes if the date was not just a twosome. "I know some other kids who would like to go too."

Mark replied, "I was thinking of inviting some others too. "I take it you like swimming. You check with your parents, and I'll call you by Wednesday."

DeeDee said, "Thank you for tonight." Mark turned and walked to his car, and waved goodbye as he drove away. The Venetian blinds closed.

DeeDee's heart wouldn't stop fluttering. She took deep breaths but couldn't wait to tell her mother everything. She had so much to share, and she knew her mother would be awake and wanting details.

"Right on time," DeeDee said to her mother as soon as she entered the house. DeeDee's father was asleep so it would just be girl talk. She didn't even wait for her mother's questions. The words rushed from DeeDee, "He was wonderful! We had a great time! He was a perfect gentleman, and fun to be with. We danced, we talked, we laughed, and he asked me out for next Friday night. He was like a little boy when it came to dance. I showed him how to start on the right beat, and how to control dizziness in turns. He said I had the reputation for being the best dancer at P.H.S. and that he needed lessons. He did just fine, and then Juan and Spacia danced. Juan is really a very good dancer. But Mark has really good potential too, and Mark kept track of time so we wouldn't be late and …"

"Slow down, sweetie," her mother said "I take it you accepted his date for next Saturday. Where are you going? Who with?"

Dee Dee was suddenly concerned. What if her parents said no?

# Chapter 10

"A BUNCH OF US are going to go swimming at the Inn where I worked all summer." DeeDee said to her mother. "I think Alice will say okay. She thought I was the best maid she ever had. The pools are big, together they are an Olympic sized pool with diving boards and...

Ann interrupted, "Have you asked her yet? And who else is going?"

"Not yet, Mom, but I will. Juan and Spacia are going and a bunch of other kids from school. It's going to be a lot of fun. We will wear our swim suits over there and then come back here to change if it's okay, and then go to Bob's Big Boy."

Ann was greatly relieved DeeDee confided in her. "I'll check with your father. Of course all the rules apply, but the curfew will be shorter. I want you home by 9:30."

"Ten?" DeeDee pleaded.

"9:45." Ann bargained.

"Yes! Yessss! Thanks, Mom!" DeeDee yelled. "I'll call Alice and then Mark right now."

"You better wait until morning," Ann said.

Ann felt guilty about not having to ask her bubbly daughter if Mark tried to kiss her. She already knew.

When Mark got home from his date with DeeDee, he saw the old porch swing gently moving with the warm breeze. He sat down to think about the evening. .He thought about DeeDee's father with all his questions. He closed his eyes and could still hear the sound of her laughter. He could feel her body pressed against his. She was warm, strong, graceful, so full of energy, yet her gentle touch gave him a sense of peace mixed with excitement. He shook his head in wonder and could not help but smile thinking of her. Then Mark became aware of a tightening in his stomach as a cloud covered the moon, and despite the heat, he shivered as he went inside to bed.

That Friday Mark arrived in a polished light grey 1947 Chevy with white wall tires. It had a brown grain dash and plush interior. DeeDee asked incredulously with a dropped jaw, "Is this new car yours?"

Mark's pride of ownership spoke before he did. "Yes, it's mine. All paid for - $250, but it isn't new. It's actually eight years old, but it only has 5,000 miles on it. I saved most of my earnings working as a busboy last summer. I've had my eye on it for a while but I just got it today."

"Wow!" DeeDee remarked. "It's beautiful." She felt privileged to be the first date in Mark's car. Spacia came out of her house about the same time that Ann joined everyone outside. Spacia was wrapped in a large towel, and barefoot. She asked the same question Ann had. "Where is everyone else? Whose cool car? Where's Juan?"

Mark answered, "It's mine. Juan will be here in a … whoa, here he is now," as Juan drove up in his blue Ford. "We will go pick up four others." Mark finished as Juan joined everyone. After all the oohs and aaws concerning

Mark's new car were over, Ann said, "Okay, it's past 6:30. Have fun." Ann reminded DeeDee, "See you at 9:30."

DeeDee had a stack of towels in her arms and wore a long t-shirt down to her knees. As she entered Mark's car, she yelled at her Mom, "See you this evening no later than 9:45."

Juan followed Mark and DeeDee as both cars pulled away. Ann waved goodbye, then considered…why would they need so many towels? Maybe just to protect Mark's new car.

The evening had begun. DeeDee didn't know what kind of a swim party it was going to be. Juan had arranged for a sophomore girl, Sue, and her date, a junior, Ron to join Mark and DeeDee. "That way," he told Mark, "DeeDee won't feel out of place with all seniors. Neither Sue, Spacia, nor DeeDee knew what was ahead of them: a crash, splash, and drive party.

The other couple in Juan's car was Lori and Lawrence. They had been going together for three years. Everyone thought they would be married before they graduated. They were known on campus as the "LoLaws."

The first stop was at The Inn. They arrived a little after 7 p.m. DeeDee felt really important going into the Inn to let Alice know that she was there to go swimming. Alice looked at the two cars containing seven other people, and said, "I thought it was just you and your date."

DeeDee's ever present smile faded. "When I called I didn't know for sure his friends were coming. Will it still be okay?" she asked.

"Well, look. The pool hours are over at 8 p.m. You have less than one hour, but don't hog the pool. Let the paying guests have priority." Then she repeated, "The lights go out at eight, and so do you, okay?'

DeeDee was relieved, "Thank you! Thank you! We will." And she ran out to tell everyone it was okay for them to go in.

Led by Juan, the eight teenagers ran to the pool, dropping their towels on the deck. Someone yelled, "Last one in buys the Big Boys!" All eight headed for the water, and entered the pool almost as a single splash. Water cut across the pool in a giant wave. The teen girls let out high pitched squeals as the boys began splashing water in each other's faces and showing off their wrestling skills. Some of the patrons were smiling at the teens. With the water levels rising and falling, the pool was full of energy and currents. Some of the other guests frowned and felt that their quiet and slow zones had been violated. They were starting to leave the poolside.

DeeDee noticed this and took Mark into one corner of the pool. "We need to be quieter. The manager said we need to be sure that we don't offend any guests."

Mark understood. "Give me your oversized t-shirt." As she began removing it, he jumped up on the low diving board, and in his strong voice said, "LADIES AND GENTLEMEN! May I have your attention please!" People on deck stopped talking. Others stopped leaving, and looked toward Mark to find where the voice was coming from. They listened.

Mark continued, "For your entertainment pleasure, my partner and I will present to you a diving contest on the high board. It will be a circus of trick diving unequaled in the whole state of Arizona."

There was a buzz in the pool. People got out and began drying themselves as their eyes remained on the diving board section of the pool. Mark motioned for Juan to come over as DeeDee handed Mark the t-shirt and said, "I can't dive unless belly flops count."

Juan asked, "Who? What? What are you talking about?"

"Look, we need to win these pool patrons over. You have several dives that are clean and impressive. You go up and do your dive. I will follow trying to beat your dive."

Juan, with a befuddled look said, "And this is going to win them over?"

"Yes, I'll be the clown like we did two years ago. Just do it! You'll see."

Juan and Mark swam every summer as kids. They loved to dive just for fun. One summer they put together a "good diver/clown diver" routine. They could have become competitive divers except both had to work during the summer as they got older.

"Okay," Juan said and climbed the ladder to the high dive. He stepped on the high diving board; the low sun glistening off his wet, tan body accentuated his physique. He took a deep breath waiting until the spectator tension began to rise. Then, in perfect form, he approached the end of the diving board raising his right leg and both arms to begin the spring that would lift him high above the pool where he would execute a clean and impressive jack knife. His body entered the water with barely a splash. The audience applauded.

Next, they saw a funny looking swimmer going up the high board wearing a wet baggy T-shirt. It was Mark. He mimicked Juan by exaggerating his every move. He stumbled on the board, then went back and started over. This time he raised his arm, then his leg. His spring was more of a jump up, but as he came down, his one leg missed the board, and he went over the side of the board head first, his arms at his side like a pelican diving for fish. His legs were bent behind him as he entered the water with a splat.

Initially, the spectators believed he might be hurt, but when he surfaced, he pumped his fist at the sky, and pulled himself out of the water. He took a bow as if he just completed a perfect 10 dive. Then he motioned for Juan to do his next dive. As Juan passed Mark to climb the ladder, Juan said, "I hope you know what you are doing?"

Juan went through his pre-dive routine. This time as he went high, his back arched and his arms spread out as his head went back. He executed a beautiful backward swan dive with another zero splash entry. People applauded as Juan got out of the pool.

The funny looking diver was already on the high dive. He lifted one foot, then the other. Then he repeated the same motion going faster, and faster. He was running in place, not going anywhere. Then he lifted his knees high and ran to the end of the board. He hit the end of the board with a spring that lifted him up and out over the pool. His legs continued to run cutting through the air as his head went back and he was in the upside down position, but his legs never stopped running as his hands were placed over the back of each hip, and his head entered the water, with a smack and a splash.

The pool patrons were now warmed to the entertainment. First, the perfect form, the perfect dive, followed by the clown, looking like a drunken bird with an unwarranted high opinion of itself.

Juan did an inward 1-1/2. The drunken big bird fainted, and fell backward on wobbly legs, head first into the pool.

Juan did an extra spring for greater height needed for

him to do a double with a 1-1/2 twist. Big bird, on his second spring, hit his derriere on the board propelling him into the air in a bent over sitting position with his legs spread pointing up. Before he hit the water, he rolled over and tucked his head over his knees to avoid the sting of a flat entry and possible injury.

The clown was clearly a good diver and the spectators responded with applause. After the entertainment, everyone enjoyed swimming. Some even tried the low board. Juan and Mark answered their questions and thanked them. At 8 pm, the lights blinked on and off. The pool was closing. People began leaving. DeeDee realized the date was almost over. She would be going home soon and she didn't even get to be close to Mark most of the evening.

She and the other girls used the restroom to dry off, pressing towels against their one piece swim suits. When they came out, the lights on the pool were off. The boys were waiting at the cars. Juan was talking to the boys, "Okay, for our crash, splash, and drive, what's it going to be, the Phoenix? Or the Arizona? Should we give the ladies a vote?" The boys were shaking their heads "no" when the girls walked up.

"That was fun," Lori said."

"But it passed so fast," DeeDee added.

Spacia looked at the boys. "What was all the head shaking about when we walked up?"

Juan spoke up, "We were just agreeing with you, lots of fun but too short."

"That's why we are going to do something about it. We are going to extend the play time." Mark said.

"How are we going to do that? The pool is closed," Spacia said.

"Not where we are going. It's time to change the rules!" Juan said as he headed toward his car with the LoLaws. "The Phoenix first." he yelled while he waited for them to get in. He opened the door to his blue Ford for Spacia, and then they sped off. Ron and Sue hurried to Mark's car. Mark got blankets out of his trunk. "My new car doesn't need a bath yet," he said as he laid the blankets down for Ron and Sue to sit on. Then he opened DeeDee's door. The moon light highlighted her smile and her laughing eyes. She was ready to get back in the car with Mark and prolong the date.

DeeDee moved over to Mark's side of the car and curled her arm around Mark's biceps. She put her head on his shoulder. Mark tilted his head toward hers. It was a perfect evening and the date wasn't over yet.

"Who was the last one in the pool at The Inn?" Ron asked.

"We all went in together!" DeeDee said, "That wave went all the way over to the other side of the pool."

"And that fat lady got knocked off her floating ducky." Sue chimed in.

"She was upside down," Ron added with laughter. "I thought we were going to get kicked out right then. That was quick thinking doing the clown diving show."

"So who is buying the Big Boys?" Mark asked.

"I'll buy the clown's. He earned it." Ron said. "Juan did a good job, too."

DeeDee was content to be close to Mark, to feel his strength, to savor every moment of their evening. Mark had never experienced these feelings of closeness and warmth before. Each time he was near DeeDee, his heart pulled him toward her. Yet that nearness also brought with it a growing knot in his stomach and a breathlessness that was beginning to feel like fear.

Mark took a deep breath and put all the feelings aside as he pulled away from the curb in pursuit of Juan. Sue spoke first, directing her question to Mark. "Maybe you wouldn't mind filling us in."

"Sure, what would you like to know?" Mark asked.

"What did Juan mean when he said "The Phoenix first?"

"That's where we are going first." Mark answered.

"Why?" D.D. asked.

"To go swimming," Mark answered.

"What if it is closed?" Sue asked.

"That's why we change the rules." Mark said.

"How do we do that?" Sue followed up.

Mark said, "Okay, listen. It is called crash, splash and drive. We park ½ block down the street; quietly let ourselves into the pool, sort of like crashing a party. Then we enter the pool, that's the splash, and then we quickly exit on a dead run to the car and drive to the next crash, splash, and drive destination."

"What if we get caught?" Sue was not smiling.

Mark said, "We haven't yet."

Ron spoke up, "I know what you are thinking. 'There is a first time for everything', but there is an answer for that, right Mark?"

Mark answered, "I've thought about it. I would prefer to give you the answer after we have done it because there is an extra adrenaline rush to help put everything into perspective, but look at it this way. What is a swimming pool for?"

"For swimming" the girls said in unison.

"What are we going to use it for?

"To swim," was the answer.

"All we have done then is change a rule. Why is there a rule? To prevent a lot of noise that disturbs someone's sleeping time. Are we going to be quiet? Yes. Why? Because we don't want to be caught, and we never are. But if we were, what would happen? We would be told that there is no swimming after 8 p.m. and that we should leave, which we would do. Are you in?"

Ron said, "I'm in."

DeeDee looked at Mark. Their eyes met. "I'm in if Sue is going to do it," she said.

Sue said, "I was just going to say I'm in if DeeDee is going to do it."

"That sounds like we are all going swimming," Mark said as he pulled in behind Juan's Ford. The senior crew in Juan's car was already to go. Spacia got out and went directly to DeeDee. They both smiled as they nodded yes. The excitement and the fright of getting caught sent adrenaline rushing through their bodies. Their breathing increased. Their legs were ready for a 100 yard dash.

Mark took DeeDee's hand. He led the group to the metal gate, and lifted the latch quietly. They filed in, dropped their towels on deck, and slipped into the water. All was quiet. Mark pretended to be dancing with DeeDee in the water as she went under his arm and twirled, then returned to his bare chest where she put her arms around his neck. He held her around the waist. The other couples created their own music and dance. Ron went under the water and came up under Sue and lifted her on his shoulders. Sue straddled his neck and shoulders. She couldn't help letting out a surprise squeal when she was raised above the water.

Mark saw a light go on in the office window. He

whispered to everyone, "Time to drive." They scurried to the ladders and stepped out of the pool drying themselves as they headed for the gate. Mark and DeeDee were the last ones through the gate. They heard someone say "Who's out there?" Holding hands they sprinted down the sidewalk overtaking the senior group. Mark opened the door so his passengers could just dive in while he started the car.

"Everyone in?"

"Everyone," someone said. Mark counted the doors slamming shut, and then peeled away from the curb in the direction of the Days Inn.

"That was close" Sue yelled. "Did you hear that man's voice?"

"He was right behind us!" DeeDee exclaimed, her heart still pounding.

"Why didn't he just turn on the lights?" Ron asked.

"He wouldn't do that," Mark said.

"Why not?"

"Guests would not like their dreams interrupted with flood lights." Mark replied. Mark reached over and took Dee Dee's hand. She was trembling. He held it tightly. With her other hand, she reached over and grabbed his forearm and pulled herself close enough to rest her head on his shoulder. She felt safe. She also learned what a new term meant. "Adrenaline rush." There was a mixture of fear, excitement, and sexuality that heightened all five of her senses.

The next splash and drive would not be so easy.

# Chapter 11

RON SAID," I HAVE never been to the Days Inn. What is their pool like?"

"It's accessible," Mark said. "For us, that's good. It's easy in, easy out. But there is a catch." Sue's and DeeDee's hearts skipped a beat.

"What catch?" Sue asked.

"Carl Jenson, last year's Student Body President worked at the Days Inn. He worked three nights a week doing quiet maintenance, such as checking the chemicals in the pools, cleaning the restrooms, walking the premises as a night watchman. Things like that. The catch is he isn't working there anymore."

"Who is?" DeeDee asked.

"I don't know. There is a 50/50 chance that the shift has changed to different days and different times. Or, that someone will be somewhere on the grounds nowhere near the pool."

"Can we find out?" Ron asked.

"Yes, when we get there, keep your eyes and ears open."

When both cars arrived, Mark gathered everyone around and explained the hazards associated with this crash, splash, and drive location. When he was finished answering all the questions, he said, "Are we all in?" as he put his fist in the center of the group. Each person put his hand over Mark's and whispered, "I'm in!"

Ron said, "I feel like we are going on a dangerous commando raid, but I'm in." There was muffled laughter as they moved down the block to the iron fence surrounding the pool.

At the gate, Mark held everyone up until they were completely still. He waited for three minutes. No flashlights, no sound, no movement. He had to tug twice before the latch lifted and the gate swung open.

"Let's go." he whispered.

The eight commandos were on high alert. There was 50 feet of lawn from the gate to the pool deck. They moved stealthily, and quickly dropped their towels when they reached the cement. They walked down the four steps into the water. DeeDee and Mark walked down slowly with her hand on top of his. When they touched the pool floor, Mark stepped behind DeeDee and put his hands on her elbows pulling her back to his chest as he gradually paddled a back stroke. DeeDee was riding with her back on his chest. Her head snuggled under his chin as they glided toward deeper water. When they reached the other side, they separated and grabbed the ladder. Mark put one arm around her waist and pulled her in close. He was looking into her eyes; their lips brushed each other lightly. Mark squeezed her hand and whispered, "We better go."

DeeDee was holding her breath, her lips eager. Mark swam away . She followed. It looked as if the seniors paired off and commanded their own private corners of the pool. Sue and Ron were sitting on the steps, the water covering their lower torsos. They watched Mark and DeeDee swimming toward them.

Mark, with just the tilt of his head, gave Ron the signal it was time to go. DeeDee was trying to find Spacia, but the pool was too dark. Mark took DeeDee's hand and walked her up the steps past Ron and Sue. He turned, looking for Juan and Spacia. They were not in the pool. The LoLaws broke apart and swam toward Mark. He gave them the come-on sign extending his arm and curling his hand toward his chest. At that moment, the serene evening quiet was shattered with Spacia screaming as water attacked her from all sides. Juan was there to put his arms around her and guide her off the lawn, but the automatic rainbird sprinklers machine-gunned strong staccato streams of water over the entire area. Laughing loudly, the seniors moved quickly through the battlefield to the other side. Mark took DeeDee across covering her head and face with his towel, then he returned for the others. When they reached the gate, they found Ron trying to lift the latch but it wouldn't budge. The five foot fence was designed to keep animals and small children out. But the seldom used gate was stuck, keeping the teen commandos in.

"Let's go over," Mark said. Juan faced Mark. They cupped their hands providing stirrups for two feet. They heard talking and looked back toward the pool. Two flashlights were searching the area.

"You go first," Mark said to Ron, "then Lawrence. I need you two to catch the girls." Both boys landed safely on the other side of the fence.

In turn the girls placed their feet in Juan and Mark's cupped hands and were catapulted over the fence coming down in the waiting arms of Ron and Lawrence.

The flashlights were getting closer. "I know someone was here," a voice said.

Mark put his hands on top of the five foot fence, and with one spring he vaulted to the other side. Juan had no trouble doing the same thing. The teen commandos sprinted to the waiting cars. Juan and Mark brought up the rear stopping only to pick up dropped towels, and someone's bra.

They piled into the cars laughing and talking all at the same time. It was pandemonium. When the noise finally started to diminish, Mark held up the bra and said, "Ron, I hope this isn't yours."

Sue gasped, "It's the LoLaws." More laughter and creative scenarios erupted about how the bra could have fallen off, followed by more laughter. "She had to loosen it to stuff in more toilet tissue." Or, "The light flashed with Lawrence's hand caught in the cookie bra." More laughter.

As they arrived at DeeDee's house to change out of their wet suits, they were talking nonstop, still excited from their adventure. Then they realized they needed to be careful not to give away the exciting parts.

As they were headed for the door again, DeeDee's mother asked, "Are you going to have time to go to Bob's Bigboy before your curfew?"

"If we just order from the car we can," Juan said.

After the stop at Bob's Bigboy, as everyone said goodbye, all the members of their unusual date agreed it was a lot of fun and worth every moment they had spent. Mark dropped DeeDee off last. He walked her to the front door. She turned and faced him. He gave her a warm embrace almost lifting her off the ground. DeeDee resisted the urge to kiss him rather than wait for him to kiss her first.

He set her down. Then he took each of her shoulders in his hands and held her at arms length. He studied her face and eyes, then brought her in close to him for another hug. He pushed her away and then turned abruptly and walked back to the car. DeeDee stood there, watching him leave. When he got to the car, he turned and blew her a kiss. Then he drove away.

Later as Mark was lying in his bed, he laughed out loud thinking of the carefree moments he and DeeDee had shared that evening. All the fun and excitement had been so rare in his life. He drifted off to sleep with the image of DeeDee standing on her porch, lips parted, waiting for that first kiss.

Two hours later Mark woke with clammy sweat dripping from his forehead, his breath short and ragged. Bolting upright, he reached out to find DeeDee. "No! No!" he yelled. He had to find her. He opened his eyes and began searching when he realized he was in bed and it had been a dream, a very real dream.

He and DeeDee had been driving near a sheer cliff by the ocean. The moon was full and the waves were crashing against the jagged rocks. Suddenly, a black figure with a large head stepped in front of his car. He braked and steered right onto the shoulder. The ground gave way and the car was free falling, turning over and over, down, down, down. He heard DeeDee scream as her car door opened and she fell into the dark churning sea.

There it was again, that empty feeling that always came after the dreams. It was always the same: helplessness, loss, intense loneliness. But this time it was about DeeDee and this time he decided he was not going to be alone anymore. DeeDee was his lifeline and he wasn't going to let fate take her away from him.

# Chapter 12

B Y THE TIME SCHOOL began in September, the word
was out. Mark and DeeDee were a couple. They dated
no one else. They went to movies, church, school dances,
and family functions together. They saw Burt Lancaster,
Tony Curtis, and Gina Lollobrigida in *Trapeze,* Deborah
Kerr in *The King and I*, and Gregory Peck and Kim Novak
in *The Man in the Gray Flannel Suit*. William Holden and
Kim Novak in a scene from *Picnic* showed them how to
kiss. They won the prize waltz at a school formal. Always,
they met her parent's curfew.

DeeDee's mother continued her vigilant peering
through the parted Venetian blinds when Mark walked
DeeDee to the door and gave her a hug, then turned
around and walked away. In small increments the hug
became longer than five seconds.

One night after a football game, Mark looked into
DeeDee's eyes and felt that familiar little girl at Wilson
Grade School looking up at him. She was no longer a
little girl. He didn't know why, but he was afraid to kiss
her even though he was passionately in love with her. For
him, that haunting fear dared him to kiss her, to risk a
connection that could leave him falling into the darkness

of his dreams with no one, nothing to hold on to. He looked again into those deep brown eyes, into her very soul and he knew he had to take the chance. He saw the lifeline that would anchor him when the freefalling despair crept in.

He tilted his head to the right, she did the same as they looked into each others eyes, and brought their lips together. Hers were full, warm, and eager. Suddenly, he felt a strong adrenaline rush. Earlier in the evening, the Panthers had just beaten West High, and he now had faced another foe within. He turned and ran toward his car, then with a loud, "Yahoo!" he leaped in a single bound over the hood of his car.

Startled at first, DeeDee saw and felt his exuberance. Her lips mouthed the words that her heart produced, "I love you!" she said silently as she watched him drive away.

The Panthers were state champions that year in 1956. Football scouts were in touch with Juan who had the choice of several schools. The Army also actively sought after him to play football at West Point. The rest of his senior year was crowded with scouts vying for his attention. Along with several other coeds, Juan continued to date Spacia, but less and less frequently until they finally decided that dating others exclusively was a good idea. Spacia had taken notice of one of the wrestlers, and wanted to be free once she caught his eye.

Mark was now wrestling which took him away on some Fridays when the team traveled to Yuma or Tucson. He watched the dynamic develop between Spacia and Barry, a one hundred eighty-one pound senior. Spacia would walk by the team members after a match and would congratulate them all, but each time she did it, she would pause a little longer with Barry and mention a particular take down that he used and how well he executed it. She caught his attention with all the terminology she mastered. Soon they were dating.

When Barry learned that Spacia and DeeDee were close friends, he suggested that Mark and he double date for a New Year's Eve celebration. Barry was much like Mark regarding alcohol. Nothing good ever comes from it, and you can have a lot more fun without the headaches.

The high school band was giving an end of the year concert at the high school which would last until 10 p.m. The non-drinking seniors were then going over to the La Cucaracha Mexican food restaurant until midnight to see the new year in. Mark's reputation as a strict teetotaler convinced DeeDee's parents that they did not have to worry about him drinking at anytime, and they were going with Spacia and Barry, two more nondrinkers. Her parents agreed as long as DeeDee called her parents right after midnight and was home before 12:30. The date was on.

When Mark picked up DeeDee, she had Barry and Spacia join them for hot apple cider. Ray talked about all the drunks on the road and how dangerous it was. Mark mentioned how the school had a special assembly for a program by the Drivers Ed teacher on how to drive defensively. Mark then revealed how he lost a sister to a drunk driver and that's why he was extra cautious. Her parents also took into account that DeeDee was 15 years old, and could stay up for a New Years Eve celebration. Both young men were nondrinkers and wrestlers who could protect their daughter.

When they arrived at the Mexican restaurant, the

parking lot was full. They drove down the street a block and found a place to park. In walking back they had to pass a dark alley. As they approached, a twenty year old Mexican man stepped out in front of the two couples. When they tried to go around him, three others stepped out of the alley. Mark and Barry placed the girls behind them and got ready for a fight. Both Mark and Barry had heard about the pachuco gangs and knew this wasn't going to be easy. The gangs usually had switchblades and other weapons. Nonetheless, both Barry and Mark knew that with their speed and knowledge, they could neutralize two of them right away, but they preferred not having to do that.

Mark whispered to Barry, "Left to right, four of them. 1.2.3.4."

"Where are you going?" the leader of the gang asked?

Mark wanted to reduce the tension, and if that didn't work, he would confuse the leader so that Barry and Mark would be the ones to strike first. Mark faced the leader, staying about five feet away. Two of the gang members stood slightly behind the leader and on his left. The other on his right. Mark spoke up, "To the La Cucaracha. It's the best Mexican food in Arizona. Come on and go with us. We will treat you."

The leader shook his head 'no' as he reached into a deep pocket of his pants and moved closer to Mark.

Mark said, "OK. Then we will get some take out for you. Right, Barry? Take out number two?"

Barry, with his big fist of iron, hit the leader with a right cross that spun his head around and he staggered back. Three other gang members, who had remained in the shadows, stepped out. Mark faced them to protect Barry's flank.

Suddenly, there was a flashing red light and a shrill siren as a squad car pulled up. The gang members took off back down the dark alley full speed. The two officers got out and asked if everyone was all right.

"You got here in the nick of time." Mark said. "We're heading for La Cucaracha. Phoenix High has a party happening there."

"We will escort you," the officers said.

Mark thought for a second and then asked if he could drive his car back to the restaurant and park in the "loading zone only" without a ticket. That way his car would be safer and so would their dates.

The officer said, "It's a good idea. I'll tag your car so no other officer will bother it. We will keep an eye on the restaurant." the officer said as he was shining his flashlight on the ground. "It looks like you met up with Dr. Cuchillo. That's Spanish for knife. Whose blood is on the pavement?

Did the Dr. use his scalpel on anyone?"

"He had his hand in his pocket when Barry dropped him with a right cross," Mark answered. "He might be hurting too much to come back tonight but we will keep an eye out for him."

DeeDee felt secure, safe, and loved. New Years came in with a bang and howls, from sober high school students who counted the clock down. They let go with horns, noisemakers, and confetti bombs. There were hugs, kisses, and dancing to Olde Lang Syne. DeeDee made her call to her parents.

The new year had begun. It would bring many changes.

# Chapter 13

THE SCHOOL YEAR MOVED rapidly. Weekend dances and dates gradually increased the feelings Mark and DeeDee were having for each other. The more they saw each other, the more they felt the need to be together. The time they shared was the happiest Mark had ever been. He looked forward to every day, holding hands, the stolen kisses, the quiet moments just looking into each other's eyes. The nights were a different story.

Mark often awoke from his same nightmare: the cliff, the dark shrouded figure, DeeDee falling out of his car as they dropped to the jagged rocks and ocean below. By now it was familiar and not as frightening. Still, the hopelessness and fear he felt were real.

One night after being awakened by a particularly real nightmare, Mark got up, walked to the refrigerator, drank some water, and got back in bed. "Okay," he thought to himself, "How would it be possible for me to lose DeeDee? She is too healthy to get sick and die. A car accident is always a possibility, but she rides with me most of the time. I'll be extra careful. How else could I lose her? Of course! I could lose her to someone else. If I'm in college and she is a sophomore in high school, there are plenty of opportunities for her to meet someone there, someone she shares a class with, maybe they even study together. She is more attractive, more mature. Those Levis she was wearing last week were tight, almost like billboard advertising. I don't think she should wear Levis anymore. I'll tell her tonight when I pick her up for the dance." Then he fell asleep, but his dream continued. DeeDee got lost. He couldn't find her. There she was with another boyfriend walking away from him. Mark woke up again with salty tears running down his cheeks, and the icy fingers of loneliness tearing at his heart.

That feeling stayed with Mark into the morning hours and all day at work. He would definitely talk to DeeDee about wearing those Levis before the dance. Mark picked up DeeDee right on time. She was her usual bubbly self. She noticed Mark was not smiling. When she asked if he was ready to do the new chicken dance craze, he said, "No."

"Are you tired? Was it a big day at the market?" she asked.

Looking straight ahead, Mark said, "No."

DeeDee tried again, "It was just a joke. I know you must have cut up 60 cases of chickens today. We don't have to dance at all. Honest."

"No, I've been thinking about something else," Mark said. "I don't think you should wear Levis."

"Oh, no, I'm not wearing Levis to the dance. See?" DeeDee said as she pulled her coat open to show her dress.

"No, I'm talking about all the time." Mark answered.

DeeDee still couldn't understand. "You mean my old ones, with the stain? Don't worry! I threw those away.

That's why I bought the new pair. They are a perfect fit. I love my new Levis."

"I'm talking about all Levis." Mark made it clear. "They are like an advertisement to every guy at P.H.S. that you are available."

"Oh, you never ever, ever have to worry about that." DeeDee assured him. "That's silly."

"I'm not silly. I know how guys think." Mark said angrily.

"I don't mean you are silly. It's just crazy to think I would do anything with someone else," DeeDee said in exasperation.

"Crazy, silly? I don't care! Do not wear Levis anymore!" Mark said in a stentorian voice.

DeeDee was getting flushed with anger. "All the girls wear Levis," she countered. "That doesn't make us sluts."

"I don't care about other girls. You will not wear those anymore. Understand?" Mark's tone was demanding and demeaning. He seethed with anger. There was silence as they arrived at the dance. Mark asked as he parked at the curb, "Do we have an understanding?"

"No!" DeeDee answered as she opened the door and got out. Mark got out on his side, stood on the running board of the car and looked over the roof as DeeDee began walking away.

"If you go in there, we are through!" Mark yelled to her as DeeDee kept walking. "Is that what you want?"

DeeDee nodded yes as she entered the dance hall.

Mark tried to dig out in anger, but his forty-seven Chevy didn't have the horses. He was blurry eyed, unable to think straight, burning with anger. He paid no attention to a light that had just turned red as he entered the intersection and then did a wide right turn.

The motorcycle officer right behind Mark did notice and came up along side him motioning him over to the side.

Mark's face had all the signs of anguish. The police officer knew something had just happened. After looking at Mark's driver's license, the officer said, "Where were you just a few minutes ago?" as he pulled his citation book out.

Mark let it all out. "My girlfriend and I just broke up and I didn't want to lose her!"

The officer listened to the whole story, then said, "You know, when I was about your age I got worried about my girlfriend going away to college. I was afraid I would lose her. So I gave her an ultimatum, me or that college. We fought and she walked away. I never saw her again. It took me many years to find someone else as smart and beautiful as she was. You don't show your love for someone by yanking a chain around their neck. Do you like how she looks in Levis?"

"She looks great!" Mark said.

"That's why she is wearing them. They are for you." The officer put his ticket pad back in his pocket. "No ticket this time if you promise two things: First, you stay alert and obey the rules of driving at all times. Second, go get that girl back."

Mark sat for a while thinking. He envisioned his life without DeeDee. What was the fear about? It was about being afraid to love someone for fear of losing them. If he didn't take the chance, he would lose her for sure. At that moment Mark decided it was worth the risk.

"You are right, Officer. Thank you for helping me see the light. I'll go get her. Thank you! Thank you!"

He was so relieved he almost broke the first rule. He started to make a u-turn in the middle of the street and race back to the church. He stopped, took a deep breath and eased back on to the road. The church was only a block away.

When he pulled up to the church, DeeDee was sitting outside on the steps crying. Mark got out, she looked up, and they both ran to each other's outstretched arms.

"C'mon, let's go where we can talk," Mark said. His tears mixed with hers as they both sat as close together as they possibly could. Mark drove to Encanto Park where he guided them to the bridge linking two lagoons. Mark lifted her like a bride crossing the threshold and put her down when they reached the halfway point. There, they declared their love for each other over and over. He loved and trusted her with his heart. This trust deepened and changed their relationship.

# Chapter 14

T HE CHANGES WERE SUBTLE as far as DeeDee and Mark were concerned. Mark thought he was behaving in the same respectful, gentlemanly manner toward DeeDee as he did on the first night he met her. Dee Dee's parents saw something else. Mark and DeeDee were seeing too much of each other. They were always making contact with their shoulders standing side by side, or holding hands all the time, or looking deeply into each other's eyes. The goodnight kiss lingered past the five second limit. Ann continued to be the watchful mother peering through the Venetian blinds.

When Ray stayed after church for a meeting one Sunday, Ann decided it was the perfect time for a mother-daughter talk. Ann asked DeeDee to help her cut up apples to put in a pie for Sunday dinner.

As Ann started the crust and DeeDee was busy peeling apples, Ann said, "That sign language you and Mark are using in church looks interesting. What does it mean when you hold up your pinkie?"

DeeDee smiled, "It's an 'I'. Mark learned it when he worked with a deaf meat cutter who gave him a card with the whole alphabet of signs."

"So you spell out words?" Ann asked.

"Yes, we say funny things about what is going on. This morning in church I signed to Mark 'I hope Sister Ellis doesn't sing.' Then he signed back 'You mean screech, don't you?' I signed, 'Yes, she seems to be in pain.' Mark signed to me, 'It's us who are in pain.'"

Ann tried to hold back a smile knowing most of the congregation saw Sister Ellis' singing in a similar light. But when she had noticed the signing she had other thoughts. DeeDee's mother had imagined more personal words of love and longing, words of plans for the future, ominous messages worthy of such secrecy.

"Some things, like church, should be serious." Ann said. "Other things, like your relationship with Mark, should be fun and casual."

"It is fun. We laugh a lot. It's not stiff and formal." DeeDee said.

"By casual, I mean not so serious." Ann explained.

"Serious about what?" DeeDee asked, beginning to understand where the conversation was going.

"You and Mark! At your age you should be dating others and branching out to learn more about life outside of Mark." Ann said as she caught herself almost yelling. She took a deep breath and spoke more slowly, "When you are older, you will have grown enough to be thinking seriously about a young man."

"You mean like the way you and Daddy did?" DeeDee said defensively.

"That was different back then. Girls matured faster and married earlier." Ann argued. "You can't compare the two."

Nonetheless that is exactly what Ann did after DeeDee had silently finished the apples and asked to be excused.

Ann started thinking about those early days with Ray. They were exciting times. The sound of his name made her smile. The warmth in his eyes sent her pulse racing. And when he kissed her... Her little girl certainly was not ready for those feelings.

Mark wrestled his way into the State Finals which were held at Phoenix High School on Friday afternoon and all day Saturday. His parents had never attended any of the matches. His father had taken a part time job and couldn't get off work to catch the dual matches after school. His mother didn't drive. His brother had a girlfriend and other priorities. DeeDee was a welcome sight at all the matches during the year.

DeeDee wanted to be there for both days for the entire time, but her mother objected, saying, "You are seeing too much of Mark." It was the first time that Mark knew there was a problem.

Because of his undefeated record, Mark got a bye for the first two rounds and then would wrestle the next two rounds, but the finals on Saturday would be a big day. He was disappointed that DeeDee was going to be busy with a babysitting job until the evening finals. He brushed it off with, "Well, that's okay, other people have lives, and if DeeDee's mother committed DeeDee to a job, then that's the way it is. I shouldn't expect the world to stop just for me. I just have to stay focused." He won both his matches on Friday with pins. He didn't get home until 9:30. When he called DeeDee, her mother answered. "DeeDee's babysitting job is an overnighter. She won't be home until Saturday afternoon."

Mark said, "I know she can't have any calls while she

is working. Will you let her know that I won my matches and that I have four more to go before making it into the finals?"

"Yes, I will tell her, and she will be at the gym for the evening finals."

On Saturday, he didn't call DeeDee. He was busy with wrestling opponents. Mark dispensed with four opponents: Three pins, one superior decision and he was in the finals. That evening, he would face the Yuma wrestler, a formidable, well built opponent with strength, and an undefeated record.

Mark watched the Yuma wrestler earlier in the day, and decided he could be out-wrestled psychologically. Mark was in the best condition he had ever been in. He planned his strategy, imagined moves and counter moves, and concluded his best chance would be to become the "buzz saw." The buzz saw wrestler was incessant right from the beginning. Every move he would make had a follow up move to accompany it and then another, right after that one. His opponent would not get an opportunity to execute an offensive move. He would always be on the defensive or backing away, or being cautious. Mark had the speed and the conditioning to keep this strategy in place the entire match. He would avoid going head to head or trying to match his strength against the Yuma wrestler's. To do so would give away valuable information. His opponent would find out that he was stronger than Mark.

Before the match, Mark looked around the sold-out gym. Excitement was building as the parents and friends of the wrestlers were drawn into the matches, yelling encouragement, hugging the winners, consoling the less skilled. Mark didn't see DeeDee, but he couldn't let that derail him as they called his championship match to begin.

No points were scored by either wrestler in the first period. Mark kept his adversary on the defensive, giving him no opportunity to execute a single offensive move. By the second period, Mark felt his opponent was getting tired. Mark started in the top position. The other wrestler got down on his hands and knees. Mark carefully went down on his knees over the Yuma wrestler, placing his right hand under his opponent's stomach and his left hand on the wrestler's forearm.

When the referee blew the whistle to start the action, Mark allowed his opponent to escape and get the first point. Still, the Yuma wrestler didn't know Mark's strength, but the unexpected easy first point caused him to worry that Mark was going to put some move on him that he couldn't defend.

It was time for Mark to lock up for the first time using both hands to force his opponent's head down and over to one side. His opponent got the message: Mark was in better condition. Now it was time to get his opponent to over-react out of fear. Mark went for his opponent's left leg knowing he would jerk it back so fast that he would have his right leg squarely on the mat. That's the leg Mark was targeting. He snatched an ankle and brought it up high forcing the Yuma wrestler to hop around on one leg trying to run off the mat. Mark, with both hands firmly gripping one leg, pulled him back to the center of the mat. Then Mark elevated the leg to his own shoulder trapping it there with both hands. He watched the footwork as the Yuma wrestler hopped up and down. When the single leg was off the mat, Mark gave the leg he was holding a quick strong tug and jerk which brought his opponent to the mat for a two point take down. Mark rode, easily staying in the top position, for the rest of the period.

In the third period, Mark was confident he could escape. No opponent all year was able to ride Mark for more than fifteen seconds. With his escape, Mark led the match three to one.

The Yuma wrestler heard his coaches yelling, "Go get him! You get the take down. Now! Go after him. Go get him!"

Thinking there were no personal fans of his own to encourage him, Mark used the Yuma coach's energy to double activate his own body. It was Mark who went after his opponent. Rather than play a cat and mouse game until the end of the match, it was Mark who seriously went after take downs. He finished the match with a take down and a winning score of five to one.

# Chapter 15

DEEDEE WAS THERE TO watch the final match. She sat with Mark's father who was finally able to get off work in time to be there. They waited until the picture taking was done, and the trophy and medals were awarded to surprise Mark. Mark's shocked expression changed to pure joy when they rushed to his side. Mark's father grabbed his son's arm and held on with both hands as he beamed with pride over his son's accomplishments. It was the first time Mark remembered really feeling his father's love.

When it was all over and the wrestlers cleared the gym of all the mats, Mark was free to go. He took her by the hand and put his other arm around his father's shoulder. "Let's go out to eat." he said. For a wrestler who no longer needed to diet to make weight, that was the top priority.

After two of Bob's Big Boys and a chocolate shake, Mark took his father back to the car he came in, gave him a hug, and watched him drive away. He then turned to DeeDee. "We need to talk," he said.

DeeDee sensed doom and gloom. It showed in her face. Mark read the response and said, "Wait a minute. When you stop smiling, there has to be a serious reason.

Let me rephrase it. I missed you Friday and most of Saturday. We need to catch up."

DeeDee's smile returned. "I'm sorry I couldn't come earlier, but my mother's best friend needed to go to Tucson for her mother's funeral and she didn't want to take her daughter with her, so Mom volunteered me to baby-sit. I missed you too."

Mark opened the car door for DeeDee. She slipped in all the way to Mark's side. When he got in, he found her snuggled close to his shifting arm. He lifted that arm to go over her shoulders and pulled her in closer to him. She looked up anticipating his parted lips pressing against hers. The kiss said, "I did indeed miss you."

"Where to now?" Mark asked.

"Well, it's going to be curfew time in forty-five minutes."

"How about we take a walk in Encanto Park? The lights are on until ten o'clock."

When they got to the park, DeeDee took Mark's arm and began their stroll into the park. They walked to the arched bridge connecting two of the lagoons. Mark stopped DeeDee at the top of the bridge and stood behind her as they looked at the rising moon. Mark started the conversation. "All of the seniors are waiting for replies of acceptance to a college of their choice. I haven't been a straight A student but with the state champion award in wrestling and football and my B+ average, I think I could get a scholarship from BYU."

"That's in Utah." DeeDee said. "Why not someplace closer, even Tucson?"

"What I am thinking about is applying to three schools and see what turns up. I also thought about

Phoenix College for two years and then transfer to ASU."
Mark said.

"I don't want you to leave," DeeDee said as a tear
started to well up.

Mark turned DeeDee toward him. He saw tears
rolling down her cheeks. Looking into her eyes, he said,
"That's what I wanted to be sure about. You see, I am in
love with you. I want us to be together forever."

"Oh, Mark, how could you not know? I love you
with all my heart." They kissed, this time for as long as
they wanted. When their lips parted, their bodies came
together. Mark could feel her warmth coming through
his clothes. She could feel his warmth rising. They kissed
again, each whispering to the other, "I love you. I love
you so much."

# Chapter 16

ASSURED OF THEIR LOVE, Mark was now on a mission. He would go to the junior college majoring in pre-dental. In just a little over three years, Dee Dee would be eighteen years old. Many girls were getting married at eighteen. If he worked extra overtime, he would begin a savings account making graduation and marriage more of a possibility in four years. By then he would be making journeyman's wages and have enough to get through dental school.

At the grocery store Mark began putting in long hours. He didn't mind the work, but he wasn't happy with the straw bosses that were put in charge after the meat department manager left for home.

One such straw boss, Jack, six feet tall and 240 soft pounds, made a remark to Mark: "When I call for everyone to go out front and wait on customers, I want you hustling or I'll have to start kicking your ass."

Mark, who thought he was joking, replied, "You and who else?"

"I won't need anyone else," Jack glared at Mark.

"You wouldn't get a chance. In two minutes you would

be lying on your back looking up at the sky wondering what happened," Mark smiled as he said it.

"Oh, yeah," Jack said, "how about we find out tomorrow at lunch time?"

Mark, realizing that Jack was serious, thought for a moment before he decided the only way to stop the bullying was to face him. Mark said, "It's fine with me. Across the street at the grassy side of South Park at high noon." Mark emphasized the time.

Another employee heard the challenge, and it didn't take long for the word to travel throughout the entire store. "Jack and Mark are going to fight at noon tomorrow." Everyone was talking about it, and bets were taken.

Mark said nothing to DeeDee about the challenge. No one at the meat department knew Mark was a state wrestling champion. DeeDee knew, but in her mind the match up would be like David and Goliath.

At noon the next day, Mark walked across the street to a shady section of the park behind a tall stand of cottonwood trees, an open space that was hidden from view from the busy street. All the employees who could get away from work and Jack were already there when Mark arrived.

Mark was surprised when the meat department manager, Bill, stepped forward away from the crowd. "The challenge was that Mark would put Jack's back to the ground before Jack can kick Mark's ass. Did I state that correctly?" He looked at Mark and Jack. They both nodded.

"Good. Everyone form a ten foot circle." Bill was going to turn this event into something positive for the store's employees and not let it breed bad blood by letting it get out of hand. He held both Jack and Mark at arm's length and said, "Let the games begin." Then he stepped away.

Jack immediately lunged forward with a kick toward Mark's thigh. Mark side stepped and caught Jack's leg with his right arm. He then ducked his head under Jack's right arm as he reached up with his left hand and firmly gripped Jack's triceps. The fireman's carry was complete. He lifted Jack off the ground and slammed him to his back where Jack lay looking up at the sky wondering how he got there.

Bill waited for two minutes while Jack struggled unsuccessfully to get out of Mark's grasp. Bill then announced, "The challenge goes to Mark." Bill made them shake hands.

Everyone was amazed how quickly Mark executed the move. They crowded around him asking how he learned the technique. "Was that jujitsu? Kung Fu?" "How did you do it? Show us."

Mark answered, "I wrestled in high school."

'Did you win all your matches?" they asked.

"In my senior year, I took state."

Bill spoke up, "Okay, everyone back to work." When only Jack and Mark were left, Bill said, "You never told anyone about your wrestling, Mark. I need to talk to you and Jack about an idea I have. Take an extra hour off for lunch and then I'll talk to you tonight after work."

When Mark punched his time card that night, Jack was right behind him. Bill came into the office. "As you know we have been having a lot of vandalism and theft in our parking lot at night. The police department is spread too thin to help us out. I have an idea but I'll need your help. Are you interested?'

Mark spoke up, "If it means catching whoever punctured Jack's tires two weeks ago, I'm interested."

Jack looked at Mark for a moment, puzzlement on his face, and then he nodded. After all that had happened, Mark was in his corner. Jack was happy to be included with Mark as a member of the new taskforce chosen by Bill. "If Mark and me get our hands on those assholes, we will turn them upside down and rearrange their faces," he said.

Bill saw humor in Mark's eyes as he said, "Good! Now here is what I propose..."

# Chapter 17

Bill's face was serious. "To stop these guys, we need two things: a sentry and two backups who can instantly be in the parking lot on a moment's notice,"

Jack said, "We won't need a sentry or any other kind of weapon when we get our hands on them."

Bill quickly looked at Mark. Mark said, "Who do you have in mind for a lookout and how will he communicate with us inside?"

Bill said, "Carlos has a thirteen year old little brother we could put on the roof after dark with a string attached to a cowbell inside the meat store. The roof is flat. He could be out of sight lying behind the two foot high roofline when he rings the bell. Jack, you would leave through the south end exit. Mark through the north exit. Converge in the middle of the lot and see what you catch. What do you think?"

"When do we start?" Mark said.

"Yeah," Jack said, "Which door do you want me to take?"

"The one you always come through after you park your car. Mark will exit the double doors where the beef is." Bill explained. "We will be ready by next Thursday."

Next Thursday came and went, as did Friday. No activity in the parking lot. Mark and Jack forgot about the whole plan.

Mark had more pressing things on his mind. To commemorate that evening when he and DeeDee talked about their future together at the Encanto Park bridge and declared their love for each other, Mark bought a music box for her. It played *Some Enchanting Evening*. They ended every date by playing the music box as they said good-bye on the porch. Her parents would hear the music and know DeeDee would be coming in the house soon. They continued to watch Mark and DeeDee's relationship. It was not wilting. It was growing, changing, becoming. As far as they knew, the young couple never fought. There were no sad times.

On Saturday Mark always tried to get off early so that he could take Dee Dee to the Saturday night church dances. It was growing dark and the Saturday rush at the store was starting to calm down. Suddenly the trend was shattered by cacophony. At first, Mark didn't know what all the clanging was about. Then he remembered the cow bell. When he saw Jack heading toward the south exit, Mark quickly pushed the north exit door wide open, hitting a Mexican man in the face. The man stumbled back and fell to the ground.

Mark looked into the parking lot and saw a man getting up from kneeling next to one of the parked cars. Mark instantly bolted for the man who dropped a hammer and hubcap and took off down the street. He passed Jack coming out of the south exit as Jack looked both ways and then ran to the north exit. The suspect Mark was chasing ran to 16th Street and turned right. Mark followed bursting with adrenaline. As he turned on 16th Street, he saw his fugitive duck down a side street. The moonless night and poor street lights made Mark depend on his hearing as he made a left turn. He could hear someone going over a metal wired fence and then running. He followed as his suspect climbed another fence and then ran into a yard but could not find a way out. Mark ran full speed at the suspect who now stood on the poor owner's small wooden porch. The suspect's back was against the screen door as he turned to face Mark with something in his right hand. Mark did not stop and instinctively grabbed the man's wrist with his left hand and delivered a fist into the suspect's solar plexus. They both slammed into the screen door shaking the house with a clattering bash as they fell to the porch. Mark saw that his suspect was a sixteen year old boy holding a screw driver.

The owner opened the house door and yelled at Mark through the screen door, "Let him go! I'm calling the police. Let him go!"

Mark stood up, his white meat cutter's apron in full view. "Please do call the police. I caught him breaking into a car."

The man continued to misread what was happening. "Let him go!"

Mark picked the boy up and slipped a chicken wing wrestling hold on him and began the walk back to the market. When he got to 16th Street where there was a little more light, Mark made sure he had good control of his captive, with only about 500 more feet to go.

As he crossed 16th Street, three young men approached Mark. He learned then that all those Hollywood fights where one assailant comes first and the others wait while the hero disposes of the first one, then turns to take on the next one while the others wait before joining in, were bogus. Mark pushed his 16 year old captive toward two of them and then got one good punch in just as a car swung in and screeched to a halt. A Mexican man with his family jumped out of his car and began yelling at those young hoodlums in Spanish. They froze saying nothing and backed away. The man continued to voice his anger as Mark decided this would be a good time to travel the final 500 feet to the store.

One of the young meat cutters, Jimmy, came out from the lot when he saw Mark. Mark explained what happened. Jimmy asked where they went. Mark said, "They came out of Roth's Tasty Shop."

Jimmy said, "Let's go see if they are still there."

Mark hesitated and then talked himself into it. The kid broke the law and needed to feel what it's like to be caught. "Let's go."

When they got to Roth's, the 16 year old fugitive was standing outside with a big smile telling a friend all about what had happened. Jimmy went up behind him, slipped a full nelson on him, and turned him to Mark. "Is this the kid that broke into my car? Teach him a lesson. At least give him a bloody nose." Jimmy held him tight. "Go ahead," he said, "hit him."

What Jimmy couldn't see was the rest of the gang members, about twenty of them, who came out of nowhere, standing behind Jimmy. They had chains, clubs, and switchblades.

"Go ahead," Jimmy urged, "do it. Do it!"

Mark said, "I don't think that's something we will do right now. Look behind you."

As Jimmy turned, a loud deafening blast from a shotgun had everyone ducking. Joe Roth, the owner of the Tasty Shop, knew that what was about to happen would not be good for business.

"The police are on their way. Everyone leave, go, get out of here. It's the police or my shotgun. Leave now!" he yelled as he waved his shotgun.

Jimmy let go of his captive and joined Mark in a quick retreat to the grocery store. No suspects were caught. All got away, but the damage to just one car made Bill's plan a success. As a result of the evening's adventure, the cowbell never had to ring again.

By the time Mark got cleaned up, he arrived late for his date with Dee Dee.

# Chapter 18

MARK HAD LITTLE TIME to read the papers or get involved in politics. Forty to forty-five hours a week cutting meat and three classes every semester barely allowed him to date DeeDee. Their time together became more precious.

His classes in psychology, chemistry, zoology, and nutrition made him more aware of what being human meant. Even his required language class in German gave him a look into another culture and other ways of seeing the world. These new perspectives shined a light on a world that was far removed from the South Phoenix ghetto.

He began questioning some of the basic precepts of the Mormon Church. He stopped attending Sunday school and sacrament meetings at Fourth Ward. Then the ward teachers came to his home, probably at his Mother's insistence, to see how he was doing.

He posed questions to them, "Why in the first Article of Faith, does it say 'We believe that man is punished for his own sins and not for Adam's transgressions' and yet, according to the church, Negroes are punished with a black skin for what Cain did to Able. Shouldn't they get the same pass that we got from Adam's transgressions?"

The ward teachers said it was a good question, but they didn't know the answer. They would find someone who knew the answer, and that knowledgeable church leader would call him.

Mark was surprised one evening two weeks later when a stake president knocked on his door in south Phoenix to deliver the answer regarding black skinned people. He said, "Before God created the earth, there was a big meeting in heaven to plan what was going to happen on earth. God wanted to give everyone their freedom of choice to do right or wrong. Satan, the contrary angel, wanted to force people to do right. So there was a vote, and one third of the host of heaven voted for God's plan, one third voted for Satan's plan, and one third couldn't make up their minds. That one third, for being indecisive was cursed with black skin when they came to Earth."

The grey haired distinguished looking church messenger seemed pleased that he was able to answer that bothersome question. He had a radiant smile and suggested that they have a word of prayer before he left. Mark went along with the idea, keeping his thoughts to himself when Brother Jensen thanked God for "coming into this house to clarify the truthfulness of the Gospel, and for helping Brother Stephens raise the question so that he too could become a missionary for your gospel and, spread the truth."

Mark became more convinced of the direction he was moving in. The concept of God that many of the churches had, including Mormons, was demeaning and probably wrong. Their God had all the characteristics of ignorant uneducated people. Their God was wrathful, angry, jealous. Their God had no concept of psychology and how the mind and body worked, no concept of evolutionary history, no idea about the various chemicals that cause mood swings, etc. The war in heaven that produced blacks sounded like a child's tale. With that explanation, Mark took another giant leap away from the church.

When Brother Jensen's prayer was done, Mark said, "Thank you for coming. You have made everything much clearer for me." From that day on, classes that shed light on the human condition, and on the great thinkers, past and present, charged him with a passionate search for truth. He was not interested in the limited variety handed down from an atavistic period full of ignorance and superstition, and lacking in the modern sciences of the twentieth century.

At the time, he had no idea that in the next thirty years this same church would be champions against racial discrimination and would be highly respected in the world for its dedication to providing the highest level of education in its many universities.

DeeDee and Mark seldom discussed the religious issue because they were so happy to be together that their topics of interest involved their plans for the future, such as their day to day efforts trying to eke out more opportunities to be together. Mark would attend DeeDee's church just to be with her. Usually he would be invited to have dinner with her family after church. That gave him and DeeDee another hour or so to stand close together, hold hands, or take a walk around the block.

Unfortunately, DeeDee's parents had more opportunities to observe the tell tale signs of a creeping intimacy that threatened the plan they hoped would pan out. That plan was supposed to provide DeeDee with her first boyfriend, the inevitable break up, their consoling love for her easing the heartache, and then her recovery with a more mature knowledge of what real love means.

Instead, Mark came over as often as he could to have DeeDee help him study for a test, or he helped her. Or, he and DeeDee washed her parent's car and Mark's car every weekend at her house. They knew if both got involved in a church play, they would get to rehearse together and see each other more often.

# Chapter 19

AFTER THE CHURCH PLAY, Mark took DeeDee out for ice cream. This gave Ray and Ann an opportunity to discuss DeeDee and Mark Stephens. Using the last name put him in another category other than "close friend."

"Did you know Mark Stephens is no longer going to Fourth Ward?" Ann asked Ray.

"That's because he is over here all the time." Ray said.

"But he is not a member of our ward, and I've heard that he is critical of the church. He has some funny ideas, and he keeps quoting scientists or some way-out theory like us coming from monkeys." Ann complained. "He has changed and I don't think it's good for DeeDee."

Ray was aghast. "He believes in that nonsense about monkeys?"

"Yes," Ann said, "and you and I know how the two of them seem to be more, you know, closer physically than ever before."

"Maybe it's time we slow things up." Ray said. "Monkeys, I can't believe it. They need a vacation from each other. In June let's spend the summer in Utah."

"I was thinking the same thing," Ann said. "Mom

is almost ninety now and she needs someone to come live with her. DeeDee could visit with all of her relatives in Utah and she could be riding horses, having slumber parties. It would keep her busy."

"Monkeys, jees!" Ray scoffed.

When DeeDee came home from school, her mother broke the news about summer vacation. "Your father and I have great plans for a really fun summer vacation. We are going to Utah!"

DeeDee didn't see what was so special about vacationing in Utah since they had done that for the last five years. Then she began to sense what was coming. "For how long?" DeeDee asked.

"That's why it is so special. We will be able to do a lot of things that we never get a chance to do." DeeDee's mother stalled.

"For how long?" DeeDee repeated.

"For three months," her mother answered.

"Three months! That's the whole summer. I don't want to go to Utah for the whole summer. No! No! I have my friends here." DeeDee protested.

"You mean Mark, don't you?" her mother asked. "Everything revolves around Mark. You have relatives who would love to see you."

"I'll send them pictures. I don't want to go!" DeeDee began crying and ran to her room.

DeeDee's mother had never heard her daughter behave that way. She went to DeeDee's room. The door was locked. She knocked. Then she said, "See what he is doing to you. He is making you unhappy. You can't even go with your parents to visit relatives who love you."

DeeDee came out of her room. She dried her eyes. "I need to talk to Spacia." And she went next door.

Spacia said, "I can't believe they are doing this to you. What made them mad? Did Mark do something?"

"No, nothing. They think we are getting too serious. I love Mark. He loves me. We've never done anything. I'm still a virgin. They are trying to break us up." DeeDee couldn't hold back the tears. "Could you call Mark," she said between sobs, "and tell him for me?"

"Sure, hon," Spacia answered. "What's the number?" She dialed, Mark answered.

"Hi, Spacia. What's up?"

"DeeDee asked me to call," Spacia said.

Mark could hear DeeDee crying in the background. "What happened?"

Spacia told him the whole story. When she was done Mark said, "Hold the phone to her ear. Hi, DeeDee. Listen, nothing can keep us apart."

DeeDee sobbed into the phone. "But" sob "it is" sob "for the whole summer." And she couldn't continue. Spacia held the phone closer to DeeDee's ear.

Mark kept trying to console DeeDee. "We are still on for tomorrow night. We never miss a date to dance. We will talk about it then. There might be something we can do to make this bearable. I love you, sweetheart."

Mark's voice was calm and comforting. He always knew what to do. She started feeling better. Spacia read the difference in DeeDee's voice and face.

"I love you, too," DeeDee said.

When DeeDee returned home, her mother noticed the difference in her.

"Did Spacia help you see we are only doing this for you?" her mother asked.

"She helped me." DeeDee answered. "Mark and I will

be going to the dance tomorrow night. We will talk about everything then."

# Chapter 20

MARK WAS ENERGIZED WHEN he arrived at DeeDee's door for their date. The screen door was all that separated him from the conversation going on inside. He heard DeeDee say in a clear voice, "Nothing you can say or do will make me happy to spend the entire summer in Utah." DeeDee's voice was clear.

"Mark is causing you all this unhappiness." DeeDee's mother said, "You were disrespectful to me yesterday. As far as I am concerned Mark Stephens is the devil's disciple."

DeeDee wanted to scream at her mother how ridiculous that sounded, but Mark was due to arrive soon and she didn't want her date with him cancelled.

"Mark will be here soon. I need to be ready," she said ignoring her mother.

Mark felt the anger directed at him. He wanted to open the screen door and yell something like "Ho, Ho! Jolly old Satan is here." But he resisted. He started to walk back to the car, but instead he walked around the block to gather his thoughts. He then started whistling and strolling back to the front door, knocking on it.

DeeDee rushed to the door ready to go. She yelled to

her mother, "It's Mark. Be home by curfew," and she took Mark by the arm and hurried him to the car.

Mark opened DeeDee's door with an extra flair by bowing, and with a sweeping gesture invited her to enter the car.

"Thank you kind sir," she said as she jumped in and slid over to the driver's side. There was little room for Mark to get in. DeeDee grabbed his arm.

Mark said, "It is all right for a girl to hang on to her youth, but not while he's driving."

"Oh, sorry," DeeDee said and she scooted over a few inches allowing Mark to get in.

Mark took her hand and kissed the back of it. He seemed to be holding something back. DeeDee noticed that Mark was not taking the usual route to the church dance. He was heading toward Encanto Park.

DeeDee asked," Did the church move the dance to the park for a reason?"

Mark said, "Noooooo, but I have a good reason for coming here," as he opened her car door and guided her down a familiar path to the high point of the arched bridge. He stopped and stood behind her with his arms around her elbows. "Does this arched bridge mean anything to you?" he asked.

DeeDee responded, "This was where we came the night after our fight when we promised to love each other forever. It was the happiest moment of my life. I hope you haven't changed your mind."

Mark let go of her arm, reached into his pocket and said, "I wasn't going to do this until you turned seventeen but circumstances changed that. It was here that we both learned how we felt about each other. Now we are facing separation, but I don't want the bond to weaken. I want you to know that my love for you will be forever and nothing and no one will change what I feel for you. Mark took a deep breath and said, "Will you, in three years from tonight, marry me?" He then took the solitaire diamond ring out from its box.

DeeDee's mouth dropped open. Her eyes searched Mark's face looking for reality checks. Was this proposal for real? DeeDee put out her right hand. "Yes," she said, "I'm so happy and so nervous. Did I give you the wrong hand? I mean it's the right hand but, yes, yes! I love you!" And she put her arms around his neck and pulled his head down to kiss him. She was trembling. Their lips met and she felt a surge of energy flow into her, filling her up. Mark held her close, wrapping his arms around her lower back.

When he released her, she said, "Here is the right hand, I mean the correct hand," and she put out her left hand. Mark slid the ring over her finger. "With this ring we seal a promise that three years from now we will marry on this day at this time on this bridge." They kissed again. It was a long dreamy kiss floating them in their imaginations to the place where they could be together forever, even if it meant running away together.

"I love you with all my heart," DeeDee said. "There is no distance long enough to change that." DeeDee was so elated; her excitement brought the little girl out. "It is so beautiful, I can't wait to show it to Spacia and..."

"You can't," Mark interrupted. "I mean, let's think about it. If your parents get wind of this, they will probably try extra hard to shut us down. What do you think?"

DeeDee imagined herself showing the ring to Spacia and how excited Spacia would be for her. Then she saw her mother's face and her father's as she told them about the ring. Mark was right. It would have to be kept a secret.

"Your music box has a lock and key," Mark said, "just keep it there, and," he said pausing, "put this in with it." He held up a $100 bill. "It will be the start of our nest egg for that special night three years from now. When I work overtime, I will save that money and give it to you."

"Are you sure?" DeeDee asked. "You need money for school and gas and lots of things."

"Don't worry," Mark said, "I manage my money just fine. Didn't I pay cash for my car?"

DeeDee nodded, "I know. Maybe I can get a job in Utah so I can help."

The word Utah strangled any enthusiasm she and Mark had. Their energy dropped to dreary. Both of them did not want any reminder of what faced them for the next three months.

"We better get dancing," Mark said.

# Chapter 21

M ARK AND DEEDEE HAD their usual dates: Saturday
night dances, movies, church functions including
an Easter sunrise service, and walks around DeeDee's
block. They took every opportunity to be alone. Their
goodbye kisses became more intense as if the kiss could
wipe away all the fears that kept surfacing. DeeDee knew
Mark was extremely attractive not just to her but to other
girls on campus. She had dark thoughts about him dating
older girls in college and finding someone smarter than
she was.

Mark listened to DeeDee's mother telling him, "You
don't have to worry about DeeDee. She is going to be very
busy every day all summer. At night they have dances at
BYU for high school students, and her cousins have lots
of friends. She can go swimming or to the lagoon where
the teens meet each other and go on the rides and dance."
Mark held his tongue.

Mark worried that DeeDee would find a better dancer
to be with and that they would enter dance contests and
have to practice and rehearse together for long hours
making constant body contact.

Neither DeeDee nor Mark wanted to talk about these

fears. Their kisses became more desperate. Mark wanted to go to Utah and warn every available male that DeeDee was his, and that they had better stay away from her. He wished there was some way she could wear the ring while in Utah, some way he could be sure everyone knew he and DeeDee belonged to each other.

DeeDee's parents noticed the changes in Mark's and DeeDee's behavior. Mark seemed more possessive, such as the time he didn't want DeeDee to wear Levis. And he was a little edgy if she wasn't there when he called. Her parents curtailed the dating. Mark and DeeDee could see each other only three times a week, then it was only two. They could talk on the phone each day for only five minutes.

Mark could not sleep. His grades suffered. His thoughts constantly turned to DeeDee. One early morning after a restless night, he dreamed of a plan to overcome the dilemma of being separated from his love, the one beautiful being he trusted to stay close to him, to be there when everyone else failed. He awoke with the visuals still alive with reality. It could work! And then what could her parents do? He wanted to put the plan into action immediately but then realized he had not even talked to DeeDee about it. It was Saturday. He could ask Emmet, a fellow meat cutter, for help, and then that night at the church dance he could lay it out for DeeDee. If Emmet said okay, then he and DeeDee could start putting the rest of it together.

At lunch time, Mark presented his plan to Emmet, who gave the idea some thought and nodded his head yes. It could work. Mark wanted to leave work early but that would leave his boss shorthanded. He would have to wait. The rest of the day he turned the plan over in his mind working out the logistics, writing down times, miles, speed, how they could get her parents to go along.

That night Mark picked up DeeDee as usual but once again he headed for Encanto Park. DeeDee knew something was cooking in Mark's mind. He was quiet. She let him ponder. When they got to the park, Mark made no move to get out of the car. He looked at DeeDee and said, "You know, I like my car but it isn't very fast. Emmet has a hot '55 Ford. He said I could borrow it for a date, a long date."

DeeDee asked, "And when would this date take place, and where would we be going?" She was starting to pick up on Mark's plan.

"It would take place on the Saturday just before you leave for Utah, June 7th, and we would go to Nogales, Mexico." After a long pause, Mark completed the sentence, "to be married."

DeeDee's mouth dropped open. Her heart jumped ahead. She took a deep breath.

"You mean married like husband and wife?"

"Yes," Mark said. "Listen, I talked to Emmet. He will loan us his car so we can, at 75 miles an hour, get there and back in a little over four hours. Here is what we can do!"

DeeDee was quiet and very attentive. She was taking in every word. Her mind was racing with questions to be asked and suggestions to make the plan failsafe. Mark was talking faster than usual.

"We will convince your parents that since this will be the last date before the summer separation, we would like to make it a longer one than usual. We would like to go to a movie at 4 p.m. to see Elvis Presley in *Jailhouse Rock* and then to dinner at a nice restaurant, and then to the church dance, getting home at the usual curfew. What we will actually do is drive to Emmet's house, exchange cars, and high tail it to Nogales, and get into a Mexican cab. Emmet says there is nothing money can't buy at the border. The cab drivers speak enough English, we take cash, tell the driver what we want, he will do the rest. We will be married and come home. I've figured out the mileage, the time, every thing. It can be done in Emmet's car, not mine. Okay, what do you think?"

DeeDee was trying to find a flaw in the plan. "The big problem is how do we break the news to my parents. They will forbid me to ever see you again."

"Sweetheart, sweetheart, we will be married. We won't have to follow their orders." Mark said.

"But they will be mad, really mad." DeeDee protested.

"Of course they will, but we will be married. We don't have to be pulled apart. They will eventually see how happy we are, and they will be happy for us."

"What if we can't get married? What if the car breaks down? What if my parents find out before we even leave? What if...."

"Sweetheart!" Mark interrupted, "I'm not going to lie to you. There are some big what-ifs and unknowns that we can't predict. But having a good, fast car puts my mind at ease about breaking down. If we can't get across the border and get married, we will just turn around and get home before curfew. At least we tried."

"Okay, let's do it." DeeDee said. "I love you and trust you to make things work out. I'll offer a compromise suggesting to my parents what a good, final, and fair date would be like for us, and let them know how good I'll be about going to Utah."

Mark got out of the car and opened DeeDee's door. "Let's go to our bridge for a moment." At the bridge, Mark held Dee Dee's hands in his, and looked into her eyes. He said, "I think we can use all the help we can get," and he bowed his head. DeeDee did the same.

Mark offered a short prayer. "Dear Father in Heaven, the plan we are about to follow is based on the one energy I know you are most fond of. That energy is love. You have placed that energy in both our hearts. We treasure it and want it to grow forever. Please dear Father, help our plan to succeed. We will never let you down. Amen."

"Amen," DeeDee whispered. Mark cautioned DeeDee, "We must be very careful to keep everything a secret. We say nothing about our plans even when we talk to each other on the phone. We tell no one. Okay?"

"What about Spacia?" DeeDee asked.

"Not even Spacia," Mark said. "At least not now. She might be a helpful backup later. For now, mums the word. Okay?"

"Okay," DeeDee said, "Now June 7th just needs to hurry and get here."

Mark took DeeDee in his arms, held her close to his heart, kissed her lovingly, and walked her back to his car.

# Chapter 22

June 7th came sooner than DeeDee wanted. She had much to do. What would she wear? At Mark's suggestion it was time to let Spacia know their plans so she could vouch for their story should it become necessary.

Also, another problem came up. DeeDee believed her mother had found the key and was aware of the contents in the music box. She noticed her picking up the music box, ostensibly to dust, but giving it a shake to hear a loose object inside before putting it back down. It was apparent to DeeDee that her mother already knew what was inside. DeeDee removed the hundred dollar bill and the ring from its container, and put the ring box back inside the music box. The rattle was the same. Then she got dressed.

"Oh," DeeDee's mother said. "You are wearing your lacy white dress. You wear that only for church and special occasions, not to dance in."

"But we are going to a movie and a nice restaurant first, and this last date is pretty special," DeeDee explained. "I'm going over to Spacia's now. She wanted to borrow some of my albums. I'll be back before Mark gets here."

As DeeDee ran across the manicured lawn to Spacia's

house, her pulse was racing as fast as her mind thinking of all the things that could go wrong with their plan and at the same time excited to be finally sharing her news with her best friend.

Spacia, in shock and disbelief said, "You are kidding me. I can't believe this. You are engaged?"

"Yes," DeeDee said, "Look!" She held up the solitaire diamond ring, and the hundred dollar bill. Spacia's pupils dilated making the small diamond look much larger.

"You really are going to do this," Spacia said. "Okay, go over everything again so I can cover for your version of the story." She was enjoying every minute of her role as co-conspirator.

Mark and DeeDee bid her mother goodbye with promises to be home before curfew. Mark in his blue sports coat and cream dress slacks, and DeeDee in her lacy white dress drove away in Mark's newly washed car as it sparkled in the sun.

Mark drove carefully and cautiously to the meat store. He went inside. He and Emmet exchanged keys. Emmet said, "She's ready to go, full tank of gas, a new oil change, and just washed. See you at my house later tonight." Then he said something to Mark that crushed Mark's optimism.

"I guess you already thought about annulment." Emmett said. Mark had never heard of the word.

"No, what's that?" Mark asked.

"Because DeeDee is under age," Emmett said, "her parents could choose to have the marriage annulled which would make it not legal. That's the law."

"Then all this would be for nothing?" Mark asked.

"That's a possibility. If her parents find out about the secret marriage."

Mark's face drained of color. His knees weakened. Emmett was a "yes" personality. He loaned his car under dubious circumstances. Now he was trying to lift Mark's spirits, but he needed to be truthful too. "You don't have to tell them until later when you think the time is right. Maybe they will go along with it then."

Mark's spirits picked up. His energy returned. He and DeeDee would have several hours to talk about "what would be the best time" as they drove to Nogales.

"Everything okay?" DeeDee asked when Mark got in the car. He started the engine and heard it roar. "Oh yeah, everything is okay."

Mark drove carefully obeying all laws, speed limits, and stop signs. Once on the road south he gradually picked up speed, getting the feel of the hot Ford. Soon they were cruising at 75 miles per hour on a lightly traveled highway. The big traffic day to Nogales was yesterday and those people wouldn't be coming back until Sunday. Mark stepped on the accelerator. There were no cars in sight going south. He could feel the power of Emmett's Ford.

"Ray, Ray," DeeDee's mother called as her husband drove into the driveway. "Something isn't right."

"What isn't right?" Ray asked as the furrow in his brow deepened.

"Mark picked up DeeDee and they left as planned, but DeeDee wore her Sunday lacy white dress and looked," Ann paused before saying it. "She looked like a bride."

Ray's expression softened. "Well, it was a special date. She wore something special, that's all."

"No, that's not all," Ann said. "I got into her music box. The diamond ring and the $100 are gone."

Ray's face flared in anger. "I knew that boy was too old for her. Someone must know what's going on. Let's call some of her friends and get it out of them." Ann made a list. Then Ray looked up numbers while Ann made calls. After a dozen calls, all they learned was what they already knew. Mark and DeeDee were having a last date. They were going to go to a movie, then to dinner, then to the church dance.

"The dance starts in three hours. " Ann said. "Let's go over and see if they are there."

Mark was in high gear now, nearing 100 miles per hour on a dip-ladened road that put Emmet's Ford airborne occasionally.

"We are making good time. We will be at the border soon. I ... Oh, no!" Mark exclaimed.

"What's wrong?" DeeDee asked. Then she looked to the side to see the sign whiz by. "Your speed has just been checked by radar." Mark instantly took his foot off the accelerator and began braking the car. He looked out the rearview mirror expecting to see flashing red lights. What he saw were four Arizona Highway patrolmen horsing around with each other, oblivious to a speeding '55 Ford. Mark and DeeDee looked at each other and breathed a sigh of relief.

"I bet that's not coffee in their mugs," Mark said.

"We better slow down," DeeDee warned.

"I'm already on it." Mark answered.

☙ ❧

Emmet was right. There were cabs waiting for the American tourists. Mark parked the car on the state side, and then looked at DeeDee.

"Sweetheart, maybe you should put on heavier makeup to make your self look older, like maybe you are trying to cover up wrinkles or something."

DeeDee got out her mirror and started going to work. Mark was in charge. DeeDee now understood why Mark earlier in the week asked her to give him one of her frumpiest dresses that was too large for her. He noticed it in her closet one day and asked if she had an older sister. No, the dress was given to her by a Utah relative. Now she would wear it. Mark had a small pillow and towels to stuff under the dress changing her small frame to that of a more mature woman . It was getting dark which helped. Mark asked DeeDee for the $100 bill. "Okay, let's find that perfect cabby."

The cabby could speak fairly good English. He understood what Mark said. He asked how old DeeDee was.

"Eighteen today." Mark said quickly. The Cabby hesitated, and then Mark took out the $100 bill. Emmet was right on. Mark could bribe his way all the way to the City Magistrate. But Mark wanted estimates. "How much will the license cost?"

"I will take you there, Senor," the cabby said, "And we will find out."

Within ten minutes, they were in front of a municipal building. Still holding the $100 bill, Mark said. "I want you to come with me to help explain what I want." The cabby was willing. The office of the City Administrator contained a desk, a row of filing cabinets, and a bench. There was another room next door.

The cabby took too long for a simple explanation. Mark started to get nervous until he heard the Spanish for fifty American pesos. The bribe was working. The administrator handed Mark a description of a marriage ceremony in English for Mark and DeeDee to read. He then went to a file and took out a single blank document in Spanish that resembled a license of some sort. Mark recognized the word "Matrimonio" and decided he was getting what he asked for. He filled in DeeDee's name where the Magistrate pointed. Then Mark put down their ages and birth dates being careful not to make an error on DeeDee's reported age. The Magistrate motioned for Mark to put the ring on her finger. Mark understood. Then the official pursed his lips and brought his hands together slowly. Mark knew what to do. He kissed the bride. The Magistrate slapped a stamp on the back of the license. Mark took the license with one hand, and with the other gave the official the $100 bill. They both released their holdings at the same time. DeeDee and Mark kissed and then motioned for the cabby, "Let's go!"

As Mark put the license in his coat pocket, the cabby said, "Go, I will be out in uno memento." Mark and DeeDee got into the cab, but could see the cabby arguing with the Magistrate who reluctantly went to his wallet and gave the cabby something.

Only thirty minutes had passed by the time the cabby drove next to Emmet's Ford. Mark gave the cabby another $10, which made him so excited, Mark thought he was going to kiss DeeDee and him.

Mark unlocked the Ford, took off his coat, and threw

it in the back seat. In moments, Mark and DeeDee were speeding north to Phoenix as man and wife.

# Chapter 23

IN PHOENIX, RAY AND Ann waited outside in their car as teens began arriving for the dance. They recognized some of DeeDee's friends whom they had called earlier. When Spacia saw DeeDee's parents, she tried to avoid them, but they had already left their car and were heading toward her. Spacia knew something was wrong.

"Are you looking for DeeDee?" she asked.

"Yes, we are." Ann replied.

"She and Mark may not be coming to this dance, you know. DeeDee said Mark's ward had a dance going too, but I will go in and look for you."

"Please do that," Ann said and then turned to Ray as Spacia went inside. "I know they are eloping to Nogales or maybe up north to Short Creek. Let's call the police."

Mark and DeeDee knew to slow down on that dip-laden road and to keep an eye out for the Arizona Highway Patrol. They also kept an eye on the time.

DeeDee and Mark had accomplished what they set out to do, and in record time. They were nearing the outskirts of Phoenix. Mark pulled over while they were still in the desert. He rolled down the windows while DeeDee removed her heavy makeup. Her smile and inner beauty glowed in the moonlight. They kissed knowing that they had just done something that would change the course of their lives forever. Everything had fallen into place and they belonged to each other now.

Mark asked, "There is something you should know. Have you heard of annulment?" DeeDee shook her head, looking perplexed. "Emmett told me about it just tonight. Because you are underage and your parents did not give you permission to marry, they have the right to have the marriage annulled. It's a legal term meaning the marriage won't count. It would be illegal."

"But we have the marriage license and ring and everything," DeeDee protested.

"It would be good if we lived in Mexico, but not in the United States." Mark replied.

"What do we do? And why did we go to all this trouble?" DeeDee asked.

"Emmett said we could keep quiet about it and then when the time is right we could tell them, and they might give us the permission we need." Mark said.

"When will the time be right?" DeeDee asked.

"I don't know!" Mark said, "But when it is right, I will know."

"I don't care. We did it and we know it." DeeDee said looking at her ring. "Here, you better keep this with you." She handed Mark the ring.

Mark said, "I feel the same way. When we get back, we will be surrounded by friends, people, parents, and we won't have another moment to be alone." They kissed again. Mark looked at his watch. "We have fifty minutes to spare."

On the phone, Ann was replying, "That's right, officer, a '47 Chevy, grey. They are probably two hours or so from Phoenix. She is wearing a white dress. He is in light colored slacks and a blue coat. She is underage. He is eighteen and very strong and skilled in fighting. He stole our baby." Ann started to cry. Ray took the phone, "Okay, thank you, officer. We will be at this number if you need us."

"I know we said we wouldn't." Mark whispered in DeeDee's ear. DeeDee pulled her dress down over her shoulders. Mark unbuttoned the back. "I love you and always will," Mark said as he attempted, unsuccessfully, to unfasten her bra.

"I love you, my husband, and I'm happy to know you don't know much about bras."

Mark made a cushion for DeeDee's head. He lowered his body over hers. Their eyes were locked on each other.

The drive into Phoenix was a mixture of happiness and terrible sadness. They were one, but they were about to be separated. DeeDee clung tightly to Mark's arm as they drove toward Phoenix. The warm wind whipped at Mark's coat in the back of the car. DeeDee reached back and rolled the window up.

Then she sat close to Mark and rested her head on his shoulder. They were silent for several minutes and then both began to speak at the same time, asking the same question, "Are we really married?" They both smiled at each other and in unison answered, "YES!", which caused giddy laughter.

"How do you feel about it?" DeeDee asked.

Mark brought her hand to his lips as he said, "I feel magnificently apprehensive, but very much in love."

"Me, too!" DeeDee answered.

"In love or scared?" Mark asked.

"Both," she said. "I know we have just done something sacred. You are my husband. I will never leave you. I love you more than ever."

Mark kissed her hand again. "I know this wasn't the fairy tale marriage every girl dreams about, but you are my wife for life. I will love you always and will fight to keep you by my side. This marriage is just as good as any other wedding ceremony."

They drove back to Emmett's house to change cars in silence, each dreaming of their future together. When Mark and DeeDee drove up to DeeDee's house in his '47 Chevy, a police car had just pulled away. Her parents rushed to the car as they drove up. All of the lights were on in the house. Spacia was there.

DeeDee's mother took DeeDee by her arm, "Where have you been?" she asked as they went inside. "We have been worried sick."

Ray stopped Mark from entering the house. "You have caused enough trouble for tonight. You can just turn around and go home."

Mark wanted to yell out, "She is my wife. She goes home with me." But that new word annulment told him to be quiet. Before he could say anything, Spacia spoke up. "I told them you went to the other dance, and you probably didn't like it, and that's when you were on your way to this side of town, but they think you got married or something crazy like that."

Mark was quietly saying, "Thank you, dear Spacia, for the perfect alibi."

Ray spoke up, "Why did you take the ring and money? Don't deny it. We have known about the ring and money for some time."

Mark was quick with his answer, "I didn't have time to cash my check today so I asked DeeDee to bring the savings for the date. As for the ring I guess she just wanted to wear it for a while. She was afraid you would read more into it than what was there so she has been keeping it under lock and key."

Her father softened, "Let's go in and sort this out."

Fortunately, DeeDee's mother had not gotten into the details of where they were until Mark was able to repeat the alibi that Spacia had presented. Ann was relieved. It had all been a misunderstanding. The next day, Mark and DeeDee would be separated for three months.

# Chapter 24

MARK AND DEEDEE'S SECRET marriage was safe or so it seemed. Mark worked long hours, and then went home to write letters to DeeDee. He was love sick. Working made the time pass faster. He lived for the letters and pictures he got from her. DeeDee's parents wouldn't allow expensive phone calls. Her letters couldn't hide her love sickness and the same heartache he felt. Her parents tried to cheer her up with varied activities such as horseback riding, swimming, fishing, a day at the Lagoon which was an amusement park where teens would go to meet other teens.

Then DeeDee misspelled a single word in one of her letters. She wrote to express how miserable she felt and how she was no fun to be around. She talked about her excursion at the Lagoon and how "honery" she felt. She meant "ornery". Mark read "horny". It shocked him. His sweet innocent bride sounded like a sex-starved, loose woman. What is she doing at this moment? Was she not what Mark thought? His lack of confidence and his lack of sexual experience played havoc with his imagination. Did that single experience that they shared coming back from Nogales unleash an uncontrollable craving in her?

He didn't know she even knew what horny meant. But there it was in black and white, misspelled but "She was horny." Mark's dark dreams and worst fears were coming to pass.

Mark quickly dashed off a letter that surprised and shocked DeeDee:

> *DeeDee,*
> *If you feel you need to have someone, go to The Lagoon and find some guy that will take care of you. I don't care. But remember, you might be pregnant right now, so don't come running to me.*
> *Mark*

She had no idea what caused his anger. When she read it, she was hurt, confused, and afraid. She ripped it up, threw it in the trash, and left the house. Her ever-watchful mother retrieved the letter and pieced it back together enough to read the part where Mark talked about the possibility of DeeDee being pregnant.

"Ray, Ray," Ann wailed, "This doesn't sound good."

"What is it?" Ray said as he rushed to her side.

"DeeDee might be pregnant!" Ann's voice began to break up.

"What?" Ray's voice boomed in anger. "Who told you that?"

"DeeDee was upset when she got today's mail. When I saw her tear up a letter and throw it in the garbage, I dug it out and tried to put all the pieces back together, but it got grease on it. Look right here. At first I thought it said: Your night be pregnant, but donut come running to me. If you look closer, it really says, You might be pregnant, but don't come running to me. This is clear. Oh, my baby, my baby!"

Ray took Ann over to the couch and sat her down. Then he got a chair and sat facing her as he took both of her hands and leaned forward. "Listen," he said, "There is more to this than that one blurry line in that letter. The best way to find out is to ask DeeDee. We know our little darling, and if she is in trouble, we need to be there for her."

"You're right," Ann said sniffling in her hanky. "When she gets home from Aunt May's, let's go somewhere quiet and private where there won't be any interruptions, and we will just ask her to tell us the whole truth." While they waited Ann and Ray discussed all the possible scenarios and what they should do.

When DeeDee got home, she went directly to her room. Her mother could see that DeeDee's eyes were red and swollen. She had been crying.

Ann followed her into the bedroom. DeeDee was lying on her bed on her stomach. "Sweetie, your father and I would like to take you for a ride to that new ice cream place in Provo." As a child, DeeDee always had loved going for a ride and getting ice cream. "We also think you would like to talk to us." DeeDee rolled over and sat up. She couldn't hold back the tears, and she ran to her mother's arms.

DeeDee's father drove while DeeDee and her mother sat in back. "Sweetie," her mother said, "I think it's time you tell us everything. We love you, and know you haven't done anything wrong." Upon hearing those words, DeeDee broke into sobs, her tears gushing over her cheeks, as all of her feelings began pouring out.

"I must have done something wrong. He doesn't love

me anymore." DeeDee opened up. The sobbing and crying made it difficult to hear everything she said. "We were afraid you were going to break us up, so we got married. We couldn't tell you the truth because you would have it anointed or something. We were going to tell you when the time was right, but now he doesn't want me, and I missed my period…

"Did you say you missed your period?" her mother asked.

"Yes, we were going to wait, but we were married and we weren't going to see each other for the whole summer. We loved each other, and now I know it was wrong," sob, "I'm sorry." DeeDee's mother held her in her arms.

"You poor darling," DeeDee's father said. "We understand. You see, I ran away with your mother on my motorcycle. She was seventeen. We got married and you came along nine months later. We're sorry, too, for not listening to your heart. You were honest about your feelings and we wouldn't accept that. Do you still love him?" her father asked.

"Yes, I do," DeeDee answered.

"Does he love you?"

"Yes, maybe, I don't know. I have his other letters, he loved me; I know he did. I'll let you read them, but this last letter he said he didn't care if I went with someone else and that if I was pregnant I shouldn't come running back to him. It sounded like he thinks I was dating someone else," she sobbed.

When they got home, DeeDee got Mark's letters out for her parents to read. After reading ten other letters, her father said, "These sound like a love-sick young man who holds you in highest esteem."

"He does love you, DeeDee," her mother said. "There

must be something else going on here. Let's call him up tonight, and you ask him if he still loves you. If he says yes, then we want you to be together. All we ask is that you get a legal marriage here in Utah."

DeeDee couldn't believe what she was hearing. She had their blessing! She and Mark would not be separated! All she needed was Mark's words that he still loved her!

Mark wouldn't be home from work until 9 p.m. DeeDee wrote down everything she wanted to say and the order she wanted to say it. Her parents would be listening in with her permission.

At 9 p.m. DeeDee dialed Mark. "Hello," Mark answered.

"It's me. DeeDee," There was a pause. "I got your letter." More silence. "It made me cry, I don't know why you wrote it."

"It was because of what you said in your letter." Mark finally replied.

"What did I say?" DeeDee asked. "I wrote to tell you how much I loved and missed you and how sad I was, and how ornery I felt. I was mean with everyone. No one wanted me around."

Mark said, "Oh no."

DeeDee said, "Oh no what?"

"You said you were ornery?"

"Yes, I did." DeeDee replied.

"How do you spell ornery?"

DeeDee said, "I'm not sure, I think it is h o r n e r y."

Mark's voice cracked. His eyes full of tears. He said, "I am sooo sorry, please forgive me, I misread what you said. I thought you said you were horny and that you were looking for someone else. Oh, my innocent sweetheart, what a fool I was to ever doubt you. Tear up that letter. I love you, I love you!"

"I already did. Now I have something to tell you! Sit down, hang on."

When Mark heard DeeDee's father's voice on the phone, his heart dropped, and then he became confused.

"We know everything, Mark, your trip to Nogales, the illegal marriage, everything. We can't say we approve of what you have done, but we believe your intentions were honorable." That one word 'honorable" caused Mark's spirits to soar skyward. "Here, let me have you talk to Ann."

Ann's voice was emotional, near the point of crying, "DeeDee told us everything. Are you ready for a wedding?"

"Yesss, Maam!" Mark replied. There was so much energy in his voice he was almost shouting.

"Well, will this weekend be too soon?"

"Nooo, Maam," I'll get off work and I'll leave for Utah on Wednesday, better get a ticket first, call Greyhound," Mark paused, his mind racing.

"Are you still there, Mark?" Ann's voice brought him back down to earth. "I'll let you talk to DeeDee."

"Sweetheart? Sweetheart? Are you there?" Mark was so eager to hear her voice he didn't let her talk first.

"It's me," DeeDee interrupted him. "I'll explain how all this happened when I see you. I'm so happy I can't think straight right now."

"Me, too!" Mark said. "Give me your phone number. I'll call you tomorrow night. I need to get a bus ticket. This is the best thing that's ever happened!" He could not control the volume. Her parents heard his voice yelling

"I love you! I love you! I love your parents! I love the world!"

# Chapter 25

MARK THOUGHT THAT HIS mother regarded him as a fully-grown man. After all, he had been working since age twelve. He never asked for money. He bought his own clothes and food. At age eighteen, he was ready for the responsibilities of marriage and family. It was annoying the way she was sending him off.

"Mom," he said, "the plan is for me to take the bus to Utah, get married there, and then DeeDee and I, as man and wife, will drive back with her parents."

"I'm just trying to help," his mother said. "Let me pin your money and the ring in this envelope to the inside pocket of your coat."

"I'll put them inside my wallet, for crying out loud, like other men do," Mark protested.

"It will be safer here," she insisted.

"But...Never mind. Go ahead, pin it."

"And don't forget the license." She said.

"The license! I haven't given that a thought. I think I put it in with the ceremony description between the pages of that thick art book in my room. So if it isn't there, it is probably still in my blue coat."

"Was it pinned?" she asked.

"No, I just put it in the pocket. Then we had that awful night at their house before she left. I haven't even looked for it. It should be with the ceremony directions," Mark said, "Remind me later to look for it." Then he left for work.

Mark's mother went to the art book and found a folded sheet. It was the marriage ceremony in English. No license.

When Mark got home, his mother said, "I looked, it wasn't there."

Mark asked, "What wasn't there?"

"The marriage license." she said. Mark started to panic. He checked the book and his coat again. He searched the car. There were two times when he was careless with his coat: When he took it off and threw it in the car and when the wind was whipping at it in the back seat as they drove into the Phoenix outskirts. He searched frantically, and then decided to calm down. It wasn't worth anything anyway, and he was leaving by Greyhound at 4 a.m. tomorrow to be married.

The Greyhound bus stopped for a restroom break in Wickenburg, Arizona. The driver said, "Ten minutes!" Within three minutes of sitting down on the throne, Mark heard two honks and an engine revving up. Before he could get his pants up, the bus left, and with it, his coat, the ring, and the money pinned to the inside pocket.

Mark was frantic. Within seconds, a local police officer drove up for coffee at the bus station. Mark explained his dilemma. The police officer didn't want to leave his coffee and donuts. Mark added the purpose of the trip to Utah. He had a wedding date! The officer said, "Lets see if we can catch the bus." Mark thanked the police officer who peeled out of the gravel parking lot.

"There are two routes to Utah from here, but I don't know which one this bus took. We will just have to flip a coin and give it a try." The officer said.

After 20 minutes of driving, the officer said, "It looks like we chose the wrong route. I need to get back to my nightly patrol."

"My coat was on the bus," Mark said. "I wonder if we can contact Greyhound and have them look for it."

"I'll give a call," the officer said. "By the way, my name is Jim."

Mark could feel that this fellow human being was taking on the predicament of this poor naïve kid and was going to be as helpful as possible. When Jim got off the phone, he said, "The bus that left you will be in Las Vegas in three more hours. They notified the driver. If he finds it, he will leave your coat at the Las Vegas terminal, and in two hours another bus will pick you up here and take you to Las Vegas and then on to Utah."

Mark thanked Jim for giving him hope. Just an hour earlier Mark was stranded in Wickenburg, broke, and without a wedding ring. The wedding probably would never happen, he thought. He cursed his mother silently for not letting him put everything in his pants pocket.

When Mark arrived in Vegas, a greyhound agent handed him his coat. Mark quickly checked the pocket. The ring and the money were still pinned to the inside pocket. This time, Mark silently thanked his mother for concealing the envelope so well.

Fate saw to it that Mark made both wedding dates.

# Chapter 26

WHEN MARK STEPPED OFF the bus, DeeDee rushed to him and jumped into his waiting arms. He twirled her around three times with her feet off the ground. A crowd of relatives was cheering as the couple embraced, kissed and embraced again as if they had to take second and third looks and hugs to be sure what was happening was real. The relatives were all smiles as they shared in the joy. Ray and Mark shook hands, ready to forgive and accept the inevitable, and Ann gave Mark a squeeze. All the while, Mark would not let go of DeeDee.

The wedding was planned for the next day. It was to be held at Aunt May's home and the ceremony was to be performed by a Mormon Bishop of the local ward. When DeeDee told Mark of the plans and asked if he was okay with everything, Mark said, "Sweetheart, when we made that trip to Nogales, I was fully married and committed to you. This Utah ceremony and marriage is for your parents. When we get back, I would like for us to have one more private ceremony that we talked about."

"Encanto Park? On the bridge?" DeeDee asked, "In the evening?"

"Yes, you remembered," Mark said. "I'm the luckiest

guy in the world, but first we have to get married in Utah."

The Utah wedding went smoothly except for the local practice of "shivaree." The custom of pranks after a wedding was a little meaner than just tying cans to the back of the car. A week earlier, a young couple had pulled back the covers on their honeymoon bed to find a dozen live toads. When they tried to separate Mark from DeeDee, it took five large farm boys to pry Mark away from her. It only happened then because Mark thought it would be better to let them succeed rather than to end up hurting someone. They felt his strength, but their ego's were in jeopardy if they didn't make Mark roll DeeDee down main street in a wheel barrel for two blocks to register at the only local hotel for their wedding night.

Such was the beginning that was destined to bring two souls together. Mark and DeeDee both felt as if some invisible guardian angel was in attendance every step of the way.

The trip home to Phoenix with DeeDee's parents was filled with angst as Mark and DeeDee sat in the back seat, holding hands and kissing each other – often. For Mark the necking was more of a test of the new relationship. DeeDee was his wife not his girlfriend. The parents had no more control of her and no right to tell her to stop all the kissing. Her parents, by their silence, honored Mark and DeeDee's new status as husband and wife.

Instead the conversation covered all of the decisions the new couple would have to make regarding where they would live, and how they would manage the budget, would they need a second car, would DeeDee finish high school? Can the new couple come to Sunday dinners?

When would Mark's graduation take place? Would DeeDee get a job?

The sixteen hour trip went fast with Mark helping Ray with the driving. When they got to Phoenix they drove directly to Mark's house where he and DeeDee took time to visit with Mark's mother. Mark related the missed bus episode in Wickenburg and how he got everything back thanks to her. Ray and Ann stayed for awhile and then Ann asked, "Where will you be sleeping tonight?"

As he got his luggage out of the car, Mark spoke up, "We are going to get into my car and canvas the neighborhood for a room for rent. Something temporary, and I believe I know of a place off Henshaw Road. Being close to work will save us gas mileage."

"Well, let us know if you need any help." Ray said. "And thanks for helping me drive."

"Thank you for letting us drive with you," Mark said as he began to feel confident that his marriage would not be annulled.

DeeDee and Ann said good-bye with tears in their eyes, giving each other big hugs, warm, loving hugs.

Mark hugged his mom good-bye and opened his car door for DeeDee. Both had big smiles as they were taking their first steps as a couple. As Mark drove to the vacant house on Henshaw, he said, "I think we can pay up to $50 a month." As they pulled up to the house, they saw 800 square feet with peeling paint in a nondescript color that might have been beige. The dirt yard was littered with trash caught by three dead bushes. The side window was broken, letting in dust and flies. It was 110 degrees and Mark could not see any kind of cooling system, not even a water cooler.

"Let's not waste our time," Mark said. "We can do

better." And they both got back into the car. The first decision of their married life was going to be a tough one: Where to live on their budget? Mark said, "We could use some cold air. Let's drive over to Food City and I'll let Bill know I can come to work on Monday."

DeeDee sat close to Mark squeezing his arm and especially his bicep. She needed his maturity to help her through this rapid, overwhelming transition into adulthood.

When DeeDee and Mark walked through the door, Bill met them as he led his employees singing "Here Comes the Bride", followed by loud clapping of hands. Everyone was yelling, "Congratulations!"

Bill took the both of them upstairs to his office. He gave DeeDee a hug and asked "Okay, what are your plans?"

Mark said, "We just drove in but I can be back to work on Monday. We have to find an apartment or something first and get moved in."

"How about a house?" Bill asked. "It's a house I lived in with my family for years, just ten blocks away. Let's drive over. It has two bedrooms, a good sized living room, and a big back yard. I've rented it but the family can't move in for a month or two. You could rent it for a month while you are looking for a place."

"Let's go!" DeeDee exclaimed.

"That's what I like," Bill said, "a wife with enthusiasm."

When they arrived at the house, Mark and DeeDee bubbled over with excitement. It had a front lawn and had been newly painted. The front porch led into a large living room with French doors. Mark was sure this rental was going to be out of reach. "How much?" he said almost too afraid to ask.

"I'm asking $40," Bill said.

"Forty dollars?" Mark asked in disbelief.

"It is partially furnished with a table and chairs, a refrigerator and matching stove, and a bed, plus the utilities are included." Bill answered.

"When can we move in?" DeeDee and Mark blurted out in unison.

"Today!" Bill answered. "Here are the keys."

"Thank you! Thank you!" the two said over and over. "This makes such a big difference. We really appreciate this." DeeDee gave Bill a squeeze and a kiss on the cheek.

He blushed a little and said, "Let's talk business. You can give me $40 for rent on your next pay day."

"Thank you. That will be next Saturday. Thank you!" Mark said.

"Now I don't know if DeeDee was planning to work this summer, but I need a wrapper to cover for employee vacations." Bill said.

"I was planning to look for a job. What does a wrapper do?" DeeDee asked.

"She weighs and wraps meat, puts the price on it, and keeps the display counter full. You can start training on Monday. It pays 65 cents an hour." Bill said. "Then you get a raise after two weeks."

"I'll do it!" DeeDee said.

While Bill finished talking to Mark, DeeDee, full of questions and excitement, went to the meat department where she watched the wrappers. She had never had such an important job before.

"DeeDee, we have to go," Mark called as he motioned

for her to break away. They stopped on their way out to buy the few groceries they could afford and headed "home" to start their new life.

The next Saturday, Mark and DeeDee took time to write their own vows and to discuss what they would wear and do at their personal private wedding at Encanto Park that evening at 9 p.m. She would wear the same white dress and Mark would wear the same coat and slacks he wore for the elopement.

There was no moon that night so DeeDee brought two candles for each of them to hold as they were married for the third time. As Mark opened the car door for his bride and gave her his arm, she handed him his candle and a lighter. They strolled slowly to the bridge. DeeDee had white carnations in her hair which seemed to glow when they lit the candles. Their senses were assailed by the sweet smell of lilac bushes growing near the bridge, by the unspoken messages shining in their eyes through the candle light, and by the taste of the love in the kisses they stole as they prepared for words that would truly bind them to each other.

DeeDee began with her vow to Mark. "I promise you all my heart, body, and soul for the rest of my life. I promise I will always put your needs first each day as I wake up in your arms ready to live every moment to the fullest. I will stand beside you through the joy and the hard times because together we are so much more than we can be alone. You are my best friend, my teacher, my husband. I love you!"

Mark followed with his vow to DeeDee. "I promise you, DeeDee, to love you for the beautiful and vibrant woman you are, to hold you, to care for you, and to honor my love for you by being loyal to you and filling our lives with learning, living, laughing, and loving you forever, until death steals us apart. This is the covenant I enter into with you on this day. I love you now and forever!"

They placed their candles on each side of the bridge and walked toward the center. Mark stared into DeeDee's eyes searching for a way to express the feeling that seemed to be erupting from his very soul. He gently took her into his arms and kissed her with a depth they had never experienced before, an affirmation of eternal love and commitment. With no reservations, Mark swept her off her feet and walked down the bridge toward their car.

# Chapter 27

AFTER TWO MONTHS IN Bill's house, the young couple rented a place in Victory Village on the Arizona State University campus. It was housing for married couples. Mark walked to all of his classes. Made from World War II barracks, the apartments were complete with an infestation of cockroaches, but the price was right: $35 a month with everything paid. Within the first month of moving in, Mark successfully spearheaded an effort to get the village debugged.

Since it had turned out that DeeDee was not pregnant, they decided to wait to start a family, but Mark was a sleepwalker. He remembered at age seven he and his brother slept in a garage with a dirt floor. One night he got up, picked up the bucket they used as a urinal and walked up the back steps. When he woke up he was outside sitting on the empty bucket crying for someone to let him in.

After two episodes of waking up in the night in the middle of trying to have intercourse with DeeDee, they decided they better try the new birth control pills so she would be protected any time. What they did not know was that the best dosage of the active ingredient was still being tested. Too much brought side effects, not enough meant no protection.

Three months after their marriage, DeeDee became pregnant. She didn't start showing for five months. When she did, the store required her to quit work, and with her mother's help, she began changing Mark's study into a nursery. Mark refinished DeeDee's old crib and dresser. They decorated with treasures from Goodwill. The day they finished repainting the rocking horse that had been through two generations of children in DeeDee's family, she started her contractions. Her labor was long and hard, but Mark did not leave her side rubbing her back, encouraging her to breathe. When Desiree arrived, Mark was totally entranced and shocked at the intensity of his feelings. This tiny, wiggly, helpless little person was his to guide, to protect with all his being.

DeeDee stayed home with Desiree, who filled her life with giggles at bath time, changing diapers, and chasing after muscular little rubber band legs in the park. Mark had had visions of a little athlete eager to follow his father to the wrestling championships. Desiree did not disappoint him or her mother as she learned to balance herself on one leg standing in the palm of her father's hand. She ran before she walked, sprinting ahead of all the boys from the very beginning. She learned to walk as her mother taught her to do barrel leap turns, ballons, and allegro traveling time steps.

Mark's schedule of work, school, and study left him only Sundays and holidays to be with his family. Still he sneaked in a little time every day to play with Desiree, to read to her before bed, to tuck her in when her eyes grew heavy, to be the last face she saw each night and the first one in the morning.

And so the years passed: working and going to school by day, each evening spent studying, guiding and watching Desiree grow. DeeDee and Mark still managed to steal tender moments together at night before they dropped into exhausted sleep.

In Mark's last year at ASU, the university held an awards ceremony for the wives of the graduates. Each wife received a Ph.T. degree for Putting Hubby Through. Mark was thrilled that the university would recognize what he knew: without his beloved wife he would not have been able to graduate. The dance and dinner ceremony was a highlight of a seven year march toward the B.A. degree.

That night they dined on a linen-covered tablecloth with flowers, and enjoyed the big band sound of the forties provided by students in the music department. It was a glorious moment when DeeDee opened the envelope to receive the official looking degree acknowledgement of her contribution. It read:

> *"On recommendation of the Graduate Faculty*
> *and on authorization of the President*
> *and the Board of Trustees*
> *here conferred on*
> *Dianne Stephens*
> *the Degree of*
> *Ph.T.*
> *for her unselfish devotion and support of*
> *Putting Hubby Through"*

Mark and DeeDee had never experienced a formal dinner before. They were not sure which fork to use, why the salad came by itself, was this all the food they were getting? DeeDee watched others to find out what to do. But Mark only saw her and all that they had shared together. After the quiet dinner music subsided, he was the first to take her by the hand when the big band swing sound invited everyone to the dance floor. For a few moments he and DeeDee were the only ones on the floor. Mark was charged with emotion, love, excitement, and the need to hold her next to him. He still did not enjoy dancing in front of others, but it was his gift to her because she loved it so much. Over the years he and DeeDee had become excellent dance partners, knowing each other's every move.

It wasn't until other couples began swarming onto the dance floor after giving them a standing ovation, that Mark and DeeDee realized that they were lost in each other's arms, enjoying the magical feelings of love and accomplishment.

After an hour of constant dancing, Mark and DeeDee went out for a moment alone on the balcony. As they gazed up at the clear starry night, Mark touched DeeDee's lips with the sweetness of that first kiss in the moonlight years before, the kiss deepening into the passion that reflected their shared love, their spiritual coupling of respect and admiration, the bond they both knew they would treasure for all eternity.

After Mark's graduation from ASU, he signed a contract with Chaffey High School in Ontario, California. In the move to Ontario the car broke down. With a new water pump they could ill afford, they were able to make it in time to find a two bedroom apartment with two bathrooms within their budget as long as the landlord was willing to wait until their first payday.

The school officials wanted a wrestling coach but his teaching assignment was teaching 10th grade English. Mark's degree was in Public Speaking. The first year of teaching was spent dodging student questions about grammar and English. Students asked, "What's a metaphor?" Mark would answer, "That's a place to keep cows." Or "What's a pronoun?" "That's a noun that gets paid." "What's syntax?" "That's a tax that God levies on bad people."

Mark realized he could not dance around forever. He knew he had to go back to school. He began work on a Master's degree in structural linguistics which took him two summers. He was then a certified English teacher, not a coach who also taught English. He stopped coaching.

Shortly after Mark received the Master's Degree, DeeDee gave birth to her second and last child, an 8 pound boy named Josh. Five year old Desiree welcomed her own private doll and helped take care of him. She spent every day giving him kisses, patting his stomach when he cried, fetching things for him, and making him laugh with outrageous faces and noises.

After Josh's birth, DeeDee was different. Her smile disappeared for days on end. She was anxious about the baby, about meeting new people, about not meeting new people. She withdrew into herself, and Mark did not know how to reach her. Every day when he arrived home, she was different. She might be so quiet and into her own thoughts that Mark could not even get her to look at him. The next day he might find her clinging to him, missing her mother, or worrying about a child's cold. She was constantly changing, looking for something to help the feelings that seemed to be crowding out the person she had always been. One day when Mark came home, she said she wanted to teach dance for the Art Linkletter studio. With Mark no longer coaching after school, he could be home to care for the children during the evening classes. Mark readily agreed hoping that maybe this could be the answer. As soon as he arrived home each day Mark would feed the children, play with them, and read to them while DeeDee attended to her dance students. Every play time was filled with balancing, moving, developing muscles and coordination. It wasn't long before their house was brimming with dancers and athletes.

Because not much was known about post partum depression, DeeDee's mood swings continued and became part of their everyday life. It made sense when she wanted to move every six months. Mark thought it was an attempt to escape the unhealthy air. She was trying to escape something else entirely.

After five years of living in Ontario, Mark gave up hope that the air would get better. He turned in his resignation to the school district, and moved the family to San Luis Obispo where the air was clean and the ocean was close by.

He had no job. With his savings, Mark rented a house, then looked for work. When he got down to his last two dollars, he put an ad in the newspaper, "I have a strong back and a good mind. I need work."

The calls came in. Unfortunately, not many were interested in Mark's "good mind." They wanted his strong back doing hard labor or dangerous work such as repairing a leaky pipe that required him to crawl under the house where the black widow spiders were, or fixing a roof on a sharply pitched three story house that other roofers chose not to do. It got him through the summer until he was offered a contract to teach English at the State Prison.

He accepted the job, but before going in, Mark took a course in Abnormal Psychology. The textbook description accurately profiled the sociopath. The sociopath has above average intelligence; he is likable, spontaneous, and disarming. His problem is he has no compunctions for right and wrong. He can kill without guilt or regret. He will steal, cheat, or lie if it serves his purposes.

Because of the sociopath's volatility, classes took fifteen minute breaks. Mark visited with his students during the breaks. One of them asked the question, "I see that all of the teachers wear clip on ties. Is that the fad outside?

"As a safety measure, clip on ties are encouraged. If someone tried to choke me, the tie would come off in his hand." Mark said.

The inmate laughed and said, "If I wanted to kill you, it would be easy."

Mark inquired, "Oh? How would you do it?"

The inmate held up a finely sharpened number two pencil which was handed out to all students. "By shoving this through your ear."

Mark then remembered a training session by an education supervisor who tried to play down danger to new teachers when he answered a question about "any trouble in the classroom." He said, "Every room has a phone on the wall. Just lift it off the hook and after 20 seconds, the guard would meander down to see what you need."

Mark thought: Twenty seconds? By then I would have a dozen pencils shoved in my ear. After meeting the sociopath up close, Mark wanted out of that environment.

He applied to Cal Poly State University and impressed the Head of the English Department with his command of three English grammars, traditional, structural, and transformational grammar. He was hired. The appointment required Mark to return to school.

# Chapter 28

Money was still tight but Mark and DeeDee saved all year and packed up the family for BYU in Provo, Utah, where Mark would get his doctorate. While he studied, the family could visit relatives and do all the things DeeDee did as a child on their summer vacations.

On the way there, Mark left his wallet at a gas station. Discovering his mistake a half an hour later, he returned to find that the station manager had found his wallet, but it was empty. With no money, Mark felt their only choice was to go home.

DeeDee looked at her husband who had been so patient and caring as she struggled to find who she was again, and she looked at her children knowing they deserved a mother who was there for them. It was time to rise up against the weight that had held her down. They needed her now. For the first time in months, DeeDee looked in Mark's eyes, took his hand and smiled. "We can do it," she said. "We can stay with my parents and I can get a job to help out while you are in school. I know we can do it.

Seeing that spark, that life in her eyes, just like the old DeeDee, persuaded Mark to keep going.

Nonetheless, when it was time for her to go for her first job interview, DeeDee couldn't eat. Because she had never waited on tables before, she was afraid of rejection. Her post partum depression worsened. She wanted so much just to stay in bed with the drapes drawn, to hide from the terrible fatigue that never seemed to leave her. Then she thought about Mark and the kids, how much they needed her, how much was depending on her. She decided that nothing was going to stop her. She jumped out of bed, put on her best dress, and came away with a job at the Restaurant on the Green by the golf course.

After her first day, she came home dancing and genuinely smiling for the first time in months. Each day, the cloud that had settled in their lives lifted a bit more as they sat on the bed counting her generous tips and laughing at all the stories of the people who came into the restaurant. Mark's DeeDee was back. Each night after they tucked the children in bed, Mark would massage her weary feet until she fell asleep.

The children thrived in the clean Utah air, and the summer ended all too quickly, as did the years that followed until the big day finally arrived when Mark was awarded his Ph.D.

DeeDee planned a surprise for Mark that day. The doorbell rang. Mark answered it. There stood a young lady dressed in cap and gown who began singing a cappella, "Congratulations to you…." The young lady then handed Mark a personalized license plate from the DMV that said, "Dr. Mark." The plate would play an important role in Mark's life for years.

DeeDee was a natural mother, but she had other

creative energies that needed to flex their muscles. She was taking dance classes in Los Angeles whenever she could because she felt that the existing dance studios in town were outdated and poorly staffed. Mark finished a 40 foot by 12 foot basement in the rented house that they soon bought. DeeDee was thrilled with her first dance studio. She called it DeeDee's Dance and Performing Arts. As he would soon find out, that studio wasn't nearly big enough.

She started with seven students. That number doubled itself every three months in the first year. Her dance studio became two studios, then three, then four. They were known as "the place to go before going pro."

DeeDee's reputation spilled over to the university as college students found her studio. She accepted a job teaching jazz and tap at the University. Her classes were full. Her Ph.D. in dance, so to speak, came when she was awarded the Bob Fosse award for Dance Educator of the Year. Actors had their Academy awards. Dancers had their Bob Fosse awards. DeeDee knew her dancing, but it was how she taught it that brought hundreds of students to her. Students were encouraged by her positive attitude, her uplifting spirit. People were drawn to her smile, her love for dance and her unflagging energy. Dance recitals for DeeDee were "shows" with props, glamour, spectacular production numbers, and even story lines written by Mark.

Mark took over most of the home duties: helping the kids with homework, cooking, cleaning. It was worth it to see DeeDee so happy, but there was that time each day after he put the kids to bed when Mark felt the deep quiet of the house as he waited for DeeDee to come home. The old nightmares returned, but he kept them to himself.

Mark was spending all his extra time helping DeeDee. The dance studios, with their thirty-one employees, provided Mark and DeeDee with little free time, and lots of headaches. The dance business paid five times what teaching paid Mark. He decided it needed a full time manager. He stopped teaching.

But success was not free. Mark had to share DeeDee, something he had trouble doing. Because of her dedication to making every student look good, she would stay overtime with a student or students until they felt the confidence that would make them look their best. She would come home at 2 a.m. drained of every ounce of energy. Mark spent hours fixing nutritious meals presented with flair to encourage DeeDee to eat when she was too tired to move. He stayed up to be sure she got the right sustenance to keep her going. He continued to massage her feet every night, nurturing and loving her as he always had.

Some nights after he finally finished caring for every one else, Mark would fall into bed only to awake breathing hard, perspiring, searching for DeeDee as the car plunged over a jagged cliff and disappeared into the vast nothingness. Afterward Mark would lay awake for hours fighting the emptiness, daring the darkness to swallow him up as well.

Life for Mark and DeeDee was busy, very busy with the dance studios becoming tyrants constantly screaming for attention. But that did not stop Mark and DeeDee from opening a dance wear shop and a discothèque following John Travolta's movie *Saturday Night Fever*. Two days before the grand opening of the discotheque, DeeDee received a phone call from her mother. Her father had died of heart failure. She flew to Utah for the funeral. The opening of the disco would have to wait. When DeeDee got home she threw herself into her work even more. Stress was part of her everyday life.

Mark continued helping DeeDee in her choices regarding her health. With her schedule, she often neglected balanced meals. She liked getting up in the middle of the night to fix a snack, such as eating peanut butter by the tablespoon. One night after DeeDee had gone to bed, Mark got the newly purchased three pound peanut butter jar with its wide lid, out of the cupboard. He took the lid off and then with a butter knife wrote "NO!" on the smooth surface of the unused jar. The next morning when he took the lid off, he saw that his message had been smoothed over and a new message in place saying: YES!"

DeeDee, with all her trips to LA, made friends with dancers and choreographers who would call her about an upcoming audition. If the audition didn't specify age limits, or gender, she would attend the audition for herself. At age thirty no one could tell her from the twenty year olds. Mark would drive down to LA to support her and to be sure she got home safely. He was surprised when she told him about Saturday's audition.

"They want swing dancers, all ages, and couples would be preferred" DeeDee said.

Mark didn't catch on. "Well, we could ask our neighbors. They danced up a storm at the New Years Eve party."

"I wasn't thinking about them." DeeDee said.

"You said all ages, didn't you? Mark asked.

"I was thinking about us." DeeDee confessed.

"Us?" Mark asked in disbelief. "Now wait a minute."

"We do the swing all the time," DeeDee interrupted.

"That's all you have to do. You can do it. It is freestyle, no choreography. You have a good look. It would be fun."

DeeDee's enthusiasm stopped Mark for a moment. Then he said, "No, I'm not ready for this."

"Just audition," DeeDee argued. "Then we'll decide. If they think you are not ready, we come home. If we get the audition, then you are ready. Please, please!" DeeDee would stand with her feet together and she would bend a little at the knees whenever she was asking or begging for a big favor. Mark couldn't say no.

When they arrived at the audition site, there were two hundred dancers lined up around the building.

"Let's go home," Mark said.

"No," DeeDee protested, "With auditions, you never know what they are looking for. They may even take us in right away.

"But we are at the end of the line."

"Just trust me, we came this far," DeeDee replied.

An agent for the audition came outside. He started going up and down the lines looking over the various prospects. He then handed out numbers to some couples, but said nothing.

Everyone was asking what this means. One lady said aloud, "I hate this cattle call type of audition. There is no consideration for us as human beings."

"Miss DeeDee, Miss DeeDee," a voice yelled. Mark and DeeDee turned around. It was Greg and Myra, two of DeeDee's former dancers who had moved to Los Angeles two years ago. They each had successfully auditioned for several other dance jobs.

"Greg, Myra," DeeDee ran toward them. Their big hugs were genuine as were the broad smiles. Teacher and students auditioning for the same gig.

Before the reunion could go any further, Mark called DeeDee. "Our number is being called!" DeeDee didn't want to leave her students, but Mark was getting frantic. "Come on we have to go. Hi guys, bye guys, talk to you later," and he guided DeeDee through the door that the agent was pointing to.

Inside, an audition obviously was just finishing. DeeDee talked into Mark's ear above the music. "See, I told you we might get in early. Look, it's the big band sound. You can do this." Mark watched and nodded yes.

Three days later, DeeDee got the call back. She was thrilled, Mark had weak knees. "We are filming on the Queen Mary in Long Beach. It's a commercial for Atlantic Bell back East. James Earl Jones is the key actor. Isn't this exciting?" DeeDee exclaimed.

Mark took a deep breath and muttered to himself, "What have I got myself into now?"

When they arrived at the Queen Mary, Mark felt very small standing on the dock in the shadow of this huge ship. Their boarding passes were ready and they went aboard. Neither of them had ever been on a cruise ship. For DeeDee, her attention was on the commercial and getting directions. For Mark, it was on all aspects of the monstrous floating city from the bridge down into the bowels of the engine. He didn't want to go to a dance rehearsal. He wanted to inspect the ship. DeeDee grabbed his hand and locked on pulling him in the direction she was going.

They followed their guide into a giant ballroom with 50 foot ceilings, hardwood floors, and tables and booths. Once again they heard, "Miss DeeDee, Miss DeeDee." Not only Greg and Myra made the audition, but two more of her dancers were also selected. They all sat around with ten other couples in a non stop talkathon of excitement and expectation.

"I heard we're not going to do the swing," one dancer said.

"What are we going to do?" another one asked. Mark's face turned white. Every dancer there felt zero fear about whatever dance was chosen. But Mark could only do the swing.

The choreographer came in and announced, "I am Joe Depree from New York. They are rewriting the script and there will be some changes. James Earl Jones will be aboard at one p.m." Then he left.

"That's all?" one of the dancers asked when the choreographer left. "He didn't seem very happy," DeeDee said. Mark saw his opening.

"It looks like we are going to sit and wait until one." DeeDee knew what he was getting ready to do.

"That was the time that Mr. Jones will be here," she said. "The choreographer might come back at any time. Don't even think about leaving."

"I just need to go to the restroom and get some exercise," Mark said unconvincingly.

"Okay, but be back here in 15 minutes." DeeDee was firm.

"I will," Mark said and then he added as he was leaving the room. "I hope I don't get lost."

For the next hour, Mark toured the Queen Mary from top to bottom: the theatre, the restaurants, the bridge, the engine room, the executive suites, the swimming pools. He spent time talking to the look-alike actors who were hired to stroll the decks to add color and atmosphere. He liked W.C. Fields, May West, and Charlie Chaplin.

Then he left the ship and toured the big Spruce Goose

airplane on exhibit next to the ship. The history of Howard Hughes was well done.

When Mark got back to the ball room, DeeDee looked relieved and then she became angry just as a loving mother would react when her 5 year old would get lost and then show up with a big smile unaware of the agony he caused his mother. Mark sat down next to her just as the choreographer came into the room. DeeDee took a deep breath and then beamed her happy, positive smile toward the choreographer.

"Listen up," Joe said. "The director has decided to replace the swing dance with the bunnyhop. That way everyone gets connected—a subtlety they think will better sell Atlantic Bell. I don't like it, but I'm sure all of you can do it." He then put on the music and chose a couple in their twenties to be the leaders. Mark and DeeDee blended in the middle. It was the same movement over and over. Just as the dancers began tiring from the repetition, James Earl Jones came in, sat down and watched with a beaming smile. Joe turned off the music and introduced James who walked toward the dancers. They quickly encircled him

"Are you going to dance?" a dancer blurted out.

"Me? Oh, no! Thank goodness!" he answered. "They want my voice. Here is the story. You are at a night club. Everything is boring – the music, the lighting, your date. The cameras will zero in on your bored, dead-pan expressions. You have no energy. Then I will talk about the wonders of Atlantic Bell and that's when the energy level picks up. You all go crazy and can't wait to join the conga line. Smiles, laughter, lots of movement, you are driven, you can't help yourselves. Life is good! Everyone connects with everyone else. Can you do it?"

"Yeah, let's do it!" the dancers yelled as they went back to the ballroom floor.

About 11 p.m. and 54 takes later, the commercial was done. Mark was exhausted. He knew DeeDee must be exhausted too, but she was not going to let anyone know it. She would be the last dancer to leave. It was a 12 hour day but the first four hours were sitting and waiting. By the time all the residuals came in from the East Coast market, Mark and DeeDee made $10,000 each. No matter how often DeeDee asked Mark to sign on with a talent agent, it was not enough money to repeat the experience.

Mark loved her as his high school sweetheart, and then loved her even more an adult lover and mate. As a dancer, she would audition in Los Angeles for a commercial or a movie. Mark would always accompany her. On their way home, drained of energy, she would lay her head on Mark's shoulder. He would extend his hand to the gearshift which gave her head more resting room on his arm. There his hand stayed while she slept, and while she slept, Mark's poetic mind would create poems about her.

The lines you create
When you dance
Are much like mine
When I write.

Experienced, sensual
You move just enough
To tease and taunt
My pleasure-centered brain.

While I, conciseness try
A couplet, a quatrain

My words have one end,
To leave you breathless.

Your dance a message sends
To stir my passion
Endless.

Our arts thus joined
We love forever
In beauty
Immortalized

# Chapter 29

FEW PEOPLE KNEW DEEDEE was forty-one years old. Her vivacious smile and well toned dancer's body concealed her age. Mark, however, noticed that DeeDee's energy level was not consistent. When she was with other people, she was the life of the party whether it was a rehearsal, a faculty meeting, or whatever she was doing. But when the meeting or cast party was over, a different DeeDee went home with Mark. She couldn't call up the high energy she left with others.

At first, Mark was hurt. To him, she didn't seem to care as much about him as she did for everyone else. Otherwise she would smile and laugh more, and want to be with him.

The first whisper of real concern came when he noticed a lump in her right beast. He urged her to see the doctor. She said she would, but she didn't. Mark became more concerned as he noticed an enlargement of the lump. She made the appointment at Mark's insistence.

The next week he walked in on DeeDee as she was talking on the phone cancelling her doctor's appointment. He took the phone away and stopped the cancellation. Then he drove her to the doctor.

The look in the doctor's eyes when he brought back the test results told it all. DeeDee had breast cancer. Mark sat rigid unable to grasp what was happening. The image of only his voice echoing in an empty house followed by dark nights with no one to hold, froze in his mind leaving him sure that he would awake soon to find it was all just another nightmare. He knew he could not bear losing the one person who, so many years ago, had reached into his very soul, compelling him to love and laugh and live.

Through his numbness, Mark gradually returned to what the doctor was saying. He listened to the doctor go over the various treatments. It seemed that there was a lot that Mark didn't understand. It was time to use his researching skills. Focusing on what he could do, helped him through those first days of helplessness and fear.

Of the many books he read, *Love, Medicine, and Miracles* by Dr. Bernie Segal gave Mark the most information. It said that the national placebo rate was fifteen to twenty percent. This meant that fifteen to twenty percent of the people would get well if they just thought they were taking a powerful drug and not the simple saline solution they were given.

DeeDee's doctor wanted her to have chemotherapy because she had lymph node involvement. She tried it once, and was so violently ill with the dry heaves that she said she "would rather die of the disease than the cure", and she stopped all conventional treatment. She said, "At least the disease is free."

The doctor explained that this was one of the side affects but that he had another drug that would take care of that. "However,' he noted, "the drug for the dry heaves also has side effects but I have something for those."

Mark asked, "What will the chemotherapy do for her?"

The doctor responded, "It will help with her chances of survival."

"How much help?" Mark asked.

"Fifteen to twenty percent," was the answer.

Then Mark mentioned his research. Mark said, "Isn't the national placebo rate 15%?" The doctor nodded.

"Wouldn't it be better to give her a harmless saline solution and tell her it was a powerful medicine? The results would be the same. She would still have a fifteen to twenty per cent chance of getting well, but she wouldn't have to throw up, lose her hair, and feel sick all the time?"

The doctor's face went red as he stumbled for an answer. Mark left. DeeDee was doing the right thing. Mark created meals for a macrobiotic diet, avoiding certain foods, such as her favorite nachos. Instead, she ate broccoli, other dark green vegetables, and she drank lots of fresh carrot juice. DeeDee created visualizations using Garfield, her favorite cartoon cat. At night with the help of pillow speakers she envisioned Garfield voraciously eating cancer cells.

When DeeDee was first diagnosed with breast cancer, she treated the diagnosis lightly. Then she had a breast removed, and the seriousness of cancer gave her a good wallop. Still, she was not ready to become a victim. There were measures she could take, plans of action to be implemented, and a busy life to be lived to its fullest. She continued her teaching, directing, and giving other cancer patients hope.

As her mother's health improved, Desiree felt free to begin her own life. She became a professional dancer right out of high school on a national TV show. The TV show had a nine year run giving DeeDee's studio added publicity. Dozens of her dancers worked on national TV shows, Las Vegas stages, and toured with stars such as Michael Jackson, James Brown, Barry Manilow, Melissa Manchester, and others. Desiree fell in love with a Las Vegas drummer, and was married the next year. When Mark and DeeDee became the grandparents of two dark haired boys, they were ecstatic.

Not to be outdone by his sister, Josh started a career as a deputy sheriff, married and had three blond sons, who also brought lots of giggles back into Mark and DeeDee's life.

Five years later, DeeDee was a survivor, alive and well, and she did it without chemotherapy. Another year passed, then two more and still no sign of cancer, until one day she had a pain in her hip. A bone scan showed the cancer had returned to her hips, skull, sternum, knees, and ribs. Mark and DeeDee went back to the previous treatments. She cut down her stress by teaching only the classes she enjoyed the most. She called on other teachers who were very willing to help her out. She returned to her macrobiotic diet. Within four months, her pain was gone.

She wanted another scan. Her doctor said, "No. The cancer may be gone but she would see a lot of destruction just like an earthquake leaves in its wake." She insisted she felt better for a reason. She got her bone scan. Mark was there when the radiologist looked at the results.

"As you can see, the cancer has worsened," the doctor said and then he paused, and switched scans. Mark noticed the date too. The doctor had them in reverse. "My, God," the doctor exclaimed. "This shows a remarkable seventy-five percent improvement."

DeeDee said, "I knew it was going away. I am feeling normal again." Who's afraid of the big C? was her attitude. She went back to work ignoring a small pain in her hip.

DeeDee's recovery continued. She did so much for others that the City of San Luis Obispo, where their main dance studio was located, chose her to be one of the torch bearers for the 1996 Olympics, being held in Atlanta, Georgia. Even though she was in pain, she would not give up the opportunity to be a model for all the other cancer victims. She high stepped the entire mile before handing the torch to the next carrier. Crowds of people lined the streets applauding as she passed by. They saw a Rockette from Radio City Music Hall with a radiant smile and a love for entertaining an audience. Mark could not take his eyes off of her. Here was his beautiful DeeDee. Every cheer was an acknowledgement of all that she had given, not only to Mark and their family, but also to the world around them. It was her day, and her smile showed how she reveled in it.

Every spare minute was spent with Mark and their grandchildren. Whether they were wrestling in a big pile in the living room or flying kites at the beach or snuggled up reading *The Cat in the Hat,* every moment was precious, filling them with memories of the past and hope for the future.

Knowing it was something they had always wanted to do, Desiree gave Mark and DeeDee tickets to fly first class to Washington, D.C. The first day they started out like wide eyed teenagers, exploring the natural history museum at the Smithsonian. By noon DeeDee was so weary she had to go back to the hotel. Each day they took in as much of the history as they could before returning to their room to rest and share quiet, tender evenings together. The last thing they saw was the Vietnam Memorial Wall. DeeDee stood there reading name after name until she could no longer speak, tears streaming down her face. Mark did not realize they were tears for the return of her pain mixed in with the loss of all the young soldiers.

A year later the pain got so intense she consented to go back to the doctor. The bone scan showed the cancer had returned. Mark and DeeDee once again returned to the macrobiotic diet and her other protocols that had worked so well. This time, it would not go away. For a year she hid the pain, never complaining. Then Mark noticed she would ask to leave early from events she loved. San Luis Obispo's downtown Farmer's Market on Thursday night was one of her favorite places, but the walk was becoming too painful. She had to have pain pills, Advil, Vicoden, and then morphine.

She became bed ridden. Rest was not helping. One afternoon she got up and began walking from room to room with a fierce look of determination. She would win! Then she collapsed on the couch unable to continue.

Day after day she would try to get up. It became impossible for her to go to the studio so Mark threw himself into taking care of every aspect of their lives. He got the teachers at the studio to take over all the classes. He could manage everything else. When he rushed home he would make healthy meals for DeeDee, taking extra care to make everything look and taste as tempting as possible. She exerted all the energy she could muster trying to eat, to do small things around the house, to hide the pain from Mark.

Every night they held each other, sometimes talking the whole night. They talked about the day they met in high school. They remembered when they first said "I love you!, the first time they made love, the day their children were born. Sometimes they spent hours looking at each other, taking in the other's scent, the feel of their skin, memorizing every part of their being. They did not want to waste a single minute. When restless sleep finally did come, Mark had to shed all the protective walls of denial he lived with during the day. Wave after wave of dark, empty dreams poured over him, leaving him weak, aching with loneliness, ready to die rather than face what was becoming his life. Each morning when the alarm blared out its warning that reality was here again, Mark would turn to touch DeeDee, starting his day with the smile she always gave in response.

In her last month, Hospice volunteers visited her several times. Mark was not invited into their sessions. For him, the miracle could still happen. It had to.

One morning at 4 a.m. DeeDee woke Mark. "Today is the day," she said, "I can't do this anymore. It's time. Call Dr. Gary. Call Mom. Call the kids. Call my Hospice nurse."

"But, sweetheart," Mark cautioned, "It's 4 a.m. Perhaps we should wait a few hours and talk about it in the morning." He could not acknowledge what the Hospice nurse knew. Her death was imminent.

She was emphatic, "No! Call everyone now!"

Mark fumbled with the light. In a mental fog he couldn't remember where his book of addresses and phone numbers was. He looked at DeeDee. She had turned over into a fetal position, her back to Mark. For the past year she had been trying to hide the pain caused by the bone cancer that was rampant now. Pain control was useless.

Still not facing the inevitable, Mark thought that she must be delirious with the pain and she probably hadn't thought this decision through. He started to lie back down.

"Now!" came the barely audible, but authoritative command. It was the only word she had to utter to let Mark know she was indeed lucid and quite conscious of the decision she was making. There would be no further discussion.

Mark made the calls, and returned to her side. As he had done on many evenings, he rocked her to sleep by grabbing the bed frame and then gently and rhythmically pushing it side to side.

DeeDee's Hospice nurse and doctor arrived by nine that morning. Her parents and her children were already there. She had been in unbearable pain, a pain one doctor compared to having one's bones broken one at a time, over and over. The liquid morphine could no longer calm the agony she was in. Her stomach would no longer tolerate it.

Dr. Gary gave DeeDee morphine suppositories to avoid her stomach. Then he gave her an injection. By noon she had fallen into a deep sleep. Later her breathing became more labored, more irregular. At nine p.m. the Hospice nurse gave her one more injection before leaving.

The local T.V. station knew of DeeDee's near death fight. They asked Mark if they could do an 11 p.m. special on DeeDee and all her accomplishments. Mark said yes. He gently eased into the bed to lie next to her, and turned on the T.V. Mark looked at her lying next to him, her mouth open, her breathing suggesting a struggle in a bad dream. The beautiful smile was gone, but he could still see in his memory the vitality of that little girl he had run into near the restroom.

The T.V. station did a fifteen minute segment on DeeDee's accomplishments and her ten year struggle against cancer. Her high profile image for the American Cancer Society and her upbeat attitude made her newsworthy.

The moment the T.V. story was over, DeeDee stopped breathing. Mark checked her pulse. She was perfectly still. He checked her respiration. Her mouth was open, but no breath was evident. He was numb. It was over. At last she was out of pain. He lay back taking deep breaths wondering how to break the news to everyone. He closed his eyes for a moment realizing the years of nightmares were now his reality. All the nights he had jolted awake, sweating, searching, crying in the lonely darkness came crashing down leaving him breathless, numb, unable to comprehend.

For five minutes as the T.V. station covered the weather. Then he turned the T.V. off. Time passed. All was quiet. Suddenly, the covers over DeeDee began to rise. Mark pulled them down. DeeDee's arms were rising to the ceiling, palms up. The hair on Mark's neck and arms stood up. DeeDee was dead, but it looked as if she might get up and leave the bed! Mark ran out and called her mother in from the next room to tell her what he just witnessed.

"Ray came to get her," her mother said.

Mark kept his thoughts to himself...DeeDee's mother felt better believing that her father, who had died 4 years earlier, came to collect his darling angel. The truth was, Mark concluded, DeeDee was in her death throes, muscles contract, gasses escape, etc. There was nothing more to it.

Later, the rest of Mark's observations began nagging at him. No other muscles contracted, and wouldn't the strong biceps, in an uncontrolled contraction, slap the hand to the face rather than extend the arm outward toward the ceiling as if she was reaching for someone or something to help her rise? Also, when Mark had come back into the room with her mother, DeeDee's countenance had changed from the grotesque grimace of a bad dream to a sweet, blissful smile. Still, he said nothing.

# Chapter 30

MARK KNEW THAT SADNESS and depression would control his life. He read two books on grieving and was not surprised that his grief followed the text book pattern. The numbness or denial had him thinking, "Everyone has to die. I'm a survivor. I'll be alright." When the numbness wore off, Mark felt responsible, guilty that perhaps he could have done more or done something different. Then he went through an angry stage shaking his fist at the heavens for letting a good person suffer and die. He called God names and challenged Him to come down and fight.

"What kind of a benevolent God are you? How could you take such a perfect being whose life was full of helping others, who loved life, and who was as close as anyone could get to being an angel? How could you let her endure so much pain and die? You are a fraud and a masochist of the worst kind!" Anyone who heard him yelling into the night would have thought he had lost his mind, but Mark fought his battles in the emptiness of his ranch far from another living soul, except the occasional coyote whose cry seemed to echo his grief.

Eventually, the anger subsided and he moved

to acceptance, which brought with it a avalanche of questions. Was this all there was to it? Mark believed that fate brought them together from the moment they first bumped into each other and that he and DeeDee would never be separated. He had trusted fate. Now all those years were gone. He was alone again.

The process left Mark feeling as though he were buried in the depths of the earth, suffocating, frozen, unable to do the simplest tasks, getting out of bed, eating, without overwhelming effort. Finally, Mark went to Dr. Gary who suggested that he write down all his feelings, all his thoughts, and get them all out on paper.

Mark sat down at his desk that night and wrote:

*It may seem foolish to be writing you a letter. I don't even know where to send this letter so it will get to you. Where are you, darling? Will we ever meet again? Is there some way you can let me know, some little clue or signal? If I knew we would be together for eternity, I would wait for you.*

*Dr. Gary says it helps to write all this down, so I'm doing it. I'm trying very hard to get the thing done but I don't see a tunnel let alone some light at the other end. Maybe you can help speed things along?*

*If only I could recapture our lives and be with you all over again. Knowing what I know now and then reliving our lives would be such a treasure. Every moment with you would be even more precious and exquisite. Maybe when we meet again and join our hearts forever, we will have a knowledge, and such a heightened sense of who we are together, that the love we share will light up a whole new universe.*

*I love you forever.*

The next day, on his way home from work about 10 p.m., Mark turned on his car radio to listen to his usual talk show coming from Nevada. He couldn't listen to music. It was too much of an emotional experience. As soon as he turned the radio on, he heard a woman's voice. She said, "If I should stay, I would only be in your way. So before I go, I want you to know, I will always love you." It was Whitney Houston. This was how she started that heart wrenching song from the movie "*The Body Guard*" with Kevin Costner. It ripped at Mark's heart – memories of the two of them in high school surfaced. His senior friends ribbed him about "robbing the cradle" when he started dating the bubbly little mascot freshman who led the football team onto the playing field with a series of back hand springs. He remembered their first quarrel when she stood up to his lack-of-confidence demand that she not wear jeans. He remembered how both of their hearts dropped when they thought their flight to Nogales would be exposed when their "speed had just been clocked by radar."

Mark remembered driving to LA for DeeDee to take dance classes. He remembered waiting for her, knowing his reward would come with their walk down the streets of Westwood, then dinner and a movie, and back to the hotel. The Daddy Reese Cookies were saved for later after Mark and DeeDee made love, slowly at first, building the fire carefully. They loved to kiss, to hold each other and toy with each other's bodies from head to toe. Mark would hold back until her passion spilled over with his, filling her up with a fiery warmth and pleasure. The next morning they would roller skate on Venice Beach.

The song on the radio generated so many memories that his eyes were blurry with tears. He couldn't drive anymore. He had to pull off the highway. He sat there linking two events: DeeDee's arms rising toward the ceiling after she died, and the uncanny timing of this song to answer specifically the questions he had just written to her.

But how did his radio station get changed from his talk radio show to a music station and then the moment he hit the button, Whitney's voice began? He recalled getting his car washed earlier in the day. One of the attendants must have moved the dial while cleaning. But still, what a coincidence! Mark decided that it was too much of a coincidence. He began entertaining the only other conclusion. DeeDee is still in existence, not with the same physical properties, but her essence or soul was communicating with him.

At the time, Mark did not know that these two events were just the tip of the iceberg. His university-acquired empiricism and skepticism were going to be challenged again, and again.

But he couldn't get these two events out of his mind. If DeeDee were still in existence, where was she? Why can't we go there and return? Is there no real death, just a passing to another place? Is this place another dimension right next to ours? Is it in a parallel universe reached with a nonlocal energy? What is the purpose of life? Death? Is there a creator? Where did he, she or it come from? Why are we here? Why do innocents suffer? Is there evil or a Satan? Are our lives predetermined? Do we have freedom of choice? Can anyone predict the future? If they can, does that take away freedom of choice? The questions wouldn't stop. Mark wanted answers. He wanted all the sorrow and crying to stop, but most of all, he wanted to know what lay beyond the veil.

The answers to these questions were in his future. He was open to new ideas, but he was also a Ph.D. who would challenge information that lacked any scientific backing. He even questioned data that he himself experienced.

When he brought the subjects up with other people, he was aware of the looks he would often get, the here-it-comes-again expression and then the diverted eyes. They would patronize him with, "You will get over this in time." This angered Mark. What he was experiencing were not senseless repetitions of coincidental events.

Mark's rationale was: What questions could possibly be more important, and if we don't ask the questions, won't our search for answers stop? A few people found his argument compelling and would engage him. They knew that if answers were forthcoming, it would be because of the driving energy that Mark and others like him exhibited.

# Chapter 31

Six months after DeeDee died, Mark was still in deep sorrow. He cried daily, and in the faint hope that it was possible, pleaded with her to let him see her again, to let him hold her so he would know that she was all right. He promised her he would keep the meeting a secret so that whatever the rules were that she had to abide by, no one would know.

One December night Mark had his first dream of her. In the dream, he saw DeeDee at a public park standing next to a chain link fence watching children play. It was a fall day. Mark came up behind her and put his hands around her small waist and spun her around. When she looked into his eyes, he could see she was overjoyed to see him. He kissed her and lifted her off her feet, then lost his balance and they fell to the ground still holding each other tightly. Autumn leaves got into her hair and on her cheek. They were still looking into each other's eyes. Then they did something that they often did in their forty years of marriage – having the same thought at the same time. They both thought: "What are all the people in the park thinking as we lie rolling around on the ground, probably that we are drunk." DeeDee and Mark burst into laughter.

Mark could feel her warmth, the fullness of her good muscle tone against his body. He could smell her hair, the perfume on her neck, and taste the Double Mint gum she was chewing. He saw how some of the red and brown autumn leaves blended with her hair. Then the thought came to him. "This is just a dream. I'll have to tell DeeDee how real it was when I wake up."

Mark woke up reaching for her in bed to tell her about this very real and unusual dream. He sobbed uncontrollably when he realized she was not there. He had awakened from his dream back into the nightmare of reality.

Later, he wondered if DeeDee visited him for one reason: to teach him how such visits would not be good for him, to have her so close and then have to part with her all over again.

The next event sent Mark in search of every piece of information he could get his hands on. It was the day before Valentine's Day, 1998. DeeDee's professional dance company gave Mark some balloons and a card symbolic of the love for DeeDee that they shared with Mark. The helium filled balloons were all of DeeDee's favorite colors together: pink, white, lavender, purple, and the contrasting red and silver balloons.

Mark appreciated the gift, but didn't know what to do with the balloons. He decided to buy a large Valentine card, write his love sentiments on it, attach it to the balloons, and send the package into the heavens. It was a silly gesture, but if it made him feel better, it would be worth the card.

The sun was shining; everything was green from a

good rain. Clouds to the west and south did not block the sun. There was a slight breeze. The forty acre ranch that they bought nine years earlier had only one tree not indigenous to the area. It was DeeDee's favorite tree, a weeping willow, the very tree where Mark had buried DeeDee's ashes. He stood just a few feet from the tree while he attached the card to the balloons.

Mark said a few words declaring his love for DeeDee and then released the balloons. Soon the package grew small. Mark took out his binoculars and focused in on DeeDee's brightly colored cluster of twelve balloons and an oversized card. To his dismay the balloons started getting larger. Mark thought, they must be falling down. Then they stopped and appeared to be in a holding pattern.

Suddenly, each balloon began glowing intensely. The red was a deep glowing red. Then came a white light so intense that it was blinding. He attributed it to the silver balloon. The purple and pink balloons took turns glowing, one shutting off while the other one flashed its colors.

For the next five minutes, the balloons stayed the same size, and put on an incredible display of colors. The reds, especially, glowed so much the entire package turned red, pulsating like an open heart. At one point, the white lights looked like a white phosphorous explosion or the high intensity runway lights of an airport at night. But these lights were glowing in the bright daylight!

The balloons were flashing colors much like the reports of a UFO seen at night. At times, Mark felt as if he were at a July 4th fireworks show. When each color took its turn, he would ooh and aaw with delight.

While all this was happening, his mind was going in two directions. The logical mind decided the balloons were trapped in a wind current and were spinning and twisting in the sun's rays. He resisted thinking that DeeDee was trying to communicate with him, but other possibilities kept surfacing.

After ten minutes or so, Mark's neck, in its tilted back position, demanded relief. Mark took away the binoculars for two seconds to bend his head down to get the cricks out. When he looked back up with his binoculars, the balloons were gone. Could they have disappeared in the thin high clouds so far above? Did he just imagine all of this? Was this a natural phenomenon? He had watched many helium filled balloons escape into the heavens on a sunny day and never witnessed such a display.

He decided to duplicate the event. The next day he bought the same number and color of helium filled balloons, and weighted a package by stuffing a newspaper in it. No card this time. He waited until 1:00 p.m. Everything was replicated as nearly as possible. He had the binoculars ready when he released the balloons. Nothing occurred. The colors were flat. No change in the balloons at all. They drifted skyward until they disappeared.

The following week Mark attended a lecture on the birth of the universe. The room was full of physics professors, engineers, one astronaut, and cosmologists. Mark cornered a physicist who knew a lot about the sun and gasses. He told him about the balloons, leaving out the part about the Valentine card, and asked him about what might have caused the glowing and flashing. The physicist thought for a moment and then said, "That is not a natural phenomenon. It would take a highly unusual electrical disturbance, perhaps in a laboratory, to make this happen."

"Who knows?" Mark thought to himself with a smile,

"Maybe this whole solar system and the life in it is a colossal laboratory experiment. One of DeeDee's dancers, after all, did say that when DeeDee entered the room she was such a whirlwind of energy that people could feel an electrical disturbance." It was his first genuine smile in several months.

During that first year of anguish, Mark managed the dance studio with the help of his able staff, but he kept to himself as much as possible. He would be going about his daily work with his usual heavy heart, functioning, taking care of business. Then a small reminder, a glance at something DeeDee once held, someone wearing her perfume, or a dance she was known for would send him running for the nearest place to hide and vent his grief. He avoided his family and closest friends as much as he could, afraid that their well intended kindness and sympathy would cause him to break down in tears. Sometimes friends he had known for years crossed the street so they would not have to deal with the sadness in his eyes. When he tried telling the few people he trusted about the balloon phenomenon, their reactions quickly indicated that they felt sorry for Mark and his grief hallucinations. He decided against saying more.

On Easter Sunday, Mark launched another card to DeeDee via balloons. Nothing happened. The balloons were flat. His disappointment and hurt didn't register for two days. Mark became depressed. He didn't know that another event was brewing, and that this one would have an outside witness. By Tuesday evening, tears flowed, and he asked DeeDee to send him a signal or clue that she was close by, "even a dream would do." That night, no dream, nothing. It began to rain.

The next day about 6:45 p.m., Mark was on his way

home from work. As he drove down the main street in Santa Margarita, he saw a huge rainbow that appeared to be over the Las Pilitas area where his ranch was. For the next eleven miles, he could see the rainbow. As he drove, he recalled gathering up the family after being cooped up during a rain, jumping in the car, and chasing after a rainbow just for fun to find the pot of gold at the end. He found out then that they were never able to catch up to those forever elusive rainbows.

As he drove closer to his ranch, Mark saw that the rainbow was indeed going to be very near his forty acres. He came around the bend and drove up the road leading to his house. He was astonished to see that one end of the rainbow was touching the roof of his house, not beyond it, but right on top of it. He could see the chimney as he looked at it through the rainbow and the hue of seven colors.

He sat there for several minutes. This rainbow was not elusive. It stayed stuck on the roof. As he drove down the driveway, he began thinking, "Is this another possible hallucination?" Then it happened. His neighbor, Carla Martinez, came running out of her house and flagged him down.

"Did you see it?" she asked.

"See what?" Mark asked playing dumb.

"The rainbow!" she said. "It was coming out of your house."

Validation! Mark wasn't imagining things. Carla Martinez was his proof that he wasn't having a grief hallucination.

Happening as they did so soon after Mark expressed a need, these events steered him onto a whole new track. He wanted reliable information and truth based on facts, but in the absence of any real scientific proof he read Tippler's *The Physics of Immortality*, Van Praugh's *Talking to Heaven*, Dr. Weiss' *Many Lives and Many Masters*, George Anderson's *We Don't Die*, Helen Greaves *Testimony of Light*, Larry Dossey's *Healing Words*, and all of Deepak Chopra's books. He discovered there was a large body of literature available and that he was not alone in having these experiences.

His quest was to know everything he could about life and death. It would be an open-minded honest journey. He would follow his curious nature. Go wherever his findings took him.

# Chapter 32

WHAT MARK DISCOVERED WAS a large body of literature that legitimized what he was experiencing. He had been having After Death Communications (ADCs). He learned that 42% of adults report having an ADC experience. Quite likely, he surmised, many others, like him, experienced them, but did not report them.

ADCs were not bizarre rare happenings. He read that probably half the world experienced them. "Why, then, have I not heard of them," he wondered out loud.

He also learned of a similar post life experience called NDEs, Near Death Experiences. The literature said thirteen million adults have had an NDE. These experiences occur when a person is pronounced dead and remains that way for minutes or hours. In some cases their bodies were being prepared for autopsy when life returned and they regained consciousness. They then told how they left their bodies, where they went, what they saw, and who they talked to.

This knowledge spurred Mark forward. He was no longer timid about revealing his experiences or reading about others. He knew DeeDee was gone and that she would not miraculously appear to him again in full body.

But he also had to accept that she may still be in existence somewhere, and that she tried to communicate with him in various ways.

Between running the dance studio and reading everything he could get hold of on ADCs, Mark had little time or desire for social events. His son, Josh, noticed this and bought him tickets to see Hal Holbrook's Mark Twain performance. Mark was eager to see Hal again since he had been instrumental in adding valuable information to Mark's PhD dissertation on Mark Twain.

For an hour and a half Mark sat on the edge of his seat, immersed in the humor and political commentary from Twain's time that still seemed so relevant. He had forgotten how good it felt to laugh and to think about the world outside his grief.

After the performance, Mark went backstage to talk to Hal. There were several other fans waiting nervously for an autograph or a word with the star. Standing in line ahead of him was a large man, 6'3", 245 pounds, dressed in a gray suit, his tie loosened. Mark felt small next to him.

The dressing room door opened suddenly and Hal Holbrook's agent stepped out, "Mr. Holbrook would like a few minutes to remove his makeup before seeing anyone." The large man ahead of him was startled when the door opened and took a step back landing on Mark's foot. "Oh, I am so sorry," he said. "I didn't realize you were there. Any permanent damage?"

"No, not to worry. I'm wearing my hard toed shoes," Mark replied.

"I'm sure Mark Twain would have had some clever thing to say about my clumsiness," the man said.

Mark was quick to suggest, "How about this one? The

true charm of pedestrianism does not lie in the walking, or in the scenery, but in the talking."

"Thank you. I bet I am talking to a scholar," the man said with a smile.

"Why do you say that?" Mark asked.

"Who else would know the Twain literature so well to be able to pull up an obscure quote so fast?"

"That's good detective work. I wrote my dissertation on Twain and Hal Holbrook's interpretation of him."

"That's commendable. I'm Jon Thurber," the man said shaking Mark's hand. "I'm with the University of Colorado. And you?"

"I taught here at the university," Mark said.

"Oh, what did you teach?" Jon asked.

"I was in the English Department. And you?"

"I have a double PhD. from New York in physics and psychology."

"Sounds like a conflict of interest," Mark noted.

"Yes," Jon smiled, "They aren't usually used in the same sentence. The combination of the two is leading me in some interesting directions."

"What are you working on?" Mark inquired.

"After my mother passed away, a number of interesting events occurred."

Mark looked startled as he said, "Oh, you mean ADCs?"

It was Jon's turn to be startled. "Yes. What is your connection with the term?" Jon asked.

The door opened again. The agent stepped out. "Mr. Holbrook will see you now, two at a time for autographs and a short visit."

Jon surveyed the group of people waiting. "Why don't we go in together?" he asked Mark.

174

"I was going to suggest that," Mark said. "It looks like we might be last, but I have a question for you."

Jon nodded and said, "Let's hear it."

"How is it," Mark asked, "that 42% of American adults can have a similar extraordinary experience called ADC and the rest of the population knows little or nothing about it?"

"The reason is," Jon explained, "Scientists see them as experiences that can not be duplicated at will. Therefore, they have no scientific value. They are anecdotes that fall into the looney bin category, some more credible than others, but useless to science because they are difficult to measure or test. Mainstream scientists have been avoiding them for fear of ridicule, or see them as just a waste of time. But I am guessing that your connection is personal."

"Yes, I have had some experiences. But Einstein cautioned that all experiences have value. What we experience is the basis for reality." Mark argued.

"I agree," Jon said. "Today, there is enough data to encourage some scientists to take a look at what may be driving these phenomena. I am one such scientist."

Mark's interest piqued instantly. "You don't strike me as a comical ghost buster. Tell me about your research. Have you come to any conclusions? Do you believe in life after death? Who else is doing research? What reading do you recommend? Would you be interested in some of my experiences?"

"I would indeed," Jon answered. "But it looks as if it is our turn to see Mr. Holbrook. Here is my card. Let's get together next week."

Mark and Jon were greeted warmly by Mr. Holbrook, who signed Mark's dissertation, thanking him for "his wonderful work." Jon mentioned Twain's popular quote,

"The reports of my death are greatly exaggerated." Hal laughed and said he had been doing the show for so long, he may have to use the quote soon himself.

Mark left Jon with a promise to call the next day. Amazingly Mark had truly enjoyed an evening without DeeDee. He had made a friend and found an ally in his quest. He had not been so excited for a long time.

# Chapter 33

THE NEXT DAY JON phoned Mark saying he had been called away and would get in touch when he got back. He gave Mark his email address and asked Mark to send him a synopsis of the events he had experienced.

Mark started thinking about all the things that had happened that could have been ADCs. On June 12th one year after DeeDee died, Mark was feeling low and depressed. He began talking aloud to her as he lifted weights. "I need you. I don't know if I can keep going. My shoulder seems to be freezing up. I'm not feeling well. I need to know if you are still there. Does time pass the same for you as it does for me? I want to touch you, to see you, to know how you feel. Are you close? Will we ever see each other again? What is your life like now?"

The next morning when Mark lifted weights in the covered area by the garage, he had noticed his shoulder was measurably better, perhaps seventy percent. He went inside to do dishes and began smelling a fragrance. It was DeeDee's perfume. He started sniffing through the house for the source. No flowers inside giving off scent, no soap suds. Was his olfactory memory playing tricks?

Mark left for work but he remembered how disoriented

and unsure of his driving he had been. He tried to focus, so he turned on his favorite talk radio station. A woman was singing:

> Cause I am your lady
> and you are my man
> whenever you reach for me
> I'll do all that I can.

Mark became so emotional he couldn't hear the words to the rest of the song. He didn't know who was singing or what the title was. Two days later with the help of his daughter, he tracked it down and discovered it was Celine Dion's *The Power of Love*.

As he thought about the rest of the lyrics, he realized this was yet another profound revelation that told him he was on to something. He could no longer deny the synchronicity of the event and the specific language used to answer the questions. To call it a coincidence ignored the obvious answer.

> Even though there may be times
> It seems I'm far away,
> Never wonder where I am
> Because I am always by your side.
>
> We're heading for something,
> Somewhere I've never been.
> Sometimes I am frightened
> But I'm ready to learn
> of the Power of Love.

The sound of your heart beating
made it clear.
Suddenly the feelings that
I can't go on
Are light years away.

Cause I am your lady
And you are my man
Whenever you reach for me
I'll do all that I can.

It was what Chopra called a co-incident, two incidents
brought together for a reason. The words were so specific
to the needs Mark expressed, and Celine sang them with
such power and force, he could not miss their meaning.

Mark decided that such communications through
song would be a natural for DeeDee given her background.
He had received many such communications. Each had
earmarks that he recognized which assured him that the
song was special and specific to the needs he had recently
expressed. For example, it had been nine months since the
Whitney Houston song *I Will Always Love You*, woke him
up to these co-incidents.

A few days after that, Mark had been thinking how
lifting the incident was for him. As he drove home, he
began talking about his feelings and how good it would
be if DeeDee gave him another communication like that.
He said these words, "I know if it is possible, you will
find a way to make it happen. It would be a real boost
to hear from you since it has been so long, but you will
choose some method that would be specific and obvious.
It wouldn't be just another love song. It will have some

special significance so that I would know it was from you."

The next morning, when Mark started his car, the music came on the radio Mark clearly remembered turning off. It was Whitney Houston's *I Will Always Love You*, the song Mark had not heard in all those months. It was clearly earmarked as an incontrovertible message from DeeDee. This incident, given the sequence of events, was exactly what Mark asked for.

Another message Mark received happened three years after DeeDee passed. Mark sold the dance business, paid off some bills, put a Jacuzzi and deck out back, and had enough money left over to pay cash for a new car. The night before he bought the new car, he was sitting in the Jacuzzi looking up at a starlit night and thinking out loud "I own the ranch and everything in it. The only thing missing is you. You need to be here to enjoy the new car with me."

The next day, Mark bought the new car and instructed the salesman to transfer the personalized license plate "Dr. Mark" to the new car so that no new plates would be sent to him. The salesman complied, and Mark drove away with his new car. Apparently someone didn't get the right information. The DMV sent Mark new plates two weeks later. The first three letters on the plate that the DMV sent were 4DD S869.

The first three letters were enough to convince Mark that DeeDee let him know she was there enjoying the car. He said to himself, "This seals it. I am convinced she is still in existence. I won't need any more ADCs to prove that."

He emailed Jon with the details of all these events. Mark received the reply that evening:

"Empirical data from the NDE research provides a foundation which holds that: Humans are composed of two parts comprising two different substances – the physical body composed of matter, and the essence composed of a nonmaterial substance which interacts during physical life to produce mind. Typically, strong emotions (even preoccupation) by those in physical form draw a departed essence to this side in an attempt to comfort us. It appears your wife loves you, knows the course your life is taking, and will be there to meet you when you, too, pass through the wormhole."

# Chapter 34

CONSUMED WITH THE DESIRE to reach DeeDee and to finally have a purpose for living, Mark filled his every waking moment with his research. But those dark, silent hours after 3 a.m. brought him back to the aching loneliness that had filled him all those years since DeeDee's death.

He remembered DeeDee, a year before she died, saying to him, "If I were to die before you, I want you to know that you have my permission to remarry." Then after a pause, she added, "but not too soon." Mark was a little surprised by her statement since it came right out of the blue. She was hiding her pain, and knew what lay ahead for her.

Mark responded, "I feel the same way. I want you to remarry, too." Then he added with a smile, "I know if there is life on the other side, we will find a way to be together."

For seven years, Mark had been living alone. Most of the time he thought he was managing the loneliness well enough. On Valentine's Day he reluctantly accepted an invitation for dinner at his son's house. Josh had bought his wife a bouquet of roses which instantly started Mark's tears. His grandsons asked, "Why is Grandpa crying?"

Josh took his father outside. "How are you doing, Pop?" Josh asked.

Mark used a sleeve to wipe away the tears. "I don't know. Some days are worse than others. I signed up for a dating service, but I have lost interest. So far no one comes even close to your mother."

"No, of course not," Josh encouraged, "but there must be a few good ladies looking for someone just like you who would love to share the rest of their lives."

"Their diseases, craziness, bankruptcies, and who knows what else." Mark interrupted. "I would be happy to leave tomorrow.

"Leave? What do you mean?' Josh asked.

"Leave this world, get it over with. I don't want to be here anymore. I don't want to talk about it." Last year Mark had signed up for an internet dating service. His heart wasn't really into it, but he knew he was just a few weeks away from permanently ending his loneliness. The few women he met, he did not ask out. His future looked rather bleak. It was in May when he vowed that if he could not find a mate, he would end his life on DeeDee's birthday in October.

Josh could see his father had given this departure some serious thought. He needed to call Desiree about their father's mental state. They definitely needed to give him more of their time to try to plug him back into the living. He thought for another moment and then said, "Let's go back in. The boys have a game for us. They have missed you."

Josh was hoping to bring him back to the anchors he helped raise as infants. Mark babysat the three boys during the day when they were small, and had developed a special bond with each one. He had been there when they woke in the morning. They had to do some work, learn something, and then play each day. Grandpa had taught them to collect firewood, to build things such as a mailbox, and to do household chores. He taught them how to use his reference books, how to read, how to write stories.

And then the play began. They flew paper airplanes and set off rockets that came down with parachutes. They played all kinds of ball games, wrestled, and explored every inch of the ranch. On rainy days their favorite game was blanket monster. They made the house as dark as possible. Grandpa put a blanket over his head and tried to find the boys who were hiding all over the house. There was always a lot of yelling, running, and laughter. This was the game Mark played that day.

As he was leaving, every member of his family gave Mark a warm hug which told him how important he was to them. When he got home, he went out to the deck and sat on the porch swing, looking at the stars and listening to the crickets just as he and DeeDee had done so many times over the years. He thought about how much he wanted to hold DeeDee again, how much his family meant to him, and how much of an effect it might have on them if he was to join her. Finally around 4 a.m. he made a decision. He decided that in the next five months, he would give his search for someone else a genuine try. Later that day he would set up meetings with two different women. On Friday, he would meet Paula, and on Sunday, he would meet Sally.

The Monday before these dates, he checked his email. There was a message from a Babs, who saw Mark's profile on the dating website. It said, "I'm not answering your profile as a potential date. I just wanted to let you know that you are not the only one out looking for a new mate after losing someone special to cancer. It was 34 years before my wonderful husband died of cancer. He also got his B.S. from ASU and his Masters from NAU. We had great times at both places. I have a second home near you out in the country but I only have five acres. Around weed abatement time, that is plenty. I just wanted to say hang in there. Some day, maybe we'll both find that someone special. Babs."

Mark replied, "Hi Babs, Thank you for your thoughtful words. Did you or your husband grow up in Phoenix? When were you there? Mark discovered that Babs and her husband lived in Phoenix just blocks from the neighborhood where Mark and DeeDee lived. They were on the ASU and NAU campuses at the same time. Babs shopped at Food City where Mark worked. Their paths must have crossed many times. More co-incidents?

Mark wanted to meet this lady in person without going through the usual dating site but he resisted the temptation and continued with emails. He liked her prose. The more he learned about her, the more he liked. He felt at ease with her. He couldn't wait. He arranged to meet her at the Golden China restaurant on Saturday at 6 p.m. He kept his Friday meeting with Paula. Within the first 15 minutes, he knew she was not the one.

On Saturday, he arrived at the Golden China early and made arrangements with the manager to be served in a seldom used room next to the main dining room. Nervously, he checked his watch every five minutes. He finally went to the restaurant entrance to wait for Babs. She arrived on time. Recognizing her from her picture, he opened the door and stepped outside as she approached. "Babs?" he asked.

"Yes, Mark?" she replied. He gave her a hug. Caught by surprise, she seemed unresponsive at first. Then she smiled and hugged Mark.

In the semi-private room, Mark and Babs traded autobiographies, the death of their mates, the dating hazards, children, grandchildren, their occupations, their likes and dislikes, even a little politics. The time passed so quickly, they did not notice it was getting dark outside. Mark did notice their waitress looking at her watch. He left her a $10 gratuity.

After dinner, Mark took Babs to a nearby city park where they walked and talked some more. Babs told Mark how she and her husband had talked about their wishes should one precede the other in death. He "wanted me to remarry" Babs said. Mark withheld the conversation he had with DeeDee regarding the same subject.

Mark didn't understand the ambivalence he was feeling. Babs was likeable. She smiled often, even genuinely laughed at Mark's attempts at humor. She had the figure of a 20 year old: narrow waist, flat tummy, long, perfectly shaped legs, and her breasts were in proportion to her size 4 figure. His sleeping libido was awakening, but he was suppressing it. Why? He decided to give her a warm short kiss, just a passing touch of the lips before the evening was over.

They held hands as they walked to the car parked in the dim light of one of the park's lamps. He opened the passenger side door and then stood in front of it as Babs moved toward him. Mark put his hands around her small waist and pulled her in close to him. She put her arms around his neck. As their lips touched, an instant stirring ran through Mark's body melting their lips together, pushing back the emptiness that had filled him for so long. He pulled her in more tightly. When they finally forced themselves apart, Babs and Mark looked into each others eyes knowing that something life-changing had just happened. Instantly, Mark felt guilt over his emotional and physical reactions to Babs. Could that be right when his heart belonged to DeeDee?

Still, Mark felt compelled to try to see Babs again. He asked, "Could you come to my ranch tomorrow for lunch?"

Babs' heart immediately wanted to say "YES, YES!", but her good sense told her to be a little more cautious, after all, they just met three hours ago.

"I would love to," Babs said, "but my girlfriend and I have plans for tomorrow,"

"Bring her along. I would love to meet her," Mark said.

"Are you sure?" Babs asked "I mean it wouldn't be an imposition?"

"Would you know later this evening?" he asked.

"Yes, she is waiting for me now at my house in Atascadero. She has decided that it is her job to make sure I get home safely. She knows about you and our date."

When he got home, Mark called Sally to cancel his Sunday date. He was feeling guilty, not about Sally but about his feelings for Babs. He had just met her. What would DeeDee think?

That evening Mark was stirred by the phone ringing. He started to pick it up right away and then he let it ring four more times. He took a deep breath.

"Mark speaking," he answered.

"Hi, it's Babs," she said. "Vickie wants to meet you."

"And if I don't measure up to her standards, am I in trouble with you?" Mark asked.

"No, we are old friends. She isn't my mother. She is a kick to hang out with. You will like her." Babs answered.

"Okay, how about I make lunch for three, and you and Vickie arrive say – high noon." Mark said.

"High noon? Sounds like a showdown." Babs chided.

"I don't plan on a shoot out and my cooking hasn't killed anyone yet. No one will forget the high noon time. I'm looking forward to meeting Vickie and having you over."

"Okay, I'll see you at high noon tomorrow." When Babs hung up the phone and began to tell Vickie about the invitation, they started jumping up and down like teenagers who just got asked to the prom, not grandmothers who were supposed to be dating sensibly. They stayed up most of the night planning what to wear, what to say, what to do. They talked for hours about the fact that despite her love for her first husband, Mark had stirred feelings in her she had forgotten existed. In such a short time, how could she see his face each time she closed her eyes, how could her pulse stir so strongly thinking about that kiss, how could she be so anxious for tomorrow to arrive.

Since the way to the ranch might be a bit tricky, Mark and Babs had arranged to meet at the park-and-ride area just outside the small town of Santa Margarita, eleven miles from his ranch,.

Mark was waiting for them when Babs and Vickie arrived. They both got into his car, with everyone talking at once in the excitement of the moment.

Mark drove slowly through the quaint one street town,

whose major industry seemed to be antique shops in old 1930's vintage houses nestled between the lumber yard, the one general store, and a small café. A right turn at the railroad tracks took them past a park filled with families enjoying a birthday party. Another minute and they were on their way sliding past the few homes and into the country. Green rolling hills were home to cattle, horses, and an occasional deer. A bald eagle swooped down from its perch to capture a frantic mouse. Everywhere they looked was open spaces, blue skies, and peaceful nature.

Mark's and Bab's minds, hearts and stomachs were a different story. As each mile drew them closer to the ranch, both of them recognized that something very important could be happening that day. Was their first date a fluke? Could it be that what they had both felt yesterday, the feeling that they knew each other, the feeling of instant electricity between them, the feeling that somehow it was all so right, might be real?

As they drove around the last blind curve and through the big wrought iron gates, Babs was struck by the majestic old oak trees that surrounded the house, making it feel safe and strong. Three dogs came rushing up, welcoming their master and his guests. When they entered the sprawling ranch style house, Babs felt the warm homey traces left by a family that had once laughed and loved there. Mark's pride showed as he gave the house tour, ending with his favorite room, his library, packed from ceiling to floor with his precious books.

After a lunch of hamburgers and lots of good home grown vegetables, Mark and Babs drove Vickie back to the car. She anxiously returned to Bab's house. When Mark and Babs got back to the ranch they sat out on the porch swing under the weeping willow tree. They spent the rest of the day holding hands, talking non stop, sharing who they had been in the past, who they were now, and who they wanted to be in the future. Both of them agreed that they had loved their spouses unconditionally for most of their lives, but they were ready to try to find some happiness in life again.

When Mark took Babs home, they both felt something extraordinary had happened. As they kissed good night, they looked into each others' eyes and saw the possibility that the human heart can hold a soul mate close forever and yet still find another place for love to bloom.

Mark's excitement over Babs encouraged him to call his son, Josh, and tell him about the lady he just met. "I know it's too soon to be talking this way, but I believe she's the one," Mark said.

"You mean the one to date for a few months so you can be sure?" Josh asked.

"No, I mean the one I'm going to marry." Mark answered.

"But what do you know about her? I bet you don't even know where she lives," Josh challenged.

"But I do and I want you to write it down," Mark answered. "Do you have a pen and paper, Mr. Detective? She and I have shared a shadow history. It's uncanny!"

"Stop stalling. What is her address and phone number?" Josh asked.

"You don't have a pen and paper yet," Mark challenged.

"OK, now I do. Tell me." Josh said.

Mark gave him the information. Then he talked for another five minutes about a possible wedding date. Before he hung up, he asked Josh, "What address and phone number did you write down?" Josh gave him the right answer.

That evening at home Mark went out to sit on the porch swing, the one where he and DeeDee had spent so many peaceful evenings talking about their day and their love, the one he and Babs sat on when they shared who they were. Doubts began to creep in with the setting sun.

On Sunday, thoughts of Babs kept Mark on edge. The house seemed darker, emptier than usual. On impulse he decided to throw a few things in a bag and head for San Francisco.

DeeDee and Mark often took advantage of a long weekend and would drive to San Francisco to get away, to clear their minds. They loved walking in Golden Gate Park, the streets of San Francisco, Pier 39, and they loved an opportunity to see a high level stage production such as *Beauty and the Beast*. Mark remembered the last time he walked with DeeDee on their way to a musical review. They had to pass an alley where six street people sat. They got up and approached Mark and DeeDee. They were dirty, greasy-haired people wearing urine stained clothes. They had blood shot eyes and yellow, brown or missing teeth. Mark positioned himself between DeeDee and them. He told her, "Don't make eye contact and move a little faster out of the shadows." Once past the alley, Mark and DeeDee heard them yelling, "Weirdoes, go screw yourselves." He remembered DeeDee asking, "What did we do to them?" Mark answered, "It's not us personally. We represent society at large. Whatever their story is—drugs, alcohol, bad home life, bad luck, they feel abandoned and angry."

As they walked on, DeeDee leaned her head on Mark's

shoulder. She felt safe with Mark. To her, he wasn't afraid of anything. He had good instincts and always managed to do the right thing.

Why then was he impulsively going to San Francisco to revisit that alley? His instincts didn't seem to be so good now. Would his head clear once he gets there? There was no turning back. He had to go. Why was he feeling guilty? He tried to rationalize his behavior. Maybe the fear he felt with DeeDee that day passing the alley burned into his memory the kind of love she had for him. To her Mark was strong, smart, and he always chose the best course of action. He knew her thoughts were "I trust him. I love him."

Maybe, he thought, he wanted to feel that love from her again. He needed to declare his love for her. The drive, the effort to revisit that spot would be proof of doubling his commitment to her. He had to go there. Mark recalled the theatre that he and DeeDee went to for the musical review, where they parked, and the alley they passed. He slowed his walk as he approached that same alley. The same assortment of misfits was sitting on boxes, two of them inserting needles into their arms. Ever since DeeDee died, Mark had no fear of death. It was just the reverse: he was hoping fate would hurry his death along.

Alone, he felt no fear. No need to rush past. No DeeDee to protect. He took his time as he looked at them. It was the smell that alerted him to something large that had just stepped in front of him. A hulking 6'5" obstacle with frizzy long hair and a beard that still had droppings of his morning breakfast attached, stood with a wide stance in front of Mark. He had a baseball bat cradled in his arms.

Mark came to an abrupt halt to avoid making contact,

and then took two steps back. Mark could see sores on the back of the man's knuckles. The large man licked his lips, then said, "What's the matter, ain't you never seen no big time baseball game? I'm gonna use your head for a baseball."

Mark wondered why the man had not asked him for his wallet. Then he realized the threatening hulk had a greater need—to see fear in Mark's eyes. Mark looked at his adversary, and could hear footsteps moving in behind him.

Suddenly, the situation became very funny. He had no fear, none whatsoever. The glaring hulk before him tried to turn up the menacing stare, but Mark could not hold back the laughter. He remembered Paul Newman in "Cool Hand Luke" who dispensed with a threatening large man by delivering a perfectly placed kick between the man's legs, and he remembered the surprised painful look on the big man's face. He laughed all the more. He resisted the temptation to do the same thing, and turned around facing four other unshaven, filthy, street people. They were threatening him with his life, and he didn't care. He looked at each one and laughed even harder. One of the unshaven ones looked like she could be a woman, but if so, what was that on her face?" As he moved toward them, their eyes looked above Mark's head, and they stepped back.

A sudden bolt of lightening blinded Mark as his brain felt the crush of the bat.

# Chapter 35

THE NEXT THING MARK sensed was the rush of wind as he traveled inside a tunnel. He looked ahead and saw a brilliant blue light. It was drawing him into it. As he reached the end, he burst through to the other side and was blinded by an even greater white flash that gradually faded to the side revealing an auditorium size hall filled with people near his age. All looked as mystified as he was as they sat in padded seats and stared with him at the podium on center stage. A woman entered from the right. She had beautiful long lines and a sensuous stride to the podium. She was wearing a long iridescent gown that seemed to radiate soft soothing light. The gown clung to her, showing her perfect curves as a toned leg peaked through a side slit. Her blond hair was pulled back to show high cheek bones surrounding large expressive eyes with long eye lashes, and natural full red lips.

Her crystal clear, even tones penetrated the entire hall. The P.A. system was tied into each chair. The words she spoke were a natural conversational style with no more effort than her being just three feet away.

"Welcome to the PMC, the Pre-Memory Complex. I am your hostess, Asha. Today, you will receive a panoramic review of where we have all been, and then you will come to understand why you are here, and where we are all going. What will pass before you in a few minutes may be alarming, but I want you to know that all of you are safe. How do you feel? Are any of you in pain?" She paused, "No? Good! I know you have questions. Some of you are wondering, is this just a dream? Where are we? How did we get here? Are we dead?"

The audience, in a collective nod of heads, indicated that Asha was reading their minds. "Let me take the last question first, Are you dead? Because none of you have any pain, if this is death, then pain does not accompany it. However, your mental anguish of the unknown is what concerns you. So let's get that cleared up right now. Technically, you are dead." Gasps from the audience were audible everywhere.

"But," Asha quickly intoned, "Your's is a near death experience and you will be returning to Earth soon. All of you are involved in life experiments on Earth. We will be covering that subject in more detail later."

"No, this is not a dream," Asha continued, "What you are experiencing is real. As to, 'Where are you?' You are home. By that I mean this dimension was your starting place." A buzz and a hum of muffled voices filled the auditorium.

Asha said, "I know, I know, all of you are saying, I have never been here in my life, but before the morning is over, your memories of this side will come back to you—slowly at first and then it will all rush in and you will feel the familiarity and comfort of home. In order for you to do that, we have to do some house cleaning. You are in the PMC, the Pre-Memory Complex. All of you have lived more than one life. Your memory banks are full. By revisiting those lives, you will be able to flush disturbing memories and call up more pleasant ones."

"First, you will experience Part One from *The Necessary Past*. Part Two will put everything in perspective, and will answer all your questions. Beside each of your desks is a pad and pen. Flip up your desk top and you will have a writing surface for any questions that come up." Asha paused as the desk writing surfaces locked into place with metal clicking sounds. "And now, it is time to part the veil."

The plush velvet curtains, with a sudden breeze, pulled to each side. A huge screen the size of a drive-in theatre but with high definition wrapped around the stage. The words "Part One: *The Necessary Past*" in large bold green letters appeared on the screen, and then moved away from the center rolling to the sides and then out of view giving the screen a three dimensional quality as they grew smaller in the distance.

The screen went black! Ten seconds passed. Just when Mark and the others began to think that there had been a projection failure, an intense white light flashed on the screen as if they were at a ground zero nuclear blast. There was no sound although their minds provided one. Their heads automatically turned away, some shielded their eyes with their hands. The intensity of the bright, white, exploding light dimmed, and pieces of dark matter emanated, swirled, and grew larger and larger as if a zoom lens camera was giving them a closer and closer view, past the cloudy cover, past the rain sizzling on a hot barren surface. There was movement below the steam. Black peaks poked up their heads above the mist. What appeared to be the green letters returning was just the shade of green that began to paint the desolate topography and to part the haze. A breathtaking dawn lit the horizon, first in orange, then the sun loomed large revealing blue ocean waves rolling up a sandy beach.

Tiny animals with tails swam, then crawled ashore and spread their wings. Four legged creatures scampered in groups then stood on hind legs to reach edible leaves. Bipedal lizard-looking creatures hunted in packs taking advantage of smaller or weaker life forms. The landscape was lush green; rain and sunlight worked their magic and the life forms grew large. The dark peaks were consumed by vegetation. The countryside teemed with life of all shapes and sizes. The camera looked at the eyes of the life forms up close. Some eyes showed intelligence and gentleness. Others were emblazoned red with rage and the intent to devour. Powerful jaws and hindquarters worked like steam pistons to claw and chomp their way to survival. Suddenly a streak from the sky became a bright exploding light, and bleached out all visible shapes.

Next, a fire covered the screen. As the zoom lens backed away, four-foot creatures were jabbing sticks at flames. The thunderclouds above looked down on the grassfire as these creatures overcame their fear long enough to show some mastery of these lethal yellow and red streaks. The creatures' eyes sparkled with the first glimmer of real intelligence. Mark saw the dawning of knowledge and cooperation, but most decidedly there was a look of tenderness and love, not just for each other, but for other objects of beauty such as a flower with delicate and colorful markings, or glorious sunsets that caused all the people to gather around and stare silently at the spectacle. The screen announced "8500 B.C. The Mesopotamia Alluvial Plains. Village Life, and the Experiments begin."

What followed were panoramic views of people

197

growing, working, living, and laughing. Laughter never occurred with the earlier creatures. Mark recognized the alluvial plain between the Tigris and Euphrates rivers where the soil soon produced the richest granary of the ancient world. Trees bore fruit, fields blossomed with cereals, malted barley yielded a brew that dulled pain, and vineyards added wine.

The food and drink were plentiful. The pleasures were returned to again and again. Overeating produced corpulence and diseases of the body. Overdrinking produced dullness, erratic behavior, and diseases of the mind. Sexual pleasures were indulged in without regard for the chosen subject be it a woman, a child, an animal, or a man. The addiction to pleasures became a problem, and another experiment began.

Some members of the audience felt an urge for a glass of wine, other appetites were mildly stimulated.

The prosperity soon stopped when warfare broke out, as military leaders became kings with an addiction for world control. The battle scenes that followed revealed the advancement of more lethal weapons.

Dates, 8000 B.C., 2500 B.C. flashed by. Pyramids penetrated the horizon, clay tablets gave way to papyrus, 612 B.C., 334 B.C. flashed by. Alexander the Great led an assault against Persia. The lens looked into the eyes of that leader. A new intelligence was emerging. Art, architecture, music, and science flowed from the minds of state sponsored planning and control. The cultivation of the fields and animals brought prosperity and city growth.

The lens moved about the globe. People looked toward the dawn over the Tigris River, and gave praise to the deities whose hands controlled the fate of the earth's inhabitants. The Gods assumed human forms and took on human emotion and human frailties. Namma, Ninmah, An. Enlil, Utu, Inanna who attended to fertility, the sky, the sun, the wind, and the sea, were replaced by other powerful Gods that had to be placated with offerings and temples. The lens looked closely at individual's faces and eyes. Some audience members felt squeamish, and skittish, but didn't know why.

The panorama soared over oceans and dropped into Celtic villages, monumental forts, pagan gods, and human sacrifice. Then back again to Greek cities where architects and artisans, playwrights, and politicians laid the foundation for western civilization for future millenniums. Chaos spawns more Gods" Ares, Aphrodite, Hephaestus, Athena, Apollo and Hades. Roman soldiers marched, cities burned, the coliseum provided blood baths that excited the citizenry, their eyes red with lust. Wine flowed freely and in excess.

Three faiths grew from the memory of a man named Abraham: Christianity, Islam, and Judaism. Background voices could be heard, "One God!" One God!" as three screens flashed images depicting the history of each religion. All three screens revealed a blood-filled history of holy wars in the name of God. Again, Mark and the others shook their heads in disgust and turned away from the slaughter. The screens looked closely at each leader from Abraham to Moses, from Jesus to St. Paul, from Mohammed to Ali and Muawiya. Each close up revealed a face in search of a meaning. Many audience members became rigid, short of breath. One man's voice could be heard tremulously repeating over and over, "one God, one God, one God." The need to know dominated their every thought. A strained, intense search of the horizon, a collapse of the body to its knees in surrender to the unknown, a determined rising with eyes toward the heavens, each leader followed a similar path with some productive changes, but with some devastating results.

In the East, Hinduism, and Buddhism merged. From the plains below the Himalayas, Siddhartha Gautama was born the son of a king. He left his princely life in search of meaning. In Eastern India, his eyes glowed with the joy that comes from not just knowing, but knowing that one knows. He was from then on known as Buddha, the Enlightened One. He taught non-violence, religious tolerance, truthfulness, and compassion.

From the Asian Steppes came the Aryans carrying with them an Indo European language and the Vedas. This collection of prayers, rituals, songs and poems mixed with other religious sects. Some audience members remembered the words to the songs and poems. There was no single leader for the lens to focus on. No set form of worship, no single dogma, just a loosely knit organization held together by the belief that everyone should strive to achieve Moksha, the ability to break the cycle of rebirth. Its open approach to this achievement encouraged newcomers.

Jesus followed with pleas for love, forgiveness, sharing, and brotherhood.

The lens took the congregation of captivated students galloping through two millenniums of war, degradation, and greed. This greed, often disguised as a lofty religious ideal, drove the armies. "To the victor belongs the spoils" was the battle cry of the crusaders. The confederate soldier believed that slavery was a moral and positive good. He died for southern perfection.

The screen changed to a prosperous shipbuilding city

of 300,000. Japanese families and workers awakened to a bright sun after spending restless nights in air raid shelters. All was peaceful. They stretched and began their day. Above, a lone B-29 dropped something by parachute. It drifted slowly down. Then the screen exploded with a huge flash brighter than any sun. Mark felt the heat striking his body as a firestorm wind blew past. His eyes closed, his lips pressed tightly against each other to keep the wind from entering his mouth. A mushroom cloud rose 23,000 feet into the sky. The noiseless flash was followed by a silent, slow measured look at the ash-strewn desolation of what was at one time a thriving city. Everything was charred and reduced to rubble. Stunned survivors stumbled and picked through flattened remains. Others lay quivering in a heap of hopelessly burned flesh. Some audience members moaned and cried.

Mark didn't want to watch any more, but the screen was relentless in its detail. Other wars, other destruction of life and limb, other horror and inhumanity would pass, before the screen finally went dead and the lights came up. At last it was done. Asha returned to the podium.

# Chapter 36

Left with so many images of death and utter destruction, Mark was incensed. Others breathed sighs of relief when the last war was over following the collapse of the World Trade Center Towers. Why was the audience subjected to this review? He wanted to erase the negative images. He grabbed his pen and pad and wanted to be first with his questions.

Asha's clear tones were concise. "You no doubt have questions. I will take them now."

Mark was eager with his question. He stood up and yelled, "What was the purpose of the review?"

Asha answered. "No need to yell. Your seats are also a microphone. Just raise your hand and I'll call on you. You asked, what was the review's purpose. Mark, you and others wanted to erase the negative images. But you also felt a familiarity with some of the inhabitants, their communities, their fears, did you not?" Looking at each other, the majority of the audience nodded yes. "Did you sense a deja vu when you knew what was going to happen before it happened? That was because you were there. You lived in that time. You felt anxieties, you experienced indulgences, you wallowed in debauchery, you protected the vulnerable, the young, the old, you believed in frightening Gods. You followed out of fear, you marveled at works of art and beauty, you chose to lead, you died violent deaths as well as deaths of sickness and age. You were sated for short periods of time, but few of you could attest to real happiness."

A woman raised her hand. Calling her by name, Asha said, "Marie, your question please." Surprised, Marie hesitated then said, "How did you know my name?"

"Is that your question?" Asha asked.

"No, not the first one," Marie responded, "but how do you know my name?"

"Most of you," Asha said, "have had more than two lives in different periods of human history. For our experiments to be successful, we must keep track of you. Your individual auras carry that information along with other important data about your experiences. It is easy for me to access that storage. Now what is your first question?"

"Who started all this?" Marie asked.

"Your pronoun "this" requires an antecedent, so I'll ask you, what do you mean by the word 'this?' Do you mean 'this' in a cosmological sense? Or, are you talking about past lives, experiments, the PMC etc?" Asha responded.

"All of it?" Marie said non stop. "I want to know who created us, you, this dimension we are in, the Earth we just left, the universe, these programs that we seem to be a part of, the...."

"Whoa there," Asha interrupted. "By the time you get through with your question, there won't be any time left for the answer." Marie smiled with the amused audience. "I'm sorry," she said. "I've never before been so hungry for information."

"No need to apologize." Asha said looking out over the audience. "How about it? Do the rest of you feel as famished as Marie?" From the audience came verbal answers such as, "Yes." "More so!" "Very hungry," etc.

"Well then, let me put a little food on your plate," Asha said. "First, let's talk about origin. Did the first part of the Necessary Past act as an appetizer? Dr. Roberts, a Ph.D. from Harvard, has an answer." Asha said as she acknowledged his raised hand.

"Thank you Asha," Dr. Roberts said. "Let me make two points, and then present my question. First, even if we were to accept that we originated in the primordial soup, if I may continue with the cuisine metaphor," Dr. Roberts said with a smile, "and that we crawled out onto land where we followed our accepted evolutionary history to become the humans we are, and second, even if we were to accept the anthropic principle that everything is bent toward life suggesting that there is an intelligence behind the design directing our course, it does not answer the prime question: who or what created the creator?"

Asha took a deep breath, "Dr. Robert's question cuts to the mother of all questions and opens the door to part Two: *Our Origin and the Grand Creation.* Let's go there now."

The curtains parted, the screen read "Part Two: *Our Origin and the Grand Creation.*" As the words faded, the audience was mesmerized with colorful and enchanting scenes of an exotic world somewhere in the expansive universe. The lens astronavigated the heavens, sailing from one galaxy to another. Whirling worlds, spinning orbs, ringed disks, cloud covered spheres, suns and moons glided by as the interplanetary travel lens zeroed in on one large, orange planet with cream colored clouds. The words 'Our Origin' covered the screen and then the lens zoomed in for a close-up into a dome shaped structure and into a large room.

Mark saw a figure that resembled Picasso's "Man with Violin," and other cubism such as Duchamp's "Nude Descending a Staircase." But these lines were more like overlapping layers of lightening in angular zigzagging movement. These colorless black and white lines were osculating, rubbing against each other. Bolts of electric sparks caused the figures to glow and recede in brightness. They were alive! They were life forms!

Their movement seemed to have purpose as they stood near rectangular shaped instruments. They caused gauges to register and lights to shine. At times, two life forms came together seeming to face each other. Small white beams of light began an interchange from the top to the middle part of the life forms, leaving one and entering the other. All of these abstract looking life forms were manipulating miniature spheres similar to those of the interplanetary trip Mark just took.

Mark concentrated on specific lines within each cubist form. For a reason he could not pin down, he began to feel a deja vu come over him. The lines seemed familiar. He picked up his pen and pad to write a note. As he did so, his hand, for a moment, glowed, and then receded as if he were looking at pure energy. He shook his head and looked up. The screen was blank and Asha had returned to the podium.

Asha began, "If anyone got a twinge of nostalgia during that session, it was because your pre-memory allowed you to remember your origin. That's right! You are looking at your original life form, before you joined in service of the grand creation experiments." A hum like blue flies filled the auditorium. "As you recall, before you recently left Earth, your species was on the verge of self-design, that is, genetic engineering. On Earth, you are tinkering with the material that will eventually determine your ultimate evolution. On this side, what you refer to as God or the Creator, reached that point of self-determination over four billion years ago. The Creator, with others, felt that their present life form, although excellent for intellectual development, was lacking something. They brainstormed, to use your phrase, and came up with certain principles or guidelines that would direct their architects of design.

"As you saw from the shingle-like factory pattern, the life forms here are not static. They have energy, but that energy lacks something your bodies have—sensations! As photonic electromagnetic beings, we have a complicated system allowing us to record unlimited information which gives us our only pleasure. It is an intellectual gift. Our architects decided to synthesize this, our original creation, with one borrowed from another life form discovered in an exploration of the second multiverse." Then after a pause, "That's right! There is more than one universe. The life form was a very primitive one that quite likely has not survived. Our biophysicists theorized, nonetheless, that with some modification and careful culturing we could create a life form that all of us could wear, or should I say, become, and enjoy. This life form is the one you and I are in now. It has come a long way toward its ultimate design, but it is not yet free of defects and disease. The experiments, of which I spoke, have been going on since the creation of the Earth's solar system. Not everything we do here is perfect. Sorry folks, the Creator, about whom you will learn more later, doesn't own any magic wands. What appears to you as magic, follows the laws of all creation which means there are some things we can not do."

At this time, hands are going up in the audience. Asha called on an older looking woman. Mark looked around the auditorium and wondered what each one was doing at the time of their Near Death Experiment. This woman looked very refined and spoke with perfect diction. "Regarding the origin of God, are you able to shed any light on this subject?"

"Thank you Rachel, for your question," Asha said, "Now we are back to the question Dr. Roberts asked, 'Who or what created the Creator?' In our pre-existence, we were in a pre-life form like those you just saw. It is indestructible. For billions of years, we have been exploring the multiverses. We were hoping to find the answer to these questions: Who are we? How did we get here? Who created us and for what purpose? And finally who created the Creator?"

"We kept hitting stone walls and could go no further. Then the creator, whom you will meet shortly…" (Again the hum of blue flies filled the room as the audience members turned to each other and exclaimed, "We are about to meet God!")

# Chapter 37

A<small>SHA CONTINUED</small>, "As I was saying, the Creator, or the life form responsible for the experiments, brought us together with a novel idea. The Creator posed this question: 'What if we could create a life form that had other means for gathering energy and information?' What if we could insert our life form into that creation? For the first time, we would be able to grow in ways that were never available to us before. Perhaps the answers to the age old questions could be found there."

Asha continued, "Not everyone jumped at the idea. Since the pure energy life form of our pre-existence was indestructible by itself, there was an unknown about joining it with a destructible life form. However, a major value to all pre-existent life forms is the value of free agency. We all have freedom of choice. Those who liked the Creator's idea, volunteered to insert, that is to take up a new body. Others said no thank you."

Dr. Peters stood and got the nod from Asha, "How are the experiments going?" he asked.

"We have made progress, but we are having trouble with the pain/pleasure principle, and our beloved 'freedom of choice,'" Asha answered. "Many of those who volunteer to insert, feel pain and pleasure for the first time and many want to abort with the first pain. Others want to repeat the pleasures to the exclusion of everything else. Addiction is common. What does addiction do to free agency? That's right, freedom of choice is taken away. This is a major problem."

"We are, however," Asha continued, "on target for the death of mortality. The bodies are lasting longer, injured body parts can be replaced without complications thanks to our progress in stem cell research. In the future, in case of an accident or whatever, all of us will have our own body parts stored and banked ready for use, without using rejection drugs since these parts belong to the patient. The Creator's *Grand Creation* will soon place us on the threshold of purpose."

A young man in his 20s stood up when Asha called on him. He seemed very serious and sad when he asked, "Why does there have to be so much destruction? Is Satan causing it?"

Asha said, "Paul, I know you lost your whole family when you were nine. You will be seeing them shortly." Paul's eyes lit up and his heart stopped for a moment as he gasped for a deep breath. At this point, Asha's voice changed. She spoke rapidly, "Oh dear, I goofed, but the cat is out of the bag now. I will have to shorten this session. I want to answer Paul's question and then dismiss you because all of you, not just Paul, are going to be met by someone you love who passed before you. They will show you around and answer more questions like these."

Mark's heart dropped, and then began racing. Could he be seeing his high school sweetheart in a few moments? His legs felt wobbly. He wasn't sure he could stand. He tried to take notes as Asha spoke, but he didn't hear most of what she said as she answered Paul's question.

"Bad things happen because mistakes are made," Asha rushed her answer. "There are accidents. The New Mexico Ranger who started a backfire did it to save homes, but information about winds didn't get to him, and his backfire burned down 140 homes, There was no Satan, no evil, just mistakes. There are genetic mistakes; there are experiments that go haywire, accidents that happen. We are committed not to entering in because the *Grand Creation*, which you will learn more about later, requires freedom of choice. To turn you into mannequins with strings attached or to make you a robot with buttons we can push, would flaw the design and render it a failure. I'm sure all of you will learn more about this later."

Mark was getting his legs back when one wall of the auditorium began parting. People on the other side in excited talk and squeals of delight waited as a surprised congregation mingled quickly with everyone on the other side.

His eyes instantly welled up and tears flooded his vision. He wiped at his eyes, and then caught sight of a beautiful young lady in a long white flowing gown that outlined a curvaceous figure when a breeze pressed the gown against her. He ran to her, threw his arms around her narrow waist and lifted her off the floor. He felt her warmth, her full muscle tone. He held her tightly, she pulled him against her. They both anticipated each other's moves—pulling back, looking into each other's eyes, embracing again, holding each other tightly, reading each other's thoughts, and then they kissed, full lips blending heart and mind together into one being. He looked at her youth, her restored body so vibrant and young. He didn't think about his own age and how strange it must have seemed to others as he embraced a young, beautiful twenty-five year old.

DeeDee took him by the hand and guided him down some stairs. "I missed you," she said. The communication had an unusual air about it. He understood every word, but it was being sent in some other fashion. He responded without hearing his voice, "I have been praying for this moment every day of my life since you left."

"I know. I heard you many times."

The conversation was crystal clear. They stopped and embraced again. The love and complete joy they felt reached out and wrapped around their hearts pulling them together more closely than ever before.

She took his hand as they stepped outside. "I know this is so strange to you right now," she said.

"As long as I have you next to me, it can get as strange as it wants. I'll never let you go again" Mark said.

There was a pause. Her face registered a worrisome thought as Mark turned to her. "We are going to be together forever, aren't we?"

DeeDee smiled broadly, "I can answer you unequivocally. Yes, our future together is for sure."

"But you didn't look so sure a moment ago."

"There's so much for you to learn in a short time. You will be returning without me—but only for a little while and then we will be together forever."

Mark protested loudly," No! No! No! I'll never let you go!"

"Listen," she whispered in his ear as she kissed his ear lobe, "let's finish the pre-memory process, and then if you decide not to go, you do not have to." Mark felt instantly better.

"That makes a big difference! Let's get on with this process," he said with enthusiasm.

They walked down marble stairs 50 feet wide. Mark turned and looked back at the building they were in. Nine fluted ornate marble columns 60 feet high supported the superstructure. Sculptures of human figures were everywhere engaging the senses—eating grapes, smelling flowers, touching and kissing each other, painting a landscape or playing a musical instrument. At the top of the gabled sloping roof was a polished bluish-white marble statue. It was as if Mark was looking at a superbly conditioned athlete leaping to the sky, but instead of having two legs, there were forty in rapid motion lifting the statue off its perch. Except for this unusual statue, Mark would have believed he was in ancient Greece looking at the Parthenon.

A heavy fragrance of orange blossoms made him turn his head in that direction, but before he could take a step he was showered with the delicate scent of lavender, lilac, and jasmine. He looked up to see the sky was so solidly blue with light fluffy clouds gliding overhead, and a landscape so rich with green turf, blossoming trees, and flowers lining every path, that Mark thought of an overzealous painter trying to out-do nature. He squeezed his sweetheart's hand. "Where are we going?" he asked.

DeeDee answered, "That's the last question in the Triad. Your PMC classes tomorrow will clarify whatever you missed today.

Mark stopped walking and turned her toward him… What is she talking about?… Is this DeeDee?… he asked himself. She seems more…"advanced" is the only word he could come up with. DeeDee was looking at Mark's studious gaze. She spoke just before he did.

"I'm sorry, honey. You meant, where are we going at this moment. I was thinking of the larger philosophical questions. You know: Who are we? How did we get here? Where are we going? Mea Culpa." She threw her arms around his neck and pressed her breasts into his chest. "You know where we are going," she said with a coquettish smile.

Mark felt her warmth. He held her tightly for a moment as he remembered the list he had lovingly compiled over the years from her daily-created malapropisms. He recalled her telling him to "unmutify" the TV when she wanted him to take the TV off mute, and how she told him that they hadn't yet passed the model homes because she didn't see any "floopies", the balloons or flags used to get your attention. Mark thought. But now, "larger philosophical questions?" "Mea Culpa?"

DeeDee was reading his thoughts. Trying to reassure Mark she said, "You will find that there is a different emphasis here – a cerebral one. My language reflects that emphasis, but," she paused and looked deeply into his eyes, "my heart and yours speak the same poetry."

Mark kissed her tenderly on the lips, and then their mouths opened as they hungrily fed the intimacy. She spoke first, singing Rosemary Clooney's "Come on uh, my house, my house uh, come on."

He finished the next line for her, "and I'll give you everything." With hearts leaping and lifting, they ran hand in hand through a park with rolling green hills and came to a walkway.

"This is my cottage," she said with pride pointing up the hill to the end of the 100-foot walkway. Mark looked at a southern style mansion, but smaller, with two tall columns supporting a covered veranda. Circular steps left both sides of the porch and curved in as if a mother's arms were reaching out to gather in her children.

Mark's eyes enlarged as he took in the charming structure with shuttered windows and large double doors. He could see the upper bedroom window and chimney above. The lawns surrounding the cottage were meticulously landscaped and trimmed. "Bread and butter," she yelled and pushed Mark toward the stairs on the left, while she began scampering up the stairs on the right. Mark took the challenge taking two stairs at a time and reached the veranda before she did. They both rushed to the center and embraced with Mark lifting her and turning two full revolutions before setting her down. Facing the double doors, Mark said, "Do you have a key?"

She nodded and politely said, "Please open." The double doors swung open revealing a curved staircase with a white banister and gold knobs. To the left was a step down living room. DeeDee pointed upstairs and Mark lifted her off her feet, crossed over the threshold, and carried her up the stairs. He was surprised at his strength. At the head of the stairs was a large mirror in an ornate gold frame. Mark saw two young people, but did not recognize the young man carrying his bride. He stopped and put her down. "This is a dream, isn't it?" She pulled him into the bedroom and on to the canopied round bed.

"By this time tomorrow," she said as she removed her one piece of clothing, "You won't have to ask that."

Their lovemaking was surreal, intense, tender, and then passionate again and again. They made love with insatiable desire, then held each other as if it were the last day of their lives. Exhausted, they lay still in each other's arms. Mark soon fell into a blissful sleep breathing her and her sweet breath, into him.

# Chapter 38

WHEN THEY AWAKENED, THEIR lips were inches apart, their bodies wrapped around each other. Mark spoke first, "I guess this isn't a dream. But if not, what is it?"

"It is the other side, it is home, it is where we all come from, where we all began," DeeDee answered.

"Why can't we see this place from Earth? How did we get here? Why are we here? Why do I have to leave? Who is in charge?" The questions began to flow uncontrollably from Mark.

DeeDee interrupted putting her hands on his shoulders at arm's length. "Let's begin with: This is not a dream. It is a reality as real as your experiences on Earth. When you are on Earth you are involved in an experiment."

"What kind of experiment?" Mark asked.

"Remember when Asha talked about joining in the service of the grand experiments?" DeeDee asked.

"Yes," Mark answered. "She said the Creator and all of us were some kind of electrical life form and that this human body was created so we could enter it. But why get into a body that hurts and can be destroyed?"

"That's what all the experiments are about," DeeDee

said. "When the Creator and others decided to design and build this life form, they did it for several reasons. First, their photon energy life form is indestructible and very adept at acquiring knowledge, but it has no physical sensations. Everything is cerebral, intellectual, and highly developed. What they created was a life form that has five wonderful sensory apparatuses that deliver sensations including the one we experienced several times last night."

"I can accept that," Mark said as he sat up in bed and placed pillows behind his back, "but what has that got to do with experiments?"

DeeDee spoke slowly with space between each word. "We… are… not… done…yet. The design is not perfect and much work is ahead of us. The project is very complex even for the Creator's intelligence. Yesterday you got a look at one of the labs and the advanced life forms working there."

Mark broke in, "And that's when a strange deja vu came over me."

DeeDee smiled, "That will happen to you more often all day today. For now, you need to know that we are not done yet. Our present prototype bodies have defects, diseases, and genetic mistakes, but the problem isn't just on your end. Before our photon energy life form, which I will call pre- life forms, can get into the flesh and blood life form or earth-form, there is a complicated transformation process that is being worked out on this end. We are making progress and we will be successful!"

"How do I fit in?" What experiment am I doing?" Mark asked.

"You are not the experimenter," DeeDee said. "You are the subject of the experiment. As the subject of the experiment, you are not allowed to know you are involved in the experiment."

"Why not?' he asked.

"It was decided that for the sake of accuracy and efficiency it was best to blanket the whole earth."

"What do you mean?'

"Cloak it," DeeDee answered. "Put everything in a double blind study. Observe, and collect data from a distance, make adjustments, build new prototypes and then place a pre-life form into the new vehicle and give it a test drive."

Mark shook his head. "After seeing the "Necessary Past" and all the destruction, I don't see how you can say we will be successful. It seems to me, we will blow all of us to kingdom come."

DeeDee got out of bed. The window light created a glow around the flowing curls of the hair he had so lovingly stroked the night before. She stepped into the bathroom out of sight. Over running water, Mark heard her speak, "The pre-life form is indestructible so we do not have to worry about that. Our earth forms, however, are not permanent, but," she paused for a moment, and then stuck her head into the bedroom, "I know I can't explain this part: We have backups."

"Backups?"

"Honey, we need to get down to the PMC. They will be able to give you a better answer."

After a quick shower, Mark dressed asking questions incessantly. "How can you afford a mini mansion like this? Do you have a job? What sort of monetary system runs this society? Where in the universe are we? Do you have seasons? Is God alive?" The questions blocked any thought of breakfast. DeeDee answered, "yes" to those questions requiring a yes or no. To the others, she deferred to the PMC.

When they reached the PMC, DeeDee tried to shed Mark's hand. He wouldn't let go. "Aren't you coming with me?" He looked frightened for the first time since arriving.

"I have to go to my job," she assured him, "but I will be back for you at lunchtime. Go on in; we will have a lot to talk about later."

Reluctantly, Mark let her hand slip out of his. She blew him a kiss. It was then that he noticed others, but not quite as many, with whom he had sat yesterday, all going through the same painful separation. He tried putting on a broad smile as he joined others shoulder to shoulder as they stepped up the marble stairs and into the PMC.

# Chapter 39

Asha was already at the podium center stage. "Good morning. You look enriched and enchanted. Because of my goof yesterday, we got a little behind. I didn't mean to let it slip so soon that you would be seeing a loved one. When it happened, I realized I couldn't hold you any longer. The lesson to be learned is that even on this side, inadvertent mistakes do occur."

"Yesterday," she continued, "we looked at the Necessary Past. Everything that has occurred was necessary to get us where we are today. We are conducting experiments to find out cause and effect. For example, what causes serial killers? Is it too much of one chemical or not enough of another? Why can some people over indulge in pleasures and substances but suffer no ill effects? How will the pre-life form with its electromagnetic photonic energy interface with the biochemical energy of the earth-life form? There is still much work ahead of us, but we are making progress. We are perfecting the five senses and have started work on a sixth sense."

A hand from the audience went up with urgency. Asha acknowledged the questioner.

"What is the purpose of the sixth sense?" asked a Freudian-looking man with a grey beard.

Asha responded, "One of the advantages of the pre-life form is its ability to take in and store information and energy. It can then instantly call it up for immediate use in solving problems. The amount of the memory banks used is huge compared to the brain of the earth-life form. The reason for this is that the earth brain gets sidetracked with all of the five senses constantly bombarding the owner with feelings of pain or pleasure. As a result the brain moves at a snails pace in comparison.

The sixth sense, in answer to your question, once fully developed, will allow us to assimilate information as quickly as we do in the pre-life form, only we will do it in the earth form with all its sensations. It is this combination we believe will open doors to finding the answers to those basic questions."

Asha turned to the curtains and with a sweeping gesture of her right hand, the curtains parted, and the screens again lit up. Asha walked toward her eager, attentive students and looked back at the screen. "You will see universal scientists at work. They will turn toward you and communicate. Do not be afraid. Let your feelings, your memories flow."

Mark took a deep breath and watched the screen. Once again, the screen took them on an interstellar journey to that huge orange sphere and zoomed into a dome shaped structure. The same life forms they saw yesterday were hovering over banks of large screens that appeared to be filled with flashes of light and color mushrooming before fading off the screen, with numbers rolling forward like a slot machine gone haywire. One of the pre-life forms stopped and maneuvered toward the lens, getting larger until the viewer was able to see between the cubist lines, between the spaces, and into the essence of the life form. Small drops of light began to emanate from within, bathing Mark's retina with warm fuzzy strokes. He felt immediately comfortable, almost as if he had sunk back into his mother's womb. All was warm, satisfying and safe. The warming sensation increased, and then disappeared into a dynamic that was immediately familiar to Mark. He was transformed into pure energy, and with it came a sense of self that erupted from a database of math, science, history, psychology, medicine, philosophy. Mark felt the intense power of the unlimited world of knowledge that assailed him.

Suddenly the screen was blank and the lights came on. Mark was blinking his eyes and felt as if a fully revved up engine inside him was turned off and was running down. The whirring vibration slowed to a stop. He felt exhausted and empty. Asha was at the podium. "Let's talk about how you just felt. Was it a positive feeling?"

A lady raised her hand amid the nodding heads. Asha called on her. "Initially, I felt warm and secure, and then I felt elated at having my personal library within such easy reach, but there seemed to be something missing."

Asha asked, "What do you believe was missing?" The lady shook her head. "I am not sure."

A gentleman stood, "I had the same reaction, but as I think about it, when I thought of planet Earth, the blue marble was lost in numbers and formulas. I never got to see the beauty of the creation. I mean, the numbers all fell into place and that was pleasing, but I didn't see the blue; although, I knew what was required for that part of the spectrum to register in my brain."

Many people were now nodding their heads.

"Excellent observation," Asha acknowledged, "and well expressed. Would you want to see the world in those terms, and only in those terms at all times?"

The gentleman was still standing. "It felt good to know so much, and I did feel powerfully energized, but the answer is no."

"So you missed the sensations themselves. You received excellent descriptions but you didn't *feel* them?"

"Yes," he replied.

Asha continued, "What if you could have both – all the sensations in addition to easy access to volumes of data?"

Now, everyone nodded affirmatively. "Good." Asha said, "You now understand the primary purpose behind the *Grand Creation*. The creator is creating a life form that will do exactly that. Once the *Grand Creation* is completed and you take up your final, eternal body, there will be no limits imposed from the outside on your ecstasies and your knowledge."

A young woman asked, "What is, and when will, the final resurrection take place?"

"When the prototype earth life-form is completed and fully tested and when the pre-life forms have been conditioned and adjusted to merge with the earth-life form, then all of us will live forever as a human being possessing a pre-life form essence. That should happen within the next 1000 years."

Someone yelled, "Is time the same here as it is on earth?"

"Yes," Asha answered, "but the difference is in the markers for measurement, that is, if you have no seasons, no daylight, no sunsets, and you never change or grow old, etc. then time has no meaning. When you measure time by these markers alone, and you step into a completely different environment where the markers do not exist, it does not mean that time stops everywhere else."

Asha anticipated the questions at the tips of outstretched hands. "I know, I know," Asha said holding her hand up with her palm toward the barrage of questions coming at her. "Time travel is on your mind. Those questions will be answered by the Creator himself after lunch."

There was a gasp and then complete silence. A murmur of whispers quickly filled the auditorium as everyone checked with each other to be sure they heard Asha correctly. God would be talking to them? Did she say the Creator? Here?

"Don't look so awestruck," Asha said, "At one time humans looked upon their doctors as if they were Gods. Then they found that in spite of a doctor's knowledge and training, the doctor made mistakes and misdiagnosed like anyone else might do. The Creator gets credit for the idea of the *Grand Creation*, but the work required for its completion is shared by many essences. Now more questions, please. By the way, the Creator will remain in a pre-life form and will be the last to take up an earth-life form body.

Mark raised his hand. Asha called on him. "What has been the biggest obstacle with the transition from the pre-life form to earth-life form?"

"An excellent question, and one that has given us the most trouble. The purpose of the *Grand Creation* is to marry two life-forms for the value each has. The pre-life form allows for maximum intellectual development, but is missing the pleasures of the senses. The earth life-form allows for the most exquisite pleasures, but does not use 95% of its intellectual capacity. What we are having difficulty with, is the overwhelming sensations that the essence feels when first subjected to the magnificent ecstasies. Addictions inevitably occur. We have not found that perfect balance between free will and addiction.

Addiction bars free will. Most of the problems on earth can be traced to addiction. The majority of your prison population is there because of addictions. I'm not talking only about drugs and alcohol. Work, food, sex, power, control of others, physical fitness, anything that brings someone so much pleasure they must indulge in it to the exclusion of everything else, is addiction. It is the obsessive behavior that will undermine the Creator's *Grand Creation*."

"This imbalance," Asha continued, "tilts stability and order toward chaos and disorder. Most of the wars you witnessed yesterday, including the holy wars, were a perversion of what is holy. Pre-life forms addicted to egomania or personal pleasures waged these wars. The debate raging on this side is whether we should tone down the ecstasy, or provide an escape mechanism that trips automatically when the essence is in trouble."

"What have they decided?" Mark asked. It was a question that stood out above the others, although everyone was yelling and pushing forward with questions.

Asha, looking a little apprehensive about losing control of her students, said "Please wait until I call on you before vocalizing your question." She pointed to Mark whose hand was now rising to the ceiling. "Your question, sir."

Mark repeated his question regarding the freedom of choice vs. addiction conflict. Asha, answered, "We are working on it. You can see the dilemma. The ecstasies are why we are here. If we take away free will and start pulling strings, we will dampen variety. Without variety, a key ingredient to ecstasy, we will reduce infinity to one long bore. One more question."

The refined older lady with perfect diction stood when Asha pointed to her. "Do the essences in the pre-life forms ever exhibit criminal behavior?"

Asha answered, "Our electric chairs are diagnostic tools. A pre-life form who has the urge to hurt someone or take advantage of other pre-life forms' trusting nature, will voluntarily use the electric chair. That analysis will pinpoint the origin of the problem and correct it.

Other hands go up, but Asha said, "We are going to take a lunch break now. Be back here in one hour. I know you won't be late. The Creator would like to chat with you about time travel.

# Chapter 40

THE WALL PARTED AS it did yesterday. There she was, among all the others who were waiting for their loved ones. Mark rushed to DeeDee's side and grabbed her hand. "What is this joke about the Creator chatting with us after lunch?"

DeeDee asked, "Did you see any pre-life forms on the screen today?"

"Yes," Mark said, "Just for a couple of minutes."

"Did you sense a communication?"

"Yes, information flowed through my body, but only briefly. Why?"

"That was the Creator, warming you up," DeeDee said. "You will have to be on his level. Don't be afraid. All pre-life forms are inherently good, especially the Creator. He wants you to be successful more than anyone because his success depends on your success . Kind of a co-dependent relationship." DeeDee said with a smile.

"How do you know he's a he and not a she?" Mark asked.

"There is no correct pronoun for the pre-life entities here," DeeDee said. "You might as well call them he/

shes. 'The Creator' will do since that term is not gender specific."

"Okay," Mark said, "I can't wait to meet the he/she Creator again. Where to now?"

"If we go back to my cottage, we will probably never have lunch. We have already missed breakfast," DeeDee added, "and we have all night for that cuisine."

"You know my appetites well. I'm with you," Mark said.

"Let's go to my favorite place, the Big Apple." DeeDee said as she pulled Mark outside and down the marble stairs.

"You mean we are going to New York," Mark asked playfully.

"Almost," she said as she took a sudden right turn and stepped onto a moving walkway.

Mark hung on to DeeDee tightly as the moving walkway picked up speed. Others behind him made comments about the wind blowing their hair.

He turned around and said, "That's a minor concern if this thing doesn't slow down enough for us to get off."

Within moments, the moving walkway began slowing. Mark wasn't sure it had stopped when DeeDee grabbed his hand and stepped to one side. "Keep walking," she said.

They disembarked smoothly almost on a slow run and then began walking again. There were shops on their side of the sidewalk. He looked up at high-rise buildings and window displays at sidewalk level. To his left was a wide walkway with moving interchanges just like a freeway only these were smaller and with no cars, just people standing or moving on them.

"In here," DeeDee said as she went through a

revolving door into a room with about 50 people. There were no windows, no chairs, and no tables. Everyone was standing.

Mark looked around and said, "This restaurant better have good food. It doesn't seem to have much of anything else."

"This is an elevator," DeeDee said.

Mark couldn't feel the usual movement of an elevator. "Do we need to push a button to get started?" he asked.

"We are already there," DeeDee said, "fifty-five stories up."

A wall parted and everyone stepped into what resembled a neo-gothic crystal palace. A hundred feet above them was an open domed web of cast-iron girders and wrought iron trusses covered with a clear skin of glass. The sun poured in warming the entire massive structure. Full grown trees reached up to the sunlight, flowering plants displayed dazzling color, a waterfall splashed at the far end where a fifty-foot cubist statue could be seen a block away.

"Wow!' Mark remarked, "I thought you said we were going to a restaurant called the Big Apple"

DeeDee smiled, "We are in it. See the stairs on each side as we walk down the promenade?"

"Yes," he answered gazing at the moving steps and the sign above that said, THE MING DYNASTY. "Are we going there?"

DeeDee answered, "We could. It is very nice in there. Your complete dining experience includes Confucian Temple dancers, Ming trees, and circo-rama screen travels over the Great Wall. But I thought you liked American food."

"I do. So, this Big Apple has different dining environments?"

"Yes, you can choose French, German, East Indian, Mexican, Chinese, Peruvian, any type of food you want, and each dining experience is complete with an elaborate setting, mood enhancers, authentic music, and native plants. All settings provide a menu of the healthiest and tastiest foods you can imagine."

"Now I'm in real trouble," Mark exclaimed. "I'm faced with over-choice. Indecision is a terrible thing."

"You must be like Mark Twain," DeeDee said, "You have such a prodigious quantity of mind, it takes you forever to make it up."

Mark smiled remembering the quote from *Innocents Abroad*. "Not forever, maybe a week sometimes. Tonight, I want something different---Indian Food."

"American Indian?" DeeDee asked.

"The Big Apple has American Indian food?" Mark asked incredulously. "I never even gave that a thought."

"East Indian then. Follow me," DeeDee said tugging his arm, and then slipping her left arm around his waist. Mark put his right arm around her right shoulder and set the stride. She kept up and then skipped so she matched his stride left for left, and right for right. Together they did the walking dance step pausing on the outstretched left foot as the right foot touched down behind them on the left side and then with a hop and a skip, their right feet, in unison, landed in front of them, and they continued their walk. Together they yelled, "You remembered!" Their laughter brought smiles from other patrons coming and going.

The façade of the East Indian restaurant called "The Vedas" was surrounded by terra cotta figures wearing gold, silver, copper, and bronze jewelry and headpieces. The figures were all engaged in some pleasure of life such as bathing, eating, and tender embraces. When Mark looked up, a dome shaped roof was the support for another structure with a steeple that soared to the top of the crystal palace. They entered through tall gates and into a courtyard. Four doorways with a marquis above each, greeted them. One said, "Rig Veda, the Music Of Life." Another said the 'Atharva Veda, and other Magic Spells." The other two said, "For the gratification of the Curious. We serve information only."

"I like the Rig Veda." DeeDee said, "The hymns of knowledge are a perfect compromise. I'm attracted to music and you are attracted to knowledge."

"What is the Atharva Veda?"

It has some of the same good food but the theme emphasis is on producing spells or manipulating your mood through substances. I know you wouldn't like it," DeeDee answered.

"And the last two for the curious?" Mark asked.

"No food there, just an authentic museum of Indian Life and Belief. We can go through it after lunch if you like," DeeDee added.

By now, Mark was picking up a tantalizing aroma of hot food. He pointed to the Rig Veda and pushed aside the veil covering the doorway. A dark-haired beauty with dark eyes in heavy mascara approached them. "Dinner for two?" she asked.

Mark nodded. "This way please," she said as she walked in front of them. She was barefooted. Her costume was silk. Mark could see rings, bracelets, beads as neck chokes, and a piercing on her left nostril. Her hair was partially covered with a white beaded hairpiece. A satin sash was tight around her small waist.

DeeDee whispered to Mark, "She is also one of the Himachal Pradish dancers." Mark and DeeDee were seated in a booth with overstuffed cushions.

The dancer asked, "May I get you some masala chai or an appetizer? I would recommend the Alu Chat."

"Thank you, please do," Mark said. "But first please tell me what each is."

She smiled and was eager to help, "Chai is a black tea with sugar. Alu Chat is diced potato tossed in onion, coriander, and lemon. Are you ready to order yet?"

"I guess I could use a little help." Mark said sheepishly. "What are Rogan Josh and Aloo Saag?" The dancer repeated the items correcting Mark's pronunciation, and described a delicious meal with barbequed lamb, and a potato, spinach, onion and tomato hot dish. DeeDee knew what she wanted and ordered the chicken Pandora style.

The dancer smiled and said, "I will return soon." Mark noticed that the dancer seemed to be looking at him with a special interest.

DeeDee leaned over and said, "Don't flatter yourself. She is interested in a high praise from you."

"High praise?" he asked.

"It's similar to a gratuity only worth more. Since there is no money exchanged on this side, one can only measure one's worth in service or accomplishment," DeeDee explained.

"You mean I have to say something nice about her to her supervisor?"

"No, no. She is the one who monitors her own work.

She will be thrilled if what she does elicits a high praise which you deliver directly to her."

"How do I do that?"

"You tell her," DeeDee said almost short of patience. "Tell her if you like her service, her costume, her dance, or whatever it is you genuinely like. She will try to repeat what she does if she receives high praise."

"And if I don't like her?" Mark asked.

"Then your silence politely tells her she was lacking somehow," DeeDee responded.

"But how does that help if I am not specific?" he questioned.

"Without the high praise, she will actively pursue help from others. We have schools here for everything." DeeDee continued, "Here, everyone works toward self improvement. The motivation is the pleasure we get by learning something of value. The value reaches out to everyone. It is such a simple idea, and everyone benefits."

Over a lunch of red glazed chicken baked in a clay oven, and the barbeque lamb and a dessert of Golag Pander, Mark had more questions.

"What is going on here? I mean I understand that on earth we are part of a grand experiment test-driving the body, but what do people do here? You are in a body. I have seen only a few pre-life forms. What is happening here, and in your answer, could you at least hint at your own line of work?"

DeeDee looked at Mark and grabbed his hands across the table. She held them firmly and said, "When you go back to the PMC, you will be able to ask the Creator, but be prepared if you don't fully understand. It only means that you aren't ready yet. I don't want to sound condescending, but when you get back to earth, you wouldn't try to teach algebra to an ant, or genetic research to a three-year-old child."

Mark nodded agreement, "But can't you give me some idea of your job and what the immediate goals are?"

DeeDee said, "I can try. I have achieved Moksha or Nirvana, that is, I have broken the cycle of rebirth, and will not be reborn again until the Grand Design's life-form prototype is completed."

"Is that good?" Mark asked.

Modestly trying to rush past her answer, DeeDee said, "Because of my previous life experiments, a lot of suffering and other challenges, I was granted acceptance into the Infinity Study."

"What's that all about?" Mark asked.

"Lets say that a very wealthy man wanted to build a utopia, a universe of basic needs and pleasure, to insure everyone of absolute happiness forever. But first, he worked from a scaled down model, let's say an island. This island will be sterilized of all disease. It will have fertile rich soil, the perfect annual rainfall, no danger of earthquakes or hurricanes, and will require no fees of any kind," DeeDee explained.

"Sounds like the Garden of Eden," Mark said.

"Yes," DeeDee answered, "One of the 110 Hindu hymns of knowledge we might hear tonight is called the Hymn of Creation and is similar in many ways to the creation story found in the Bible." She continued, "This is that mini-utopia. We are in a re-created earth form but one that has all the latest updates and re-designs. Our job is to identify the requirements necessary for such a Garden of Eden to be successful. What I do is help those who are having difficulty adjusting when they get here. I make them feel safe, loved, and cared for.

"Fascinating," Mark said, "If last night and what has happened so far today is any indication, I would say we are right on track." The "we" reference seemed so natural now that Mark had begun seeing everything with his involvement tied in.

"Look at the time," DeeDee stressed. "I have to get back to work, and you have some important matters to digest."

As they were leaving the restaurant, Mark thought how strange it seemed not to leave a tip. He looked for that dark haired beauty to let her know how much he enjoyed her dance and her help with ordering his meal. Finally, he caught sight of her on the far side of the restaurant. She looked up just in time to catch Mark looking at her. He smiled and then gave her a thumbs-up signal. A radiant smile spread across her face.

"See how easy that was?" DeeDee said.

As they started to leave, Mark took her hand and gave it a tight squeeze. He stopped walking and looked deeply into her eyes. Just for a moment the enormity of what was happening took his breath away. He was really here with DeeDee, holding her hand, eating with her, looking at her smile.

"I love this world!" he exclaimed, "And I cherish you, my beautiful love, for Eternity. My heart is so full. All I want to do is hold you close and tell you over and over I love you, I love you, I love you!"

DeeDee placed two fingers over his lips. "My feelings for you are stronger than ever, my dear husband! Tonight we will celebrate."

# Chapter 41

At the PMC, DeeDee and Mark embraced. She assured him once again that she would be back by six p.m. Reluctantly, Mark let go of her and turned toward the marble steps. A few others were starting to arrive. It was ten minutes to one. Mark went to his same desk, picked up his pen and pad, and looked around. He noticed that there were not as many people. He wrote down a question. "Why are our numbers dwindling? He turned toward the lady sitting next to him and said, "I don't mean to alarm anyone, but have you noticed there are fewer people here?"

"Oh, didn't you know?" she asked. "That's because of the nature of their NDE. You must be a coma victim so you have more time here. Those who had a temporary heart stop don't get to stay too long."

Mark thought,…'So that's it, the Louisville slugger knocked me unconscious. I'll have to thank him when I get back…'

Asha returned to the podium. "After lunch is a paradox. First, you grow in breadth, now you can grow in depth. Yesterday I told you that the Creator would be here to answer some of your questions. I misspoke. The Creator will not answer some of your questions. The Creator will answer all of your questions and will do so within this next session. You will not again, in your stay here, sense such conciseness, clarity, and completeness. To make this happen, the Creator will appear in and speak to you as a pre-life form. Contact with your own pre-life form memory will provide the language and understanding that the Creator will use. I was asked to forego a lengthy introduction, and I will. Close your eyes, take ten deep breaths, and release. Then open your eyes slowly."

Mark followed directions. When he opened his eyes, the auditorium was dark. A small glow on the stage began to expand like a spotlight growing larger. Mark felt warmth coming from the stage. He let it caress him, making him feel safe, comfortable, and awake. The spotlight on the stage transformed into cubist lines that began to flit and zigzag. Mark felt a vibration in him as if an engine was starting to rev itself up. The pulsing light on the stage fell into perfect sync with pulsing energy in him.

The pre-life form had now grown large, dwarfing the podium. It moved toward the audience members who sat motionless, eyes fixed on the dynamic transformation taking place before them. The pre-life form was instantly familiar to Mark. Mark smiled and could feel acknowledgement being received. This time he was ready. When the small drops of light left the pre-life form, Mark returned them. They were absorbed by the pre-life form whose goodness and intelligence radiated love, wisdom, and security.

All of Mark's questions were at once formulated and teleported directly to the pre-life form. Answers like waves came rolling in front of Mark, laid out clearly so he could understand their beginning and development, and how bits and pieces of knowledge, some acquired by contributors, and some acquired by accident, fell into place. Everything was happening so fast and yet with such clarity that there was never a question about validity and accuracy. The language was exact, the implications of the meaning clear. Formulas, equations. mathematical descriptions would fly by with instant intelligibility.

Mark looked into mirrors facing each other and saw himself and an infinite number of mirrors facing each other. When one image moved, they all moved. Photons live in many worlds at once. Matter interfaced as pure energy, and existed elsewhere. The veil masqueraded as more mathematical equations, but with a new twist: conscious thought now parted the veil making time travel possible. Like pages being turned by the wind, universes flipped by. Occasionally, a flash flew from a turned page—a universe was gone. Mark saw time travel as the thumbing of the pages backward or forward.

The pages flipped backward. Mark saw himself in another life almost 3,000 years earlier. The pages flipped forward. He knew he was in the past by what he was wearing. The garments were radiant long linen. His were violet. Others were white. The two panels of linen were seamed up the sides and across the top with openings left for the arms and head. Over his shoulder draped a heavier cloth, which he wrapped around himself, and then clasped it at his hip with a gold broach. His sandals were gold with gold-leathered straps, and his hair curled close to his head…ancient Greece and fashions met in the future…he thought. Next, the pages rushed forward. This time, he was the same age, but he was in different clothing. He wore a wig, a long waistcoat, and a skirted coat with turned-back cuffs, tight breeches, and stockings.

He looked pale, the sky was cloudy, and the fog was rolling in. London, he thought, three hundred years ago.

When all was done, Mark felt the whirring, vibrating engine inside him start to slow down. He couldn't think of another question. Even the question that arose as Mark imagined other universes, had an obvious answer. That question about a whole solar system being lost, a peril that comes with freedom of choice, became academic when one knew that a fatal mistake did not mean the entire experiment was lost. Exact mirror image copies existed to carry on. The anthropic principle was even more far reaching than Mark had imagined. Now he knew what DeeDee meant by "backups."

As quickly as the cubist figure appeared, it returned to a diminishing spot on the stage. Mark had to take a deep breath. A great burden had been lifted off his shoulders. The lights came on.

Asha returned to the podium. "Stunned?" she asked.

Everyone sat there for a moment stupefied. Their understanding of what had just occurred stormed over them for a moment as they sat there in a daze looking for the words to describe what they just experienced. They all began to talk at once. "Incredible! Electrifying! Fantastic! Inconceivable! Awesome! Magnificent!" came the shouts and then thunderous applause rocked the room.

Asha smiled, "I know this was the most extraordinary event in your earthly lives."

Mark's head was spinning. He saw himself living on Earth in two time frames, over two thousand years apart, but here he was in his earth body in another dimension talking to God. A feeling of warmth spread over him as he began realizing he was in a very special place, a safe beautiful world where all its inhabitants could live without jails, wars, weapons, anger, or hatred. No one needed to be wealthier than others, nor did they need to control or command those around them. No police, no courts, no hospitals for the terminally ill, no deaths, no funeral parlors. A stop at a hospital would take fifteen minutes for a body part replacement or a boost in certain neurotransmitters. There was much joy and laughter. Everyone was busy at a task of their choosing for the common good. This was a truly a heavenly place where everyone could live forever with infinite variety.

# Chapter 42

THE MEETING ADJOURNED, AND Mark rushed out excitedly. DeeDee was waiting. She looked apprehensive.

"How was your day?" she asked.

Mark was buzzing with excitement. "I can't believe this is happening. I talked to God! It was incredible. It was so effortless to grasp and understand concepts." They sat on a bench in a spacious park with rolling green hills. Each small valley afforded the visitor privacy. Mark continued, "I could even understand the inner workings of a quantum computer. My mind was so open, so quick to absorb, it was fantastic, but so much more. I was touched by a peace, a fulfillment, an essence beyond anything I could have ever imagined. "

DeeDee said, "That feeling is with us every moment of our existence here. It is good to watch the new arrivals experience it. It helps us not take it for granted. Did Asha talk about the decision?"

Mark replied, "About going back?"

"Yes," DeeDee said.

"That's a no-brainer," Mark said beaming. "Unless

you can go back with me, I'm staying right here next to you."

DeeDee went to a wooden box resembling a birdhouse, turned around, and said, "That decision will always be yours, and yours alone. All I ask is that you don't make the decision until tomorrow." Mark felt better and was willing to wait knowing what his answer tomorrow would be. Looking at the box, DeeDee lifted the roof, and then looked at Mark. "This park is like a drive-in theatre. I can dial up some of the world's best movies. Do you mind if we watch one of my old time favorites?" Mark was ready to hold his sweetheart close and watch anything she wanted.

"Do we get to do a little necking?" Mark said with a smile.

A pleasant warm evening breeze outlined DeeDee's top against her breasts. He watched as she pressed the numbers under the roof. Flowers scented the air. A large screen rose above them. DeeDee chose an old black and white film that she and Mark had seen many times during the Christmas seasons: James Stewart in *It's a Wonderful Life*.

Too content to think about how strange everything was, Mark put his arm around his love. As he watched the movie, he remembered the sweet innocence of courtship during that period in the forties. He wouldn't mind seeing the hilarious scene of the gym floor parting during the dance revealing the swimming pool below and how everyone fell or jumped in. DeeDee wanted him to see something else. She squeezed his hand at specific times during the movie.

Mark recalled how James Stewart's character committed suicide. An angel allowed the character to experience the world as if he had never lived. As a result, he wasn't there to save his younger brother who fell through the ice, which meant his younger brother never grew up to join the army and receive the Congressional Medal of Honor for saving the lives of a whole transport of troops. DeeDee squeezed Mark's hand. The angel explained that if one were not around in the first half of one's life, a sequence of events would mushroom into a larger impact on society. Therefore, by taking himself out of the second half of his life, the same mushrooming of events and domino effect would take place impacting many innocent people. Mark's breathing increased as he became aware of DeeDee's intentions.

DeeDee said, "Relax, Hon, the decision to return will always be yours. It's just that the more information you have, the more firmly will you own your decision, making it the right choice for you." Mark was wary. DeeDee continued, "I'll request an extra day for you. It's important that you have enough time so that you don't have to regret a hasty decision."

"How about a year?" Mark asked.

"You being in a coma for a year would devastate our children and grandson's emotionally and financially as well. No, if you choose to go back, sooner would be better." Mark nodded, "Two days then. Where to now?" he asked.

"I want to take you to the MV Center." DeeDee answered.

"I know that doesn't stand for Motor Vehicles because I haven't seen a car yet," Mark said.

"How right you are! It stands for Memory Visits. On Earth, it was called the Akashic Record." DeeDee took his arm and led him up a flight of stairs to an open platform where others were standing or leaning on a protective rail. Mark saw a long plastic-looking tube with a snake-like silver streak inside. It was winding its way up from a distant valley. It grew larger very quickly and glided to a smooth stop. He and DeeDee stepped into it as others disembarked on the other side. DeeDee still had hold of Mark's arm, gazing into his eyes. Mark saw and felt the adoration, the love, the warmth of interlocking hearts, and pulled her close to him.

"What do we do at the MV?" Mark asked playfully, "Motivate Venus, the Goddess of Love?"

"I go there often," DeeDee replied, "alone, so that I never forget our children." Before she could start another sentence, the letters "MV" flashed on the screen up front. "We're here," she said.

"Wow, if we were that close, why didn't we just walk?" Mark asked.

"We just traveled over 20 miles," DeeDee said.

"No way! I didn't even feel movement, or hear wind."

"That's because we traveled in a vacuum," DeeDee replied. They stepped off as a voice thanked them for traveling on the "Power Void,"

The MV Center was made of layered discs stacked on top of each other like pancakes with ten to twenty feet of space between each disc that was 200 feet in diameter. The last disc created a rooftop for star gazing. A steel tube ran up the center of each disc serving a dual purpose: to support the building and to house the elevators, restrooms and restaurants. The fifty layers, with the space between, put the last rooftop at over 100 stories.

When they reached disc fifty, DeeDee took Mark by the arm and pulled him into a large room. The ceiling seemed to open into the sky. A young man directed his remarks to DeeDee. "The memory visits you requested are in the server. Just dial them up by date. Everything will replicate itself exactly as it happened. Call me if you need assistance."

"Thank you," DeeDee said as she punched in some numbers.

Mark sat next to DeeDee as the bare room began its transformation. The sides of the room began changing colors, and then shapes of trees, hills, and ground cover appeared. The scene was three-dimensional. The sky was blue. Everything started to look familiar. Mark closed his eyes. As he opened them again, he saw the view from his garage. He saw the driveway and the basketball standard he and his son erected for his grandsons. He heard the boys' voices. There they were! As alive and real as he could possibly imagine. He saw his son and the boys involved in a basketball game. He looked at DeeDee. Her eyes were on another figure in the scene. Mark looked in that direction to see himself waiting to be thrown the ball. He was drawn to that image which he could view from every angle, and he felt himself being overtaken by a magnetic force drawing him into the figure. The ball came to him, and he passed it to one of his grandsons who went in for a lay-up. It was blocked. His son now had the ball and was taking it back for a three point shot.

At this point, he looked back toward DeeDee. Now his view was toward the garage, and he saw DeeDee sitting on the tailgate of the truck watching the game. This was not the DeeDee who entered the MV Center with him a few moments ago. This was the DeeDee five years earlier. He left the figure of himself, and went over to look into her eyes.

Meanwhile the ball game continued. Mark heard his own voice giving directions to his grandsons. DeeDee's eyes were full of tears. Her beautiful countenance couldn't hide the pain that prevented her from playing with her son, grandsons, and Mark. She had only four more months to live. She knew she was going to die. Mark could see she would do anything to be able to participate and be able to go on living to watch her grandsons grow and develop into fine young adults making valuable contributions to life. He felt a tug on his arm. It was DeeDee, the one with whom he entered the MV Center. She said, "Come, sit beside me. You will see yourself. The memory will seem so real, so alive, but we are visiting, not becoming."

Mark felt her squeeze his arm. He sat down as the scene changed, revealing a three-year old Zach helping his grandpa build a brick wall fence. The three year old was putting bricks in a wheelbarrow so Grandpa Mark could move them closer to the wall under construction. Mark whispered to DeeDee, "I remember this day. He lifted 52 bricks altogether. I felt guilty breaking the child labor laws, but I couldn't get him to stop. As long as the job wasn't done, he wasn't going to quit."

DeeDee looked at Mark and asked a serious question, "Is he a good worker today at age twenty-one?"

"The best," Mark said, "never complaining. Just does his work until the job is done."

For the next hour, Mark watched as one scene after another dissolved and a new one transformed the room into another memory: Fishing at the lake, learning how to bait a hook, all the guys rolling a log over to see what creepy crawly things ran from the light of day, learning how to make a blade of grass play a tune, hiking the hills, and looking at rainbows and sunsets. Nick even taught his grandpa how to catch lizards with nooses made from grass stems. Mark watched as each grandson got his lesson on how to read, long before kindergarten's first day. Eli arrived at kindergarten ready to be his teacher's special assistant, helping other students learn to read.

DeeDee squeezed Mark's hand and asked, "Are they good students?"

"All get 'A's and 'B's," Mark replied.

There went his other grandsons. Mark remembered that day Desiree came for a visit bringing her two boys, Chris and Lucas. Chris was the oldest grandson, and at age twelve his purpose in life was to become a maker of movies. He was a walking camera looking to capture a moment of humor or drama to put in his film. Lucas was the budding athlete and stunt man in Christopher's films, but he soon tired of Chris' commands and relentless directions and went off to play in the tree house.

By now Mark knew what the visit to the MV Center was all about. He looked at DeeDee. Her eyes looked deeply into his. He turned away knowing that the logic in what was taking place was going to take him away from her.

When the hour was up, the room returned to its original size and color. DeeDee started to speak. Mark put his finger over her lips. "Okay," Mark said, "so if I wasn't there, maybe someone else would have filled in for me."

"Maybe? Maybe someone with selfish motives would thwart their positive growth. Maybe nothing would happen and they would be withdrawn and backward. Maybe, maybe, maybe! The fact is we cannot know, but if…"

Mark finished her sentence, "If I were there, I know

they would get a boost from me." DeeDee could see the impact the scenes were having on Mark.

Mark shook his head and smiled at DeeDee. "You knew all along, didn't you?"

"I knew you would make the decision by yourself," DeeDee replied, "and you have."

"Do I still get two days?" Mark asked.

"Yes!"

"You promise me it won't be long, and we will be together forever?"

She stood facing him, and pulled him up placing his arms around her small waist. With her arms around his neck, she pulled his head down till their lips met. Perfectly synchronized, their hearts and thoughts melted together first in a joyous meeting, and then in a rising heated passion. They quickly boarded the next silver streak and headed for DeeDee's cottage. Their passion continued past midnight.

The next morning, Mark awakened to feel his love still asleep next to him. He put his face close to hers, and breathed in her air. He wanted to absorb her into his system and steal away with her. He kissed her forehead, and stroked her hair. She was so young and beautiful, so knowledgeable. He started thinking about changing his mind. DeeDee opened her eyes.

"We have two days. You will change your mind several times, but we both know what you will do, don't we?" she asked.

"Yes," Mark answered, "You present a flawless case. I can't leave our kids and grandkids."

"The truth is the persuader," DeeDee said. "It is all around you. Once your heart opens to it, indecision evaporates. So what would you like to do, I mean, besides that?" DeeDee said making reference to their lovemaking.

"Well," Mark said with a smile, "besides that, I have a lot of questions."

"Such as?" DeeDee asked.

"For example, there are no locks on any doors. Don't you worry about intruders?"

"The principle is so simple. Do unto others, as you would have them do unto you. The reason it doesn't always work back on Earth is because many people have not reached the level of development required before they fully grasp the concept. Here, no one would think of breaking into someone's home or intruding on their privacy."

"Why not?" Mark asked.

"Simply because by doing it, they take away their own right to privacy. The assault on others is an assault on themselves."

"You said it was simple," Mark acknowledged. "So that's why everyone here is so civil and considerate."

"You catch on quick," DeeDee said chidingly.

"I take it there is no theft for the same reasons," Mark said.

"That and another reason," DeeDee answered, "Our source of power is free and infinite. We use fuel cells which generate current."

"How does that work?" Mark asked.

"It's really very basic. On Earth you are just beginning to utilize these chemical reactions between platinum catalysts and negative and positive poles. Essentially, hydrogen, which is found most everywhere, can replenish our supplies of energy forever."

Amazed at DeeDee's answer and how quickly it

triggered memory storage units like those that the Creator activated in Mark earlier, Mark said, "I hope I can remember all of this when I get back."

"What you take back with you is a shadow notion that there is something about power and hydrogen which has nothing to do with bombs. You will not know where it came from, but you will sense that you need to do something about it. Many inventions, discoveries, and cures have made it back to Earth this way. How else could Democritus in 400 B.C. come up with the notion that matter consisted of indivisible particles called 'atoms'? Anyway the other reason is there are no poor here. Why steal something that you can have free by stepping into any department store?"

DeeDee continued, "On Earth, the social structure consists of a horizontal layering which causes people to want to be on top. You know bigger homes, higher up the hill, more money, more expensive clothes, cars and so on. Here the social structure is vertical. No one is above another. The only requirement is that you make a contribution to the rest of society. Other than that, your life style is your choice. I don't like mansions, although I may have one if I choose it. I like cottages. Owning a mansion is stripped of all pretenses, and class distinction. There are no status symbols. There is no ostentatious or subliminal motive for owning anything. There is no ulterior motive to be above anyone else. Everyone stands vertical and looks straight across at each other with equal respect."

"We are all equal?" Mark asks.

"Not at all," DeeDee said. "Hard work deserves recognition. An athlete, for example, or a team that trains hard and comes away victorious by winning or breaking a record, deserves praise. An opponent, who does not win, looks up to the winner and joyously joins in high praise. The winner is their hero. They hope to achieve the same quality of play themselves. No one gets more money or more perks. The reward is in the performance itself."

Mark was lying on his side facing DeeDee who was also lying on her side with a pillow under her head. Mark asked many more questions. "What about love, marriage, courtship, children? Is there divorce, breakups? Do we age?"

"Slow down, honey," DeeDee said, "Let me take one area at a time. Because of the choice we made millions of years ago regarding the method we would use for reproduction of the earth-form, we have tried many different life experiments: polygamy, bigamy, monogamy, group marriages, single parent families, and same sex marriages. All of the various possibilities have been tried."

"What did you find out?" Mark had to know if his bond with DeeDee was in jeopardy. His hand traveled over her shoulder and down to her hip.

"First, in eternity there are different reasons for entering a relationship. These reasons vary with different partners. Initially on Earth, multiplying and replenishing was vital to the success of the *Grand Creation*. Offspring had to replace bodies that were fatally injured in an accident, or were diseased, defective, or aged. Children were inevitable. Here, reproduction is not necessary. We do not die. We do not age. We come together for the ecstasies that the pair bond provides." DeeDee stopped Mark's hand as she spoke.

Mark looked unsure, "And what an ecstasy it is!" He pulled her into him and kissed her with an urgency fueled by the knowledge that he only had her for two more days.

DeeDee was quick to correct his misconception. "Not all couples come together for that ecstasy. We like it. It's great for us," DeeDee responded before giving him another lingering kiss. Then she continued with her explanation. "Others might come together to create poetry, or to put on dramatic stage performances, or to be involved in other applied arts. We are tolerant of every relationship because all of us have reached a certain level of mature development wherein we do not take advantage of or hurt one another."

DeeDee continued, "What's important is that you and I are eternal soul mates. We have been together in many lives. We always find each other and overcome all odds to be together."

"I knew there was something special about us." Mark agreed, "So, there are no children, right? Because the place would get overcrowded?"

"Wrong," DeeDee said, "We haven't confirmed this yet, but apparently there is no limit to the universes."

"Then there is more than one universe!" Mark exclaimed.

"We know there are other universes, but we aren't sure if they stretch into infinity. That's because we haven't nailed down the ultimate of all questions. As pre-life forms, we created the flesh and blood body. This meant not just dealing with photonic, electrical, and magnetic forces, but adding biochemical components as well. But the question all of our scientists, both earth-life form and pre-life form, are working on, night and day, is, who or what created us? Or better phrased, how did the first universe come about?"

"Oh, my God," Mark said incredulously, "The same question, but at a whole different level. When the Creator came to talk to us yesterday, I thought that we had met the entity with all the answers."

DeeDee said, "The debates and studies regarding this perplexing question are ongoing. Tomorrow we could drop by the Centrum for Essential Hypostasis. The best minds are working overtime to put together the most credible explanation."

"I would love that," Mark said.

"Good! Then we will go," DeeDee said. "What would you like to do tonight?"

# Chapter 43

B Y NOW, MARK WAS sure DeeDee was aware of his rising passion. Her intellectual strength was a new dimension in their relationship. The energy flowed from his mind to every part of his body, charging every nerve ending, making him intensely aware of the essence of her being, filling the emptiness that had been his life for so long.

As they lay there, Mark took a big breath and sighed deeply. "Is everything perfect here, I mean, are there no problems, no issues, no conflicts? I remember you telling me that we are not done yet. I got the impression you meant we were not perfect. Which is it?"

DeeDee continued to snuggle with Mark, then turned over propping herself up on her elbows as she looked into his eyes. "When we get to the Centrum for Essential Hypostasis tomorrow, you will get a better understanding of what I am about to say. Not all pre-life forms are happy with the Creator's design. Some would prefer to remain as a pre-life form, and forego the ecstasy of the earth-life form. In fact, they observe so much pain and suffering on Earth due principally to the addictions created by the ecstasies, that they believe it is a waste of time and cerebral energy to pursue the *Grand Creation.*"

"So, what impact does this have on the *Grand Creation?*" Mark asked.

"Prior to the Creator's Grand Design, we pre-life forms were one in our pursuit of intellectual development. We believed we would eventually have an answer to the ultimate question. We never questioned our motives because each of us was an extension of the larger mass. Although we have an individual identity, we see ourselves as a single unit in search of all facts, all truths, all theory, and thereby eventually be able to identify the summum bonum or the ultimate purpose of existence, of life, in whatever form."

Mark's mind began racing for answers. Aristotle discussed this subject in his <u>*Nicomachean Ethic,*</u> and as Mark remembered from his Doctorial work, many other great thinkers agreed with Aristotle. The ultimate purpose was to be happy.

DeeDee continued, "The *Grand Creation* redirects a lot of psychic energy away from the pre-life form's primary intellectual focus, thus splitting or at least fracturing the oneness that all pre-life forms had at one time. Also," DeeDee continued, "giving the earth-life form freedom of choice, means that the physical matter making up the earth-life form's body can be destroyed by various possible accidents, thus necessitating birth and more children. However, stem cell research is our answer to that objection. Opposing pre-life forms object to this research, and the debate rages on."

"So how does this impact you or me?" Mark asked.

DeeDee hesitated for a moment before answering, "One of the pre-life forms by the name of Kardoff volunteered for a life experiment as a priest. When his earth-life form body gave up due to the onset of old age, he returned to this dimension, but chose to abandon the *Grand Creation*. He remains in a pre-life form refusing to take on another life experiment even though ten were offered to him."

"And…" Mark asked.

"He has been visiting me." DeeDee blurted out.

Mark took a deep breath. Then asked haltingly, "What do…Does this mean….What do you mean visiting you?"

"He comes to my cottage and we communicate," DeeDee said. "He remains in pre-life form, but he is conflicted. He knows his presence can warm my body and make me tingly all over. Yet, he rejects the ecstasies of the earth form."

Relieved that she hadn't been violated, Mark asked, "So, how does this create a problem?"

"He is on the verge of doing something no pre-life form would ever do," she answered.

"And what might that be?" Mark inquired.

"Finding pleasures in having power over others," DeeDee said. "He wants to have control over me, and I think somehow it is partly sexual."

Marks eyes opened wide, his neck muscles stiffened. "What do you mean partly?"

DeeDee took a deep breath, gathered her thoughts together, and said, "This is what I think is happening: All of us, as pre-life forms can choose to help the Creator in the *Grand Creation*. When our life experiment is over, we can sign up for another one, or we can return to the pre-life form."

"What about you and all these people here? They are

not pre-life forms and they haven't signed up for another life experiment.

"But they have," DeeDee said, "Do you recall my talking to you about the Infinity Study?"

"Yes, you said it was like a mini-heaven that was being tested to see what sort of problems needed to be solved before the final life-form changes take place."

"Exactly," she said, "and that's what I am experiencing with Kardoff."

"Why do you call him a him? You said pre-life forms were he/shes," Mark asked somewhat accusingly.

"Let me explain. Kardoff's life experiment was as an ascetic priest. He was denied sexual pleasure. The purpose of his experiment was to find out if a spiritual demeanor could channel sexual urges to the higher good. Again, this is the debate going on in the pre-life form world where the balance between corporeal ecstasy and cerebral development has yet to be decided. Anyway, when one returns to the pre-life form existence, one is supposed to cast off all the trappings of the earth-born instincts. In Kardoff's case, and this is why I assign him a male gender, his extreme conflict between male sexual urges and his spiritual denial of all earthly pleasures, has carried the earthbound energies into his pre-life form essence. This interferes with the usual debriefing processes that free him of all earthbound desires."

"How did this happen?" Mark asked understanding very little of what she said.

"My theory is it has everything to do with motive. When he chose not to do another life experiment, it was due to his deciding that the *Grand Creation* would not be good. Now, in returning to pre-life form existence, he is motivated to bring with him from the earth-life form whatever he can to cancel the Creator's work. He is using the denial of sexual stimulation to interrupt the infinity experiment."

"I'm not sure I understand." Mark confessed.

"I know it is complicated," DeeDee acknowledged, "but let me try another route. When pre-life forms refuse to go back for another life experiment because they have chosen to reject the *Grand Creation*, they go through a process that was created to erase all their ecstasies so they may return to their original pre-life form existence unfettered. In Kardoff's case, he took pleasure in denying himself sex. This confused the memory banks and he was able to retain his earthly pleasures in his pre-life form. Now, with motive, he can use this anti-sexual ecstasy to create havoc, but what is most significant is his willingness, almost pleasure, in controlling others with an ecstasy that his life experiment denied him."

Mark remembered the electric chair Asha talked about. "What about correcting the mutations with the electric chair?"

"That's what I have suggested, but he won't go." DeeDee answered.

"Can't you make him go? Why don't you turn him in?" Mark suggested.

"Because," DeeDee hesitated, "the way he makes me feel, I have a hard time reporting him, and he is confident that I won't." There, it was out. DeeDee had fallen under the spell of a pre-life form, and she didn't understand why.

Beginning on the first day he saw DeeDee at the PMC, Mark had felt somewhat inferior by her superior knowledge and intellect. It didn't interfere with his love or his love making because she let him know that it was natural for her to have the advantage, and that he would soon catch up. Now, he saw her as vulnerable. She needed his help.

"How would you go about reporting him?" Mark asked.

"Well, first, I have to try to correct the problem. If that fails, I talk to the Creator."

Mark had a plan. "When does he come to see you?"

"When I am alone, usually at night."

"Does he appear to you?"

"Yes, first I feel him like a warm vibration. Then I see him, and the communication is just like the one you experienced with the Creator. I understand why he doesn't believe the *Grand Creation* is a good idea. There are many unknowns involved."

Mark said, "Does he just intrude? Isn't that violating a pre-life form law?"

"Yes, but at first I gave him my permission, and now he just comes."

"Let me understand this," Mark said, "You don't say no because you are trying to correct the problem yourself, and you believe you can do this with communication." DeeDee nodded as Mark continued, "You are aware that part of the reason you don't say no is that you like the warm vibrations which are mildly sexual," DeeDee nodded again. Mark continued, "Kardoff teases you in the same way an ascetic priest recognizes sexual tension, but knows there can never be a climactic end to it. There is pleasure in its denial, and Kadoff uses this to control you."

DeeDee felt relieved, "You speak with such understanding, and I was feeling guilty over nothing. I love you so much."

"Okay, sweetheart, let's free Kardoff of his control. Can you invite him in tonight?" Mark asked.

"I think so, but he only comes when I am alone."

"Can you revert to your pre-life form?" Mark asked.

"I'm not supposed to do that in this Infinity Experiment," DeDee said.

"Why? What would happen?" Mark asked.

"I would lose in the process. My life experiments have made me what I am today. I like the feeling. I don't want to risk anything," she protested.

"Okay, here is what I want you to do," Mark outlined his plan, "Tonight…"

# Chapter 44

THAT NIGHT AT THE planned time, DeeDee began her thought processes. She lay down on the bed, focused on her cerebral pre-life form centers, and asked for Kardoff to appear. She had to imagine the warm vibrations going through her body, and stimulating her. Within moments, her body picked up sensations. She knew he was beginning to materialize. She closed her eyes, and willed him into being. A light formed at the foot of the bed. Vibrations began to excite the atmosphere. She heard a popping sound, and opened her eyes. Kardoff, in his pre-life form, stood in front of her. His energy was zigging, zagging, moving about. Then the following rapid-fire communication took place in less than a second.

"Please transform to an earth-life form," DeeDee said.

"No."Kardoff replied.

"I need equity. Please transform."

"No."

"We need to communicate in the same language," DeeDee said.

"We are," Kordoff said.

"But I am not a pre-life form. It's different," DeeDee objected.

"You change," Kardoff commanded.

"You know I won't," DeeDee said.

Kardoff sent out warming vibrations. She took a deep breath and opened her eyes. Then she said:

"You are unsure of your stand against the *Grand Creation*. You are afraid."

"You know pre-life forms have no fear because they cannot die," Kardoff answered.

"Your ideas lose life without primary experience."

"I've had primary experience on Earth."

"You are afraid of discovering the truth," DeeDee said.

"What truth?" he asked.

"That your stand is based on false memory that was tainted in the reversion process," DeeDee said with resolve.

The rapid fire of thoughts stopped. There was a pause. Then the photons slowed, the light diminished, and the spot on the floor flattened. She closed her eyes; then opened them to see a priest from the 12th century standing before her. It took some time before her speech and thoughts started coming at a pace that didn't seem so slow.

"You are a handsome devil," DeeDee said.

"So, you are going to tease me the way I teased you," the priest responded.

"Now we have parity," she said.

"But to what advantage?" the priest asked. "Both of us have vows to keep, and urges to control."

"You were successful at it, were you not?" DeeDee asked.

"Yes, painfully so," the priest answered. "The life experiment would have been more efficient without the restless libido."

"You say that because you never experienced many of the earth-life form's intense ecstasies," DeeDee said making eye contact with the priest.

"Is that why you had me transform to your level, so you could provide me with one of those ecstasies?"

"You will have your experience soon enough," DeeDee said.

"Or not," said the priest. "I wish only to return to my pre-life form, not waste my time struggling with addictions. Feelings distract from all the true work of a pre-life form."

"Since when did the 'true work' of a pre-life form include intrusion on another's privacy?" DeeDee asked.

"You invited me in," the priest answered.

"Only the first time," DeeDee replied.

"We both know you wanted me every night," said the priest with a devilish innuendo tone.

"And we both know that you are using an earth-life form pleasure to control me," DeeDee said with an emphasis on "control."

"Precisely why the *Grand Creation* has a fatal flaw. Were you to remain in pre-life form, you would be immune to such control."

"But aren't you out of character? Pre-life forms know better than to attempt control of another," DeeDee said. There was a pause as the priest struggled for an answer.

"What I learned from my life experiment is that there is no better way for evil to triumph than for good men to do nothing. I intend to speak out!" DeeDee realized how distorted Kardoff had become. The reversion process had created a pre-life form with its usual powers of strength and knowledge, but with the negative feelings and superstitious belief system of a 12th century priest.

"Evil? You are suggesting that the Creator's work is evil?" DeeDee asked accusingly.

"You know what I mean," the priest said. "This idea is going forward because no one objects. Such silence will allow a foolhardy, wasteful experiment to continue unabated."

DeeDee left the bed for the first time, and walked out of the room. She looked over her shoulder at the priest and said. "I see your point. Let's continue this downstairs. I need some refreshment. Would you like something to drink?" The priest nodded.

"What is your pleasure?"

"The same as you."

DeeDee went to her Arctic, slid open the door and felt the cold air rush out to her. She poured her favorite juice drink into two large tumblers and placed them in the spin compartment. Crushed ice and cream slowly mixed with the juice mixture, until three fast spins brought it all to a halt. Karloff was sitting in a new, comfortable, full cushioned chair in the living room. It was covered with an attractive throw created by Kolour, the painter who understood succinctly the influence various color combinations have on mood. She handed one tumbler to the priest, then sat down on the love seat across from him. He stretched his legs toward DeeDee. The priest had become wary, and asked, "Just like that? You see my point of view? What caused that miraculous insight?"

DeeDee took a sip of her drink, "You! You are a pre-form. But listen to your answers. Your point of view is 1000 years old." The priest started to get up. DeeDee said,

"Please, let me finish, and finish your drink. It will be the last memory you have. And now," DeeDee said in a loud voice, "let there be light!"

With that, the room went dark! The priest sat for a moment in the dark. He felt a whirring vibration, and realized what was happening. He started to leap from his chair but felt large strong hands reach from behind around his forehead and restrain his movement. Someone else wrapped tape around his wrists, fastening them to the arms of the chair. Before he could raise his legs, they too, were taped to the chair. The whirring got louder as the current warmed his back, and then advanced away from the center moving to his head and to his feet at the same time.

Mark and DeeDee found each other in the dark. As they embraced, they watched as the priest's aura was outlined by buzzing photons, sparking and snapping.

"I hope you are right," DeeDee said. "If he doesn't reflex instantly, he will feel much pain, and we will have failed."

Mark replied, "He will automatically revert to a pre-life form where he will feel safe. By the time he realizes what he has done, the orderly edge in the electric chair will have made the corrections to his pre-life form."

The room began to glow as the pre-life form came into full view still attached to the chair. A single bright ball of light began tracing every edge of the pre-life form darting in a straight line, up and down, and then taking right angle turns before swirling, spiraling, around and around. Soon the process was over. The power was restored, and Mark and DeeDee saw a pre-life form standing before them. DeeDee quickly adapted to receive the incoming messages that Kardoff sent. Mark turned the power off to the chair.

"It looks as if we have parity again," Kardoff said.

"The advantage belongs to us both," DeeDee said. She then asked, "What do you know about the last five minutes?"

The moment of silence seemed like a lifetime to both DeeDee and Mark. If they failed, or if the forced use of the electric chair enraged Kardoff, the consequences could mean that DeeDee and Mark would lose the soul mate privilege.

"I believe that you met my negative with a negative, but I can not retrieve details of my earth-life form memory. What registered is I had a life experience which left a specific impact on my intellect. Namely, I do not wish to support the *Grand Creation*."

"Why not?" DeeDee asked.

"It is not worth the effort," Kardoff replied.

"What do you propose to do about it?" DeeDee's heart began beating faster as she asked this telling question.

"Now it makes sense," Kardoff said, "First, I must apologize for my behavior. I recall wanting control of you, and not being able to control that urge. Somehow, and I believe you and your soul mate were responsible, that negative was negated. Again, I apologize."

DeeDee breathed a sigh of relief. Kardoff appeared to be fully reprocessed. The best part was he didn't have memory of how it was accomplished.

"Your apologies are accepted." DeeDee said. "We can thrash out our differences tomorrow at the Centrum."

"Until tomorrow then," Kardoff said as he faded away.

DeeDee and Mark embraced, then they walked

toward the bedroom side by side with their arms around each other's waist.

# Chapter 45

In the morning, Mark awakened to the tantalizing aroma of hot toast and chocotae.

Similar to latte but without the caffeine and calories, chocotae had 100% of all the body's daily requirements. DeeDee brought Mark's breakfast to him in bed. Mark couldn't take his eyes off of DeeDee as she brought in the tray. She was wearing just a thong and a bra. Mark said, "If you are offering coffee, tea or me, leave the tray in the kitchen. I have an insatiable appetite for the me."

"That's dessert. First, you have to drink your chocotae," DeeDee said sounding like a mother. Mark drank his without stopping. Ignoring him, DeeDee took a bite of toast and a sip of her chocotae. "Today at the Centrum, we will hear The Dialogue on 'Ecstasy versus Addiction."

Mark had only one thing on his mind, "I'm ready for dessert," he said.

DeeDee smiled. "It's a wonderful ecstasy," she said. "Do you think you have control of it, or is it utterly addicting?"

"Am I addicted?" Mark asked with a grin, "Isn't that the way of love? Two people who can't be apart? They must have each other? What's wrong with that?" asked Mark.

"It's a matter of balance," DeeDee said. "I recall the joke about a man who goes to a psychiatrist. The psychiatrist asks, 'What seems to be the problem?' The man says, 'I like pancakes.' The psychiatrist responds, 'I like pancakes too.' The man excitedly answers, 'You do? I have rooms full."

Mark chuckled, "But isn't that balance built in already? We have to rest in between. Our organs demand it. There has to be a regeneration period."

DeeDee said, "Yes, but remember the ecstasies are essential to our happiness. Some of us feel that the intensity of ecstasies should not be diminished."

"Which leads to addiction and loss of free choice," Mark rebutted. "I like it the way it is with us."

"If we get started down that passionate path now, we will miss the dialogue at the Centrum. Are you willing to do that?" DeeDee asked.

"I see your point. Priorities in a true addiction get rearranged always honoring the addiction first. Is this dialogue going to get ugly?" Mark asked.

"You mean like American politics?" DeeDee responded.

"Yes, they attack each other and make up lies to put their opponent in a bad light," Mark said.

"Not here," DeeDee said. "The focus is always on verifiable facts, and logical use of those facts. If someone is found in a deliberate lie and misuse of facts and logic, it will hang over them in future debates reducing their effectiveness as a debater. What we know is that if you paint your opponent as a nutcase, you take away any future opportunity to be able to agree with him. Why would you and a nutcase agree? Ad hominem attacks, glittering generalities, any of the propaganda techniques to mislead or deceive will be a strike against the perpetrator. It just isn't done!"

"On Earth," Mark added, "too many people don't recognize the deception and how it is being applied. They frequently vote against their own best interests. They want to believe in something so badly they ignore evidence that is obviously going against their own conclusions."

DeeDee capped the discussion, "And then you have the well-developed selfishness syndrome. The end justifies the means. Do whatever you must to gain more and more money. We are far beyond such impoverished morality."

"Come on. Let's get to the Centrum before the dialogues start. We will have time for each other later," Mark conceded.

Mark and DeeDee arrived at the Centrum for Essential Hypostasis in time to admire the architecture, artwork, and the gardens. Just as Athens symbolized Greek culture, and pointed the way to becoming the birthplace of Western democracy, the Centrum symbolized a new consciousness, a new direction in eternity. It was a mini-city on a hill with dozens of buildings. Its gardens not only enhanced one's eye for beauty with their color, fragrance, and exotic plants in a myriad array of shapes and sizes, but virtually all of the plants, including the flowers, were edible. Patrons would never savage the gardens looking for full meals, but would selectively taste a petal or bud, or share a fruit or vegetable with another.

In the Greek tradition, the architecture and sculpture fused as each building symbolized an intellectual adventurousness. The balance between supporting members and the load between the unbroken vertical and horizontal lines, spoke of calm, reason, intelligence. Sculpture was architectural decoration, and was painted to highlight the subtle elegance and grace of the building while giving the observer a look at pre-life form abstracts. Each pre-life form sculpture had an individuality, as the zigzag of lines gave the statue movement and power as well as form, in varying degrees of lighter more rapid movement to quieter, heavier stratum. The earth-life form too, was exalted in austerely erect poses but with vitality, poise, and restraint. Statues and paintings of people involved in common day activity as well as ecstasies, were abundant. Balance and purpose was everywhere. The Centrum was the hub of beauty and intellectual strength. More than one dialogue, more than one group discussion, more than one lecture or demonstration was going on at the same time.

Mark and DeeDee found that the dialogue on Ecstasy vs. Addiction was in the Theatre of the Round. Stadium seating gave all observers a good view. Below, four pre-life forms moved about. Mark and DeeDee recognized Kardoff. The audience was a mixture of pre-life forms and earth-life forms.

Mark looked at the back of the chair in front of him, and read a sign facing him. "What does it mean?" Mark asked, "Choose a communication mode?"

"We can receive the dialogue in earth-life form or pre-life form parlance," DeeDee answered.

"Let's go with the pre-life form. It is quicker and with perfect clarity." Mark suggested.

"True, but it may lack the earth-life form language for sensations. Remember, most of the pre-life forms, including the Creator, have not had a life-experiment," DeeDee responded.

"Kardoff had a life experiment," Mark said, "and the Creator must know a lot about it."

"Yes, but Kardoff's memory of the details was erased. He can recall no ecstasy. And the Creator is here only to introduce the subject," DeeDee said. She let Mark push the earth-life mode button as they each slipped on their ear buds.

In clear tones, a woman's voice announced, "The dialogue question today is: Should addiction to ecstasies be regulated? The affirmative will be represented by Kardoff from Alpha Centauri. Kardoff has had one earth-life experience. The negative will be represented by Char from Mars Interior. Char is a multiple life experimenter. And now, the Creator will open the dialogue."

Mark recognized the pre-life form energy of the Creator from the aura emanating from him/her. The language was comfortable and familiar to Mark.

"Thank you for your presence," The Creator directed energy at the affirmative team, and said, "Our collective input will help us make the best decisions. Let's take a look at the past for a moment. For approximately 13.7 billion years, we have experienced a long and fruitful life with no fear of a non-existence. Our one motivation has always been to add to our data banks, and to discover our origin. All life is good. One would think there is no reason to change the status quo. Let us take a look at the present. We experience a fruitful life with no fear of non-existence, we continue adding to our data banks, and we continue trying to discover our origin. In short, our future will look exactly the same with no progress toward the eternal question. What I propose will not radically deter us. It is an enhancement, a growth that may well lead to our origin."

The Creator continued, "In our extensive exploration of multiple universes that continue to expand, we have discovered other life forms, one in particular, that intrigued our scientists. Granted, it was an extremely primitive, rudimentary life form, but it exhibited a characteristic that at first perplexed us because we had never experienced it. The term pain/pleasure was invented to describe the reactions this wiggly creature displayed. Experiments to divulge the origin of these reactions led us to a greater understanding of the makeup of these creatures. Unlike the electrical, photonic, magnetic makeup of our life-form, their matter was quite different, which gave birth to these unusual reactions to certain stimuli. We began manipulating the matter to develop a better understanding of its complexity. These data gave birth to the *Grand Creation* proposal.

If we are ever going to break the cycle we are in, if we are ever going to answer the ultimate of all questions, we must not only be recorders of information, we must look for new ways to get information that escapes us. We must push into new frontiers, frontiers that evade us because we do not possess the sensory apparatus to experience them. The act, the choice to create a new life form is not revolutionary, but when we create a new life form into which we transform ourselves, a portal opens through which we have not passed before. Inevitably, we will experience new territory, new dimensions, and perhaps discover our origin and the purpose of our creation."

Coming forward the Creator continued, "I am aware that not all of us wish to see my design become a reality. However, in keeping with the free agency principle, no one has been forced to participate, yet the *Grand Creation Project* is well on its way toward its natural conclusion.

We will soon know how viable the concept is, which brings us to our dialogue today. We have created an earth-life form, and we inserted, no, we have joined our soul with that body, and we have done so without danger of nonexistence. The body may die, but we continue in our non-local energy. The purpose, as everyone must now know, is to feel the ecstasy of the senses. The cerebral development appears to slow down once the senses are fully activated, but that may be deceptive. The senses may be leading us to a fuller understanding of our ultimate purpose.

For now, I have requested this session to resolve the conflict between ecstasy and the free agency principle. It is a dilemma that needs resolving before the *Grand Creation* project can go forward. We have the same goals. Let's walk together toward them." The Creator moved away from the center podium. A voice said, "Kardoff will now lead the affirmative."

The pre-life form Kardoff moved to the center. Mark heard a voice he had not heard before. He whispered to DeeDee, "I thought we would hear the priest's voice."

"Thank goodness no!" DeeDee said, "All memory of that life experiment was erased."

Kardoff opened with, "The self-recognition principle obligates me to be helpful to the Creator, and I will. But for the record, I must honestly express that I hold severe reservations about the efficacy of the *Grand Creation*. I continue to recognize the Creator as an extension of me, but the project with its emphasis on self-serving ecstasies threatens our unanimity. I have completed one life experiment, and I know this: the fact that this session was called, clearly demonstrates the dangers of pleasure and satiation to our sovereignty as a whole. With that said, I will offer the Creator the only logical course to take. Pleasure must be regulated to prevent addiction. Because addiction abrogates the free agency principle, the sacrifice of that principle for pleasure is reversion and decay." Kardoff moved away from the center. The voice announced, "Char from Mars Interior will now rebut Kardoff's remarks."

Char's pre-life form energy was lighter in both color and weight. A higher pitched voice said, "Kardoff's life experiment was erased by the orderly edge. I, on the other hand, have had ten life experiments, and they are all with me today—the good and the bad. Thus, I speak from primary knowledge. The ecstasies are why this project was conceived. I have lived in both worlds, and I believe with all my heart that what the Creator is trying to do will be embraced by all of us, including Kardoff, once all the pieces of the puzzle are in place."

Mark whispered to DeeDee, "All her heart? How is that translated in pre-life form language?"

DeeDee whispered back, "In my intuitive logic."

Suddenly, Kardoff spoke as sparking emanated from his pre-life energy. "All of us have watched the earth-life forms inflict pain on each other as they pursued these so called glorious feelings of personal pleasure."

He continued, "Can you imagine our cohesive world of solidarity, our organic unity, and our present entelechy being battered continuously? Each one of us leaving the whole to be lost in, or dominated by these feelings?" Kardoff's voice revealed the distain he was feeling.

DeeDee wrote to Mark in her notebook "Good, Kardoff is feeling something."

Mark nodded and whispered to DeeDee, "What is entelechy?"

"It refers to a vital agent or force directing growth or life."

A voice interrupted, "We are not here to debate the *Grand Creation*. That took place before it was approved. Please focus on the specific question regarding regulation of ecstasies." Kardoff's pre-life form diminished reluctantly and moved away from the center.

Char moved to the center. Unusual static began popping as her energy glowed, then began to flatten. The process took several minutes as DeeDee and Mark watched the photons begin to adhere and form a shape. Flashing, glowing, then receding, the earth life-form of a stunning young lady emerged. In perfect proportions, Char stood before the audience, her radiant smile and white teeth projected health and beauty. She was wearing a long lavender gown which parted below the knee revealing her open toed black sandals and narrow ankles.

"You met my pre-life form. You heard my voice. I now stand before you, my essence unchanged, my intellect as efficient as before, but more versatile, my data banks are accessible, but in greater preponderance because I have experienced ten life experiments which have opened a whole new world requiring a language that can not be fully understood by pre-life forms for whom the language has no experiences. To all of my pre-life form extensions, I propose this question: If you could be assured that the creation project will not threaten you with non-existence, that ecstasies will never overpower free will, and that our all encompassing omnifariousness will not be fractured, would you commit fully to the *Grand Creation*?"

Kardoff moved forward. "Char's question is based on a gargantuan 'IF,' and is designed to elicit just one response.

The dialogue today is indicative of the treacherous ambiguity of the answers possible."

Char stepped forward. "The creation design change will not continue if ecstasies become addictive. What is ambiguous about that?"

Kardof replied, "It is the essence of the ambiguity. Do you reduce the ecstasy or do you insert a safety valve in the earth-life form which shuts down its system, thus negating the exercise of its free agency?"

Char replied, "As pre-life forms, we never harmed each other nor do we try to control one another, Why is that?"

Kardoff answered, "We have reached a mature state intellectually which makes perfectly clear that such behavior is foolish and counter to an open society."

Char followed quickly with, "Why do you believe it to be impossible for that same intellectual maturity to develop for the earth-life form regarding addictions?"

Kardoff, said with confidence, "Because the ecstasies get in the way. We are now back to our starting point. It is a dilemma that will forever block the *Grand Creation's* completion."

Char suddenly stood on one leg, her other leg reached up to the side of her ear. She held that leg against her head, and stood relaxed and motionless. Then she arched her foot until she stood on just her toes of one foot. The battement was complete. "Why am I able to do this?"

Kardoff replied, "There are many reasons. For one, you obviously practiced it before hand."

"Why would it take practice?" Char asked.

"Because you have to compensate for your bi-lateral symmetry which requires balance on one leg instead of two," Kardoff answered.

"So, we are talking about balance here," Char inquired.

Karloff''s voice was louder, "Control! We are talking about control!"

"And who has it?" Char shot back as she lowered her leg in a slow restrained move to the floor.

Kardoff realized he stepped into Char's trap, and responded, "Ballet is not the dance of life!"

Char replied, "No, but control and balance is. We will find a way to balance the ecstasy without inducing addiction. Or we will not go forward until control is established."

Kardoff stammered and sparked, "But you… There is no proof… You said… I mean…"

The voice announced, "The dialogue is now over. The audience may participate with your vote and comments. A sudden wave of energy flowed thoughout the audience as discussions erupted.

DeeDee said, "As a dancer, I understand control and balance. It will be possible to enjoy all sensory experiences at their highest level without losing our freedom to choose."

Mark smiled broadly, "We agree. Let's make that our contribution."

DeeDee said, "We just did. The system recorded and sent our thoughts to the central bank to be tabulated. We can wait for the results, or go on home and call them up later."

Mark was smiling even more, "Let's get back to that delightful cottage of yours." Then it struck him. This would be the last evening with her.

# Chapter 46

ALL THE OUTDOOR LIGHTS lit up DeeDee's cottage as DeeDee and Mark approached the walkway. "Your cottage almost seems alive when it does that," Mark said. "It's as if it waits all day for your return, and then jumps for joy when you come in sight."

DeeDee opened the door with her voice command. As it swung open, Whitney Houston began singing, 'I Will Always Love You'. Mark's heart was caught off guard. He remembered the song and the impact it had on him when he first heard it three months after DeeDee died. Because of his uncontrollable grief, he saw his doctor who told him to write a letter to her. He did. The song answered his letter.

"Then you did send that to me," Mark said.

"Yes, and all the others that raised your suspicions," DeeDee replied.

"But everything could be considered just coincidence," Mark said, "Why didn't you just show up at the foot of my bed some evening and we could have talked? Then I would have been certain of the messages."

"All messages have to be cloaked. The *Grand Creation*

would be in jeopardy if we removed all doubt about an afterlife," DeeDee answered.

"If everyone could see beyond the veil, many life experiments would be aborted, and we would lose valuable data. People would quit when things got too rough. Suicide would be seen as a mere passing, a way to escape a difficult life experiment. But if all communications are in that twilight zone, no one is absolutely sure about a post existence, so they hang on as long as they can."

"Makes sense," Mark said.

Instead of lifting her up and carrying her to her bedroom upstairs, Mark took her hand and guided her to the step-down living room. They sat on the plush couch in front of the fireplace. As Whitney's last song ended, DeeDee pressed a button on the control panel built into the chocolate table in front of them. Instantly, a crackling fire put out a warm glow on the room.

"Talk about spontaneous combustion," Mark said, "I can already smell the wood burning. Doesn't this use up a lot of trees?"

"It's all atmosphere," DeeDee said, "Synthetic, but very real to the senses. Actually nothing is burning at all, so enjoy it."

"You gave me so much hope when I was down. The flashing balloons were your idea, too?" Mark asked as he put his arm around her shoulder, and she rested her head on his chest.

"You made it possible when you sent me the Valentine card with the balloons," she said.

For the next hour, Mark recounted all the co-incidents that he identified. He wanted to know how she did it. She explained how the Director along with the ADC Advisory board was involved. They had to be certain that the co-incidents remained in the twilight zone, and would never compromise the cloaking principle. All After Death Communications had to be approved. The quantum computers easily handled all the details to interface with Earth bound events.

"And the license plate I wasn't supposed to get, the one that said 4DDS689? You did that too?" Mark asked.

"I heard you saying how I should be there when you bought the new car, to enjoy it with you. You thought I was the only thing missing. I had to let you know I was there all along. Did you notice you haven't received another ADC since that one?"

"Yes, I wondered about that. I just assumed my grief hallucinations were calming down, and that I was past a need for any new signs," Mark said.

"What you were beyond was a need for reassurances about an afterlife. You knew I was still in existence somewhere."

"What was the 'S' for?" Mark asked.

"That was there to introduce us to where we are right now," DeeDee said, "Why didn't you carry me up to the bedroom?"

Mark took a deep breath, and said, "Because I want you to know how much I love you, not you the seductive temptress, not you the object of all my sexual desires, but you the beautiful woman who has captured my heart. I want you to know that if I have an addiction, it is not an addiction to sex. It is an addiction to the alluring concept of love that you embody so exquisitely. You give your love unconditionally. What people and I have learned from you was so valuable. You taught us how to grace the world with the beauty of ourselves doing good deeds."

Mark was reading an answer in DeeDee's eyes as he

spoke. The S is for sex. Mark had come to grips with that ecstasy. Tonight, he would forego the sexual passion to show her his passion for agape, that is, his worship of her and his devotion to love, and his respect for all that she had become. She is Kama, the eternal light that gives his life meaning.

Her eyes showed the joy and appreciation as he revealed to her what his love for her meant. Before he began the first word in the next sentence, she started the sentence for him and they both whispered in unison, "I love you." They embraced with exquisite tenderness. She pulled back, and with a big smile said, "So that's what you meant when you chose those words for my memorial bench plaque downtown."

"You mean you were there sometimes sitting next to me?" Mark asked. DeeDee nodded.

"Can you, that is, are you there all the time, I mean do you know my every thought?" Mark asked.

"I can not invade your privacy. You have to invite me in. Remember Kardoff?"

"Will I remember everything when I get back?"

"Not all the details. You will have impressions, feelings, hunches, all of which will influence your choices, your way of life."

"Will I remember this moment?"

"In your dreams, yes," she answered.

That last night, they talked, held each other, pressed their foreheads together with noses touching, and talked some more. By 5 a.m., they fell into a deep slumber lying on the floor before the fire.

In the morning, Mark had second thoughts about going back. DeeDee was already up preparing breakfast.

"You didn't tell me what this trip is going to be like," Mark said nervously as he entered the kitchen.

"We don't have to be at the bus station or catch a flight anywhere, if that's what you mean. You can leave from here, sometime before noon," DeeDee said.

"Will there be pain?" How long will it take?" Mark asked.

"If we do some sort of a countdown, the anxiety will create tremendous anticipatory pain. It will be better if you don't know. When you do re-enter the earth-life form, you will have a headache, but the excitement you generate in our children and grandchildren when they see your return, will mediate the pain. Remember, I love you and we will be together forever."

She handed him what had become his favorite drink. He took a sip and reached out to take her hand. His hand closed over hers, but he didn't feel warmth or solidity. His head spun, and he reached toward her with both arms. Hers were also reaching toward him. He felt his body being sucked backwards away from her outstretched arms. Blinding streaks of light rushed past him as he tumbled downward, his speed picking up, and then suddenly he felt himself slowing. Soon he floated above, then plunged down into his body with a sudden jolt! His head assaulted with pain from all sides. Mark opened his eyes slowly, squinting at the glaring light that seemed to be pulsating from the right side of the hospital bed. Fighting his way out of the haze that enshrouded him, He realized that what he was seeing was the energy coming from all his family members, who were holding each other, in laughter and tears, smiling, celebrating the life that was slowly returning to them.

The unquenchable euphoria, the hopes finally

answered, the outpouring of love that radiated from his family brought a momentary recognition that this part of the *Grand Creation* had achieved its goal of combining body and soul, pleasure and purpose, feeling and intellectual joy. As that realization slipped away as quickly as it came, Mark became aware of pressure on his left hand. He turned his head painfully and met Bab's gaze. With tears streaming down her cheeks, she said simply, "Welcome back!"

Meanwhile at the Center for Essential Hypostasis, DeeDee, with a tear in her eye but a smile on her face, nodded yes. The screen she was looking at began to record data, to compute, to analyze. Turning away, DeeDee said, "Let the next phase of Mark Stephen's experiment begin."

**The End**

A retired English professor, Lee Norman wrote this book after witnessing a series of extraordinary events following the death of his wife to cancer. He has written articles for national and local magazines, as well as local newspapers. He lives on California's central coast with his second wife.